The Last Legend:

Glitch Apocalypse

A novel

by Timothy L. Cerepaka

An Annulus Publishing Book

Annulus Publishing, Cherokee, Texas, 2015

Published by Annulus Publishing

Copyright © Timothy L. Cerepaka 2014. All rights reserved.

ISBN-13: 978-0692375877

ISBN-10: 0692375872

Author: Timothy L. Cerepaka

Formatting by Timothy L. Cerepaka

Contact: timothy@timothylcerepaka.com

Cover design by Travis Miles at ProBookCovers.com

Acknowledgments

I would like to thank my uncle, James Wilhite, for helping me get this manuscript into publishable shape. I'd also like to thank the rest of my family for supporting me while I wrote this novel. You guys rock.

PART ONE:

THE APOCALYPSE

Chapter 1

Our Aircraft machine—the *Starry Night*, large, black, and rather bulky, but adequate for our traveling needs—passed over the forests and fields below like a ship sailing across the Deep Ocean. We had been journeying northward for some time now, traveling across the Six Continents, crossing each landmass with the grace of a child skipping across stepping stones sticking out of a lake.

Not that I thought it was much of a good idea. I sat in a wobbly metal chair, staring out the clear glass windows as the clouds and birds and forests zipped by underneath us. My friend, Jill Franklin, had told me that we were going back to my hometown, Long River, which was located on the First Continent, in order to get some extra supplies and equipment for our inevitable confrontation with the Lord of the Silver Blades himself.

Don't ask me why she said we needed to do that. Though I was by no means against returning to my quaint hometown, it was about as far away from the Lord of the Silver Blades' castle as a place could possibly be. We had come so close—so very, very close—to saving our world from the Lord's wrath, yet instead of heading directly into his throne room in his castle in the city of Three Hundred Towers, Jill thought we needed to go back to the place where all of this started.

I shook my head, but at the time I had not voiced any objections to her plan. As incomprehensible as the plan seemed, over our journey I had learned to trust Jill's premonitions. Always, it seemed to me, her premonitions turned out to be correct, even if at first they made no sense whatsoever. I well recalled how, not more than a few days ago, she had taken us all the way to the Third Continent, up Black Blade Mountain, to a secret cave where the legendary Starblade—the most powerful sword ever crafted—was located. That Starblade had come in handy more than once on our journey to save the world, including one instance where Jill used it to defeat a whole pit of Giga Snakes.

Getting bored of looking at the same old scenery, as beautiful as it might have been from this height, my eyes wandered over to the interior of the Aircraft. Having originally been built for the avian Angelians, who were taller and ganglier than the average human, the ceiling was quite tall and the seats were well above the floor; in fact, my feet didn't even touch the floor as I sat in my seat. The walls, floor, and ceiling were covered with smooth metal paneling, bare save for the small lights shining from the ceiling.

Sitting on the opposite side from me was another of my friends, Julius Manna. Unlike me, he was fast asleep, his massive arms curled over his thick chest, looking almost like an oversized baby taking a nap. Not that I would ever say anything like that out loud, of course. While Julius was a good friend of mine and had a good sense of humor, he was also a Warrior, easily the strongest among us, and was not above using violence when he got angry (I once saw him wrestle an Omega Goblin and win, which had taught me to be thankful that my friends were not psychopaths who hurt anyone who looked at them funny). Saliva leaked out of the corner of his mouth, trailing down his chin and onto his lap. His massive ax, known as Skull-cruncher, lay on his lap like a dog.

Then I looked over to the cockpit. Jill Franklin, dark-haired and light-skinned, sat at the control seat, her strong hands gripping the wheel tightly, occasionally pressing a button or flipping a lever to make sure we were on course. Despite the fact that the Lord of the Silver Blades was now the proud owner of all six Omega Crystals and had threatened to use their power to conquer the world the last time we saw him, Jill looked perfectly at ease, as if we were taking a stroll down the street to the local butcher's shop, rather than sky-hopping across six continents just to return to a small town in the middle of nowhere. Then again, if she had been freaking out, the *Starry Night* would probably have crashed and we'd all be dead, so I supposed it wasn't much of a problem.

Sitting next to her in the backup pilot's seat was Alicia Bangs, a Healer who, thanks to her tall height, was about the only one of us who fit comfortably in the *Starry Night*'s seats. Her white robes reflected the bright light streaming in from the windshield, making it a bit painful to look at her directly. She looked just as at ease as Jill did, if not more so, as Alicia was a huge Aircraft fanatic, despite having had a childhood on the ground in the Second Continent, and knew more about Aircraft than even many

Angelians did. The only reason she wasn't piloting was because Jill was a superior pilot to her, which was odd because Jill had only been flying the *Starry Night* for a few months now and hadn't ever even flown an Aircraft prior to taking the helm of this ship. Just another mysterious part of the Hero who is Jill Franklin, I supposed.

The inside of the *Starry Night* was very quiet, save for Julius's incessant. Jill was not one to talk and Alicia was usually too excited by the prospect of flying in a real Aircraft to say anything. Because I had no one to talk to, I had to keep all of my worries and concerns to myself, knowing from experience that Jill, with a flip of her dark hair, would just laugh and tell me not to worry, that she knew exactly what she was doing and that everything would be fine if I just trusted her.

Which I did. I really did. She had been too correct over the past few months for me to ever even think of distrusting her. Her actions had saved not only my own life, but the lives of Alicia, Julius, and thousands if not millions of other people all over the Six Continents. She took every surprising turn of events in stride and always seemed to have just the right plan to take down any enemies who crossed our path.

So when Jill said, "We're here," I got up from my seat, straightened the creases out of my Bard Cloak, and walked over to the cockpit to get my first glimpse of my hometown, Long River. It had been quite a while since I had last visited my home, and for a moment I wondered how old Butcher Jim was doing, the town's local butcher and a good friend of mine.

I stood on Jill's left, peering through the windshield, watching as my hometown became clearer and clearer. I saw the butcher's shop, a square brown building made of stone from a local quarry; the item shop, an equally square but bright blue building owned by a man whose name I had never thought to ask but who I had seen every day standing behind the counter; and of course, the Performance Hall, owned by Harold, which, while not as grand as Performance Halls found in such beautiful cities as Twin Crystals or Magisteria, was such a familiar sight to me, with its open double doors and spire, that a wave of nostalgia flowed over me like an ocean wave.

Alicia frowned as we drew closer to it. "Sure is small."

I almost laughed. Alicia came from Wide Plains, the largest city in all of the Six Continents. Of course she would think Long River small. "It's not a bad place."

"I know," said Alicia. "Still, what do you do in there? Watch the moss grow on the trees?"

Annoyed, I leaned against Jill's chair and said, "Actually, you awake to the chirping of the birds and the shining sun. Then you have a wonderful breakfast of fresh-picked berries from the blackberry patches that grow in abundance in the woods, followed by bathing in a crystal clear stream of water. During the day you see squirrel, deer, raccoons, and a variety of other animals, engaged in the kind of silly antics you expect from such creatures. And at night, you peer through the thick branches of the trees at the stars in the sky, wondering if the Five Stars themselves might be looking down on you that night."

Alicia stared at me. "I was asking what you *do* down there, not what you see."

I sighed and said, in plainer terms than I normally used, "I usually just went to the Performance Hall and entertained any visitors we had there. Sometimes I'd visit Butcher Jim's shop and buy some bacon so I could have something good to eat in the morning."

"Ah," said Alicia. "Sounds boring. You don't even have any Aircraft races to watch."

"Well, neither does Wide Plains," I pointed out. "Besides, when you live in a small town like I did, you learn to appreciate the small things in life. It is why I am a Bard, so I can not only focus on the small things, but bring them to life using story and song so others may enjoy them as well."

"Are there any Healers down there?" Alicia said. "I don't see a Healer's House. What do you do if you get injured or sick?"

"We heal ourselves," I answered. "We have plenty of medicinal herbs and plants with which to treat our injuries, though a Healer does occasionally come from the next town over to make sure we're not all dead."

Alicia still frowned. "As a Healer, I don't like the sound of that."

"Well, as you are not from around here, your opinion doesn't matter," I said. "What matters is—"

"Hey, guys."

It was Jill. She was looking straight ahead at Long River, not looking at me or Alicia, but despite that her tone of voice caught both of our attention. I did not recognize her tone at first, as it was not a tone I had ever heard her use before.

"What is it, Jill?" I said. "It better be important because I was just telling Alicia here about how we do things in Long River."

"Look at Long River." She still spoke in that same unrecognizable tone, a tone that worried me greatly. "Something is happening to it."

That was when I recognized her tone: It was surprise.

And what frightened me most about it was that Jill was *never* surprised.

Therefore, I had to look out at Long River, as she ordered. At first, I didn't notice anything out of the ordinary; the town's layout looked the same and, now that we were so close, I even saw a few people walking along its streets, though from this distance it was impossible to tell who they were.

"I don't see—" I said, but then something happened.

How to describe it? I don't know. First, I saw Long River, sitting peacefully among the trees of the Long Forest. Then the town … it blinked in and out of existence several times. It was like someone was trying to wipe off a stubborn stain out of a white shirt, but even that didn't quite describe it. I had no idea what I was looking at because I had never seen anything quite like it.

Alicia must have seen it, too, because she sat up ramrod straight in her seat and said, "What the hell is that?"

"I don't know," said Jill. She was still surprised. "This has never happened before."

A large, black, empty hole opened in Long River and one of the people fell through it. But then the person appeared again, right before the hole, and then walked into it again. The process repeated over and over, each time making my heart break and my mind question its own sanity.

"Is it the Lord of the Silver Blades' sorcery at work?" said Alicia, leaning forward over the control panel, as if that would help her make sense of what she was seeing. "Is he attacking the town with some strange magic?"

"Can't be," said Jill, shaking her head, her tone as surprised as ever. "The Lord of the Silver Blades is in Three Hundred Towers. And he never attacks Long River, not even once."

I would have questioned Jill's tense—"He never attacks, Long River, not even once"—but I was too distracted by the strange distortions going on below to care. The item shop had somehow duplicated itself, making a perfect copy that stood right on top of it like the owner had built a second story. Even more bizarrely, the ground around the shop was built into the pseudo-second story, which would have sent me running away screaming like a maniac if I had not been completely, utterly paralyzed by the fear creeping up my spine.

Then I heard heavy footsteps behind me and I looked over my shoulder. Julius was awake, rubbing his eyes and yawning as he dragged his ax behind him like a toddler's favorite toy. He seemed to have heard the commotion because he said, "What's everyone getting so excited about? Are we under attack by a dragon or something?"

Jill shook her head, but she didn't even speak. Like me, she was too shocked to say anything; at least, that was the explanation I had. It was the only one that made sense. This was the first time I'd ever seen Jill surprised by anything. No wonder she seemed to have lost her voice.

Julius walked up to Alicia's chair and peered over it at Long River below. "Uh … is Long River supposed to look like that?"

"Of course not," I said, though my tone was more afraid than annoyed. "It just started happening. We don't know why."

Julius looked at Jill, just as he always did in these kinds of situations. "Jill, what's going on?"

"She doesn't know, either," I said, putting my hands on my cheeks. "She said she's never seen anything like this before. Says it's never happened before."

"The Lord of the Silver Blades?" said Julius. His fingers tightened around his ax handle.

"No," said Alicia. "It's ... something else."

"And Jill doesn't know?" There was fear in Julius's voice now, the kind of fear I had never heard in it before. "Jill's gotta know. She *always* knows."

"But she doesn't know this," I said, gesturing at my hometown, which was looking more and more like some kind of nightmare the longer I looked at it. "She said so."

Julius grabbed Jill's shoulder with his large hand and said, "Jill, please, you had to have some kind of premonition or something, right? Like you saw this coming at some point and you were prepared for it?"

Jill knocked Julius's hand off her shoulder and actually glared at him. "Weren't you listening to Dale? I. Don't. Know. This is the first time I've ever even seen something like this."

"There has to be something we can do about it," said Julius. "Like, I don't know, maybe use magic to fix everything?"

"Magic won't help," said Jill. "Besides ... we're too late. Look."

Right before our very eyes, Long River—beautiful Long River, quaint Long River, petite Long River, my wonderful hometown—vanished into thin air. It was replaced by a flat black square, with only what appeared to be the outlines of houses and people on its surface. Like all of the color had drained from my home and my friends.

Jill stopped the Aircraft in midair, right before we flew over the black emptiness that was once my hometown. Her shoulders slumped, she just stared at the large black space where my home had been, looking completely lost.

"Where did it go?" I said. "Jill, where did Long River—"

"It's gone." She said that with a finality in her voice that crushed my soul. "Dale, I'm sorry to say this, but your home—and everyone and everything in it—is gone. And there's nothing I can do to bring it back."

Chapter 2

"Gone?" I said. "No, it can't be *gone*. Jill, you must be mistaken."

Jill shook her head. She didn't even look up at me, as if she was ashamed to do so. "I'm not. While I've never seen this particular thing happen before, I know a glitch when I see one."

"A what?" I said. "What's a glitch?"

Jill suddenly looked like she had just said something she shouldn't. She immediately flipped some switches and pulled some levers and turned the wheel. As she did so, the *Starry Night* slowly turned in the direction of the wheel until we could no longer see where my hometown—*my* hometown—once proudly stood.

"You know what, Dale?" said Jill, keeping her eyes firmly on the windshield. "You were right. We've wasted enough time as is. We should go and confront the Lord of the Silver Blades and save the world. Just like we always do."

"Just like we always do?" I said. "Jill, we've never defeated the Lord of the Silver Blades before. Sure, we've fought the Lord before, but we've never actually defeated him. You sound crazy."

"I'm not crazy," said Jill, her voice harried. "I'm just—"

"She's in shock," said Alicia, putting a sympathetic hand on Jill's shoulder. "Most likely from seeing ... whatever happened to Long River back there. No doubt that's causing her a lot of confusion."

"Yes," said Jill, nodding too quickly. "That's it exactly."

I grabbed the wheel, holding it as firmly as I could, causing Jill to look at me in surprise. I couldn't hold back the tears fighting to leak from my eyes, which made it hard to look at her, but I did anyway because I was not going to let Jill avoid the question.

"Dale, what are you doing?" said Jill. "Didn't you just hear what I said? We've going to defeat the Lord of the Silver Blades."

"What about Long River?" I said. "Jill, I think you know what is going on here, but for some reason you're not telling us."

My tone must have been sharper than I thought because Julius —who through my tears looked blurrier than normal—said, "Dale, take it easy. Jill already said she doesn't know. And like Alicia said, she's in shock and you are, too, obviously, so maybe we should just take a moment to—"

"To do what?" I said, glaring at him with all of the anger that I could. I wiped the tears from my eyes with my other hand and said, "Just ignore the destruction of my hometown? Pretend it never happened? Act like defeating the Lord of the Silver Blades and saving the Omega Crystals will somehow right everything, make it better? Just shut up, Julius."

"Shut up?" said Julius. An angry scowl crossed his face. "Why don't you say that to my face, Bard?"

"M-Maybe I will," I said, stuttering not because I was afraid but because I was on the verge of breaking down. "Maybe I'll even knock your lights out."

Julius's laugh was a short bark, like dog. "That's rich. You can't even use a weapon. What are you going to do, sing at me?"

I almost lost control just then, but then Jill stood up and said, "Both of you, stop arguing. Or I'll make both of you walk all the way back to the Sixth Continent. Would either of you like that?"

"But he started it," said Julius, pointing at me like a child. "I was just defending you from him."

"It's fine, Julius," said Jill, though her voice shook somewhat. "I can take care of myself. It's not a big deal."

"Not a big deal?" I said. I gestured at the back of the *Starry Night*, the side which was now facing the blackness where my town used to be. "My hometown is *gone*. Everyone is *dead*. I'd say this is a *huge* deal, but I guess I can't expect you to care about it, since you're not from there like I am."

"Dale, please calm down," said Jill, putting a soothing hand on my arm. "I know you're in shock and I know you're upset, but getting angry at me or Julius won't bring back your home."

I slapped her hand off my arm and glared at her, the tears now flowing freely from my eyes. "Then what will, Jill, what will?"

Jill just looked at me, her eyes full of sadness. "I don't know, Dale, but with this happening, I think I owe you, Julius, and Alicia an explanation."

"Jill, don't," said Alicia. "You don't need to explain anything to us. After all, none of us have any idea why this happened or what's going on. Your heart's in the right place, but—"

"Not that," said Jill, interrupting Alicia. "I still don't know why that happened, but I have a hunch. But I can't share that hunch with any of you until you know the truth about me and the world itself."

"The truth?" said Julius. "What do you mean? We already know who you are, Jill. You're our leader and one of the best fighters I've ever met. You're an ordinary girl from a small town called Green Grove who has done more to help the world than any king or government ever has. What is there to explain?"

Jill looked down at her feet, ashamed (as she should be, I might add). "That's the surface truth. What you and me and everyone else is programmed to believe."

"Programmed?" I said. The tears were drying up now, but I still sniffled. "You make us sound like a bunch of robots."

"Jill's just in shock," Alicia said again, like a broken record. "She's—"

"I'm not in shock," Jill said, her tone harsher than normal. "I'm being straight with all of you. About my premonitions, about the nature of the tragedy that struck Long River, about Kinar and the Six Continents and everything that lives within them."

"But didn't the Five Stars give you your ability to see into the future?" said Julius. "I mean, that's what you've always told us, right? The Five Stars granted you a power that no one else in the world has. Even the Lord of the Silver Blades can't see into the future. It's why we've been so successful at defeating our enemies. Right?"

Jill chuckled bitterly, as if Julius had just shared a grim joke with her. "The Five Stars didn't grant me my ability to see into the future. No one did, because I *can't* see into the future. I'm just as future-blind as all of you are."

Stunned silence filled the cockpit, broken only by the rumbling of the ship's engines. Even I stopped sniffling and crying, unable to comprehend what Jill just said.

"But … you can't?" said Julius. He sounded lost, as if he had been given the wrong directions to his intended destination. "Then how do you explain how you are almost always able to accurately predict what happens next?"

"That's the thing," said Jill, her eyes locked on the pilot's seat. "It's not a prediction on my part, not really. The events we experience, the minions we fight, the puzzles we solve … they're as predictable and reliable as the rising and setting of the Twin Suns every day. All I am doing is recognizing the patterns and adjusting my behavior in accordance with them."

"Patterns?" said Alicia. "You sound like you have experienced this stuff before. Like … you're from the future or something."

"I'm not a time traveler," said Jill. "I'm not anything special, really. I've just experienced everything—from the day I left Green Grove all the way to our inevitable victory over the Lord of the Silver Blades—so many times now that I could do it all in my sleep."

"But … how?" said Julius, running his hands through his hair. "That's not possible. We haven't even gotten to the Lord of the Silver Blades yet. So how can you know we're going to beat him?"

Jill turned back to the control panel and flipped some switches and pressed a couple of buttons. Immediately, the *Starry Night* began moving forward, gradually picking up speed. A quick glance at the coordinates she had entered into the ship's map system told me that she had set the *Starry Night* on auto-pilot on a direct course for Three Hundred Towers, which puzzled me as she never used auto-pilot.

Then she turned to look at us, a solemn frown on her face. "I set the ship in auto-pilot so we'd have time to talk without interruption."

"I'd say," said Julius. "You still sound like a mad woman to me. I mean, you can't experience what hasn't happened, you know?"

Jill stepped from around the pilot's seat and walked to the back of the ship, not looking at any of us as she did so. If I wasn't so angry and confused, I would have felt sorry for her because she was clearly upset herself and trying to figure out the best way to tell us what she was trying to tell us. All I cared about was learning why my hometown was gone.

"It's difficult to explain," said Jill. "Mostly because, until now, I've never had to explain it to anybody. Not to mention I don't entirely understand it myself."

"Do your best anyway, Jill," said Alicia, unstrapping herself from her seat and standing up. "We're your friends. We're listening."

Jill folded her arms behind her back and sighed. "Originally, I was just like you three. I didn't know what tomorrow or the next week would hold in store for me. And in truth—as this disaster clearly showed—I don't know what tomorrow or next week holds in store for me. I know only as much as I do, again, because I've seen the patterns and signs."

"You keep talking about patterns and signs," said Julius. "What do you mean?"

"I mean that things are supposed to happen in a certain order," said Jill. She still was not looking at us, which annoyed me more than I'd like to admit. "I wake up in the morning, find my mother dead, learn that the Lord of the Silver Blades killed her because she used to be his lover but had spurned him in favor of my father, go on a quest to save the world, meet all three of you at various times, fail to defend the Omega Crystals from the Lord, go to the Lord's city, and defeat the Lord and save the world. That's not even counting the various mini-bosses we must fight or side quests we can go on. Like I said, I know it all."

"Are you talking about destiny?" said Julius, sounding like a young child who was trying to bring adult concepts down to a level he understood. "Like, the Five Stars told you about this or maybe showed you a vision of the path you're supposed to take or something?"

Jill turned around, now looking at us. She looked a little annoyed, though whether she was annoyed at her inability to clearly explain what she meant or at Julius's failure to grasp it, I wasn't sure. All I knew was that she had no right to be annoyed at us, not when my hometown had been destroyed and she still hadn't given us a satisfactory answer as to why, instead babbling on about 'patterns' and 'signs' and all of that crap I could care less about. I couldn't help but wonder if she was going insane or just messing with us. Neither option made me feel good about this.

"It's not destiny and it's not the Five Stars," said Jill. "I mean, it's sort of like destiny, but it isn't. It's like … look, I am being controlled. Every move I make is not really my choice. It feels like my choice, heck, even looks like my own free choice, but in reality, there is a being above me—above all of us—who meticulously plots and charts out my every move, who knows what is going to happen before it does. A being who exists above the Five Stars, even."

"Okay, now you're getting silly," said Julius, leaning against Alicia's chair. "Jill, everyone knows that the Five Stars are the highest possible beings in Kinar. There's no one above them."

"That's wrong," said Jill. "I know it's hard to believe, but it's true. The Five Stars ... I'm afraid to say, but they have no real power over this world, may not even exist for all I know. But this being does, this being who exists outside of our universe, who knows the exact course of events and knows how to control me in order to prepare me for these events."

"Really," I said, not bothering to tone down the skepticism in my voice. "If so, he doesn't sound like a bad being if he's helping you overcome these problems. If anything, I'd say he sounds quite benevolent ... assuming you aren't just going insane and he actually does exist, that is."

"He does," Jill insisted. "Why else do you think I have the Starblade? He knew of it, knew exactly when it would be available. When it became available, he sent me to Black Blade Mountain to retrieve it because he knew it would make defeating the Lord of the Silver Blades so much easier. And I know that it will help us because I've used the Starblade to kill the Lord of the Silver Blades several times."

"You keep talking about stuff that hasn't happened yet like it has happened already," said Julius. He looked at Alicia and said, "Ali, do you think Jill is going crazy?"

Alicia had always been the gentlest and least skeptical of all of us, but right now she eyed Jill the same way a hunter eyes a mad deer. "I don't know. Jill has always seemed sane to me, but —"

18

"I may be crazy," Jill admitted, "but I don't think I'm wrong. I've gone through this life so many times that I am absolutely sure of what I say."

"So you're talking reincarnation, then," said Julius. "Like that old story about the turtle and the king, right?"

"Not reincarnation," said Jill. "I don't die and come back in another life. This is the same me, going through the exact same sequence of events, again and again and again, the only differences being minor, such as gaining certain items or equipment or defeating enemies in a slightly different way."

"This is making my head hurt," said Julius, putting his hand on his forehead. "Jill, isn't there a simpler way to explain this?"

"I don't know how to make it any more simpler or plain," said Jill. "That's what I'm trying to do, but like I said, I've never had to explain it to anyone before and I don't completely understand it myself."

"Let's assume that your story is true," I said. "Can you pinpoint when, exactly, you became aware of this, er, being? When you became aware that you were reliving the exact same life again and again, just with minor variations of no real consequence?"

Jill folded her arms across her chest. "It was … a while ago, which I can't pinpoint exactly because I don't know how to keep track of time between sessions. For some reason, I started recognizing that I was doing the same thing over and over again. It frightened me at first because I thought I was going mad, but then I slowly came to the realization that I was as sane as anyone else and that it was the world itself that was 'mad,' for want of a better term. After a while, I accepted that this was just the way things were."

"Why didn't you tell us about this, then?" I said. "Why did you wait until … until whatever that thing was that happened back there, happened? Don't you trust us?"

"I do," said Jill. "It's just I wasn't sure anyone would believe me. It's a hard to believe story. Even I am not always sure of it, but it's the only explanation I have, the only one that makes sense."

"Well, it sure as hell doesn't explain what happened to Long River back there," said Julius, nodding toward the back of the *Starry Night*. "Is that the result of this 'being,' too?"

"No," said Jill, shaking her head. "The being is not malicious. I think this is a glitch."

"A what?" I said. "Is that some kind of animal?"

"No," said Jill, rubbing the back of her head. "A glitch is … well, do you remember how I defeated the Skeletal Warrior back in Black Blade Mountain? How I teleported behind him and struck him in the back with my light magic?"

"Yeah," I said, nodding. "But what does that have to do with the destruction of my hometown?"

"They're of the same nature," said Jill. "But different. That teleportation I did … it's not 'supposed' to happen, I think. It violates the laws that govern our world, but it's there and it can be exploited if you know how to do it. I once heard the being who controls me call it a glitch."

"Wait, you can hear him?" I said. "Does he ever talk to you?"

"No," said Jill. "He never talks to me directly; actually, I don't think he even knows I can think independently of him. I just sometimes hear his voice, but I never really understand anything he says. Sometimes, when things aren't going the way he wants them to, he'll curse and even scream, but most of the time he's quiet and I don't know what he's thinking until he makes me do it."

"Back to the topic of glitches," said Alicia. "Is that what happened back in Long River?"

"I think so," said Jill. "But it's not a glitch I've ever seen before. Most of the glitches I exploit are harmless, and even beneficial, if you know how to use them right. But this one … it's dangerous. I don't know why it happened or if there is a way to reverse it."

"There must be something we can do," I said. "Isn't there a mage we can talk to who might know the secret to fixing this 'glitch,' as you call it?"

"No mage can fix a glitch," said Jill. "You misunderstand. It's not magic. It has nothing to do with magic of any sort. The best way I can think of to describe it is that it is a flaw in the design of the universe itself."

"But the universe doesn't have any flaws," Julius objected. "The Five Stars designed the universe to be without flaws, right?"

"I don't think the Five Stars created our universe," said Jill. "I think someone else did, but who, I don't know. All I know is that this glitch might be harmless."

"Harmless?" I said in disbelief. "You just said it was dangerous."

Jill walked over to my chair and sat down in it, sinking her face into her hands as she said, "The glitch might only last as long as the universe is … again, it's hard to describe, so bear with me … as long as the universe is active. If the being who controls me resets the universe, then maybe Long River will return."

I sighed in relief. "Oh, good. Well, what's to stop this being from resetting the universe and fixing everything?"

Jill looked up at us, her eyes hollow. "That's why I'm freaked out. He hasn't, which means he either does not know of it or knows that resetting the universe doesn't work. Which means that this is a very serious glitch."

I gulped. "Does that mean we're all going to die?"

"I don't know," said Jill. "How many times do I have to say that? We might die or we might live. The being who controls me might try to fix it or he might ignore it."

"What will happen if he ignores it?" said Julius. "Will the problem go away on its own?"

"I don't know," said Jill, glancing out my window. "And I *hate* not knowing. I want to destroy the glitch, but I just don't know how to deal with it."

"Is that why you set the *Starry Night*'s course for Three Hundred Towers?" I said, gesturing at the map system in the control panel. "To escape something you can't deal with, you're going to handle something that you can?"

"Essentially, yes," said Jill. "But it's deeper than that. Defeating the Lord of the Silver Blades will force the universe to reset. That might fix your town, but it's just a theory and I could be wrong."

I had never seen Jill look so lost and confused. She was slumped forward in my chair, looking more like a cornered animal than a brave Hero. Though my heart was still heavy with mourning of my hometown, I wondered if my earlier outburst toward her had been unfair. She didn't know what was going on and she didn't have anything to do with it. It wasn't right of me to judge her so, even though I was now almost certain that she was crazy.

"Well, then," said Julius, pushing himself off of Alicia's chair and walking forward, a grin spreading across his large, handsome face. "I guess we have a plan, then. Defeat the Lord of the Silver Blades and force the universe to 'reset' itself, whatever that means."

"Will it hurt us?" said Alicia. "This resetting the universe that you talked about."

"No, it won't hurt at all," said Jill. "You probably won't even realize it happened. We will defeat the Lord of the Silver Blades and then, after the universe resets, we will be in the last spot we saved right before we defeated him."

"Saved?" said Julius. "Saved what?"

"Our progress," said Jill. She patted her pants pocket and said, "Remember my journal I carry along? Every time I write in it, it's the universe's way of 'remembering' where we were. It's why I do it so regularly, especially before boss battles."

I didn't believe that writing down your location in a journal would essentially act as a reminder to the universe of where you were, but I had a policy of not questioning people whose sanity was gradually slipping through their fingers like grains of sand and Jill's had clearly lost all of hers years ago.

"Whatever you say," said Julius. He smashed his fist into his other hand and said, "I just can't wait to smash that Lord's face in. He may not be responsible for Long River's destruction, but I'm going to pretend he is anyway, just to give me more motivation to break his face."

"Same here," said Alicia. "I mean, I can't actually hurt him, but I'll be sure to use my healing abilities keep you and Jill strong enough to fight."

I looked down at my hands. Until now, I had not realized just how small and pathetic they were. I had always accepted that I was not much of a fighter, that I couldn't even throw a punch very well, mostly because it had not seemed like a terribly big deal.

Now, however, it *was* something of a big deal. If defeating the Lord of the Silver Blades was indeed the only way to restore Long River, then I wished I could help. As a Bard, I was incapable of fighting, though my Bard's Cloak did give me the ability to use songs in battle that could inflict certain status conditions upon my enemies. Whether any of those songs would actually work against the Lord of the Silver Blades was another question entirely.

Nonetheless, I stepped forward and said, "I, too, will do my best to support you in battle. I will do whatever it takes to bring back my hometown, even if that means killing the Lord of the Silver Blades with my own bare hands."

"Glad to see you are all behind me on this, at least," said Jill. Then Jill's eyes widened in horror, as if she saw something we didn't. "Watch out!"

Puzzled, I looked over my shoulder and started. Through the windshield, the blue sky had been replaced by a purple, blurry flat wall that we were flying directly toward. I had never seen anything like it, but somehow I knew that it was from the exact same source as the glitch that destroyed Long River.

Alicia lunged for the controls, but it was too late. The *Starry Night* crashed straight into the purple blur, throwing all four of us off our feet and onto the floor. I crashed onto the floor of the *Starry Night* face first, smashing my nose and teeth against the metal paneling.

But I couldn't get up. The *Starry Night* was now rapidly spinning through the air uncontrollably. Raising my head as high as I could, I saw the sky and the ground flash by the windshield, taking turns appearing and disappearing. We were falling, and falling fast, and it would not be long before we crashed.

So I ducked my head onto the floor and put my hands on my head. At that exact moment, a loud sound of snapping wood tearing against metal panels roared in my ears, and then there was a jerk and I went flying into the ceiling. I slammed into the ceiling headfirst and everything went dark.

Chapter 3

Ugh … what happened? My head hurt … my back felt like a snapped twig … my knees and elbows seemed to be shattered … and my whole body felt like a giant had stepped on it. I tried to remember what had happened, but nothing came to mind right away. All I remembered was being thrown around like a rag doll, making me feel sorry for rag dolls that belonged to careless little children.

I forced my eyes open to get a look at my surroundings. I found myself lying flat on my back looking up at the ceiling of the *Starry Night*, my eyes burning as I gazed into the lights shining down on my face. Lowering my lids slightly, I turned my head to see how everyone else was doing.

It appeared that I was the only one still conscious. Jill lay face down on the floor in front of my chair, the Starblade poking awkwardly through its sheath, but it had thankfully not pierced her leg. Julius lay behind Alicia's chair, on his back like I was, but he had a large bump on his head. As for Alicia, she was lying awkwardly on her seat, her arms hanging off the chair's arms and her head tilted backward. Blood leaked out of the corner of her mouth, but aside from that, she appeared fine.

THE LAST LEGEND: GLITCH APOCALYPSE

I struggled to sit up, but my whole body hurt like crazy, not to mention the slightly tilted nature of the *Starry Night* made sitting up feel unnatural. I hadn't been in this much pain since we took on the Toxic Dragon in the Fifth Continent. All I wanted to do was rest, but I couldn't and I wasn't sure why until, without even so much as a hint, it all came back to me.

The destruction of Long River, Jill's confession, the purple blur ... it all came back lightning fast, as though a dam holding back a raging river had broke and the river was flooding the valley of my mind. Tears welled in my eyes again and I almost started crying again before I heard some movement nearby.

Jill was moving. She had propped herself up with her hands, shaking her head as she did so. Her dark hair was messy and everywhere now, covering her face, but aside from that, she didn't seem to be in quite as much pain as I was. Or maybe she was just stronger than me and so could handle it better.

"Jill, what happened?" I said, craning my neck to get a better look at her. "Are you okay?"

"I'm fine," said Jill, brushing her hair out of her face. "Just in a lot of pain, but I'll be all right. I've suffered worse."

I sighed in relief and looked around. Through the windshield, I spotted tall trees standing all around us, appearing slightly tilted thanks to the way the ship had crashed. Their thick branches and thicker leaves blocked out most of the sun, making the place much darker than it should have been.

"Did we crash somewhere in the Long Forest?" Jill asked, rubbing her face as she spoke.

"We must have," I said. "The only question is, in what part did we crash?"

"Only one way to find out," said Jill. "Let's wake Julius and Alicia and see if we can get the *Starry Night* back in the air."

"Afraid I can't be of much help," I said. I tried to move my body, but stopped the minute the pain in my back burned. "I'm in some pretty terrible pain at the moment and am essentially useless."

"Nice excuse," said Jill. "Get up. I'm not going to carry you if the *Starry Night* is too broken to fly."

While Jill got to her feet and walked over to Julius, making sure to watch her feet as she did so to avoid falling in the direction that the *Starry Night* was tilted, I slowly sat up. It hurt to do so, but I soon learned to ignore the pain and in a few seconds was sitting up as well as I ever could. Still, my arms and legs felt like lead and my head ached badly, but at least I was not dead. I would heal eventually.

A couple of minutes later, both Julius and Alicia were awake. Alicia quickly looked us over to make sure that none of us were suffering from any major wounds and pronounced herself satisfied that we were all in decent shape despite the bumps and bruises we had all sustained.

"By the Five Stars, what happened?" said Julius, rubbing the bump on his head. "What did we hit?"

"The Glitch," Jill said. She was standing in front of the control panel, checking the switches, levers, and buttons to make sure they were in working condition. "For whatever reason, it conjured a solid purple wall in the sky, which knocked us down into the Long Forest."

"How did we even survive that?" said Alicia, clutching her staff to her chest. "We fell a pretty long way, didn't we?"

"We did, but remember, we're not normal," said Jill. "The being … I imagine he must have saved us. Kept us from dying."

"Because he cares about us?" said Julius.

"Because he would be bored without us," said Jill. Then she cursed and slammed the control panel with her fist. "It's broken. The damn controls are broken."

I gulped. "Can you fix it?"

"If I had the right parts," said Jill. "And if I was a professional Aircraft engineer. But I do not have the right parts and I'm not a professional Aircraft engineer, so no, I can't fix it."

"Can't fix it?" said Alicia. "Does that mean we're stuck here? What if the Lord of the Silver Blades uses the Omega Crystals to destroy the world, now that we can't get to the Sixth Continent quickly enough?"

"The Lord of the Silver Blades won't do anything with the Omega Crystals until we get to Three Hundred Towers," said Jill, turning away from the control panel, a frown on her face. "It's the Glitch we have to be afraid of. It might attack us, do to us what it did to Long River."

I rubbed my hands together anxiously. "Then what are we standing around here for? Why don't we abandon the ship and go to the nearest town? I think Barnua is close by, isn't it?"

"Depends on where we crashed," said Jill. Then she glanced at the control panel, a reluctant expression on her face. "But we can't just abandon the *Starry Night*. It's our only reliable method of transportation. Without it, we'd have to walk across all six of the Continents to reach Three Hundred Towers. And with the Glitch active, there's no guarantee we'd make it there in one piece."

"Are you saying we're stuck, then?" said Julius. "'Cause I don't want to die at the hands of something I can't even punch."

"Jill, we'll have to leave the ship behind," I said. "We don't have the parts necessary to fix it, nor do we have the time. We'll just have to make do with what we have."

Jill sighed. "I guess you're right. Besides, it's not like we're totally without transportation. I do know of one way to travel between the Continents without an Aircraft, but it is dangerous and could kill us all if I don't do it right. At the very least, it could take us where we don't want to go if I mess up."

"We'll have to use it," I said, adjusting my Bard's Cloak, which had gotten tangled around my body after I had fallen. "Because our only other option is to sit here and wait for the Glitch to kill us."

"How far away is this other transportation method, Jill?" said Julius, picking up Skull-cruncher and hefting it on his shoulder. "Hours away? Days?"

"I don't know," said Jill. "We first have to get out of here and figure out our exact location. It might be close by or it might be far away, though once we figure that out, it shouldn't take us long to find it."

"Then let's go," said Alicia, glancing nervously over her shoulder at the windshield. "I feel like a sitting duck in here, especially with the Glitch around."

Exiting the *Starry Night* was not easy. The exit—a door located near the back, where the engine was—was blocked off by some of our supply barrels, which Julius and Jill had to work together to move. Then we discovered that the door was blocked off by something outside, possibly tree branches, but a few well-placed punches by Julius later and the door slammed open with a loud, but immensely satisfying, *crunch*.

Jill went out first, explaining that she wanted to make sure that the Glitch was not nearby so none of us would get 'glitched' by it, as she said. She didn't really explain what would happen to us if we got 'glitched,' partly because she clearly didn't know herself and partly because I remembered in vivid detail just how Long River had looked when it got 'glitched' and I wasn't in any mood to dwell on the thought of that same thing happening to us.

After Jill did a quick search of the area, she told us it was safe to go. We climbed out of the fallen ship and then turned to look at it. The black paint was scratched, probably from the tree branches that scraped it when it fell. It was leaning on its side, the right side in the mud, the left side slightly elevated above the ground. Nearby, one of its wings was stuck in a tree, like a samurai's blade stabbed in a dummy. The starry designs on its hull were covered in mud. It certainly looked like it would never fly again, which was rather sad, as it had been a good Aircraft.

Alicia looked at the *Starry Night* with sad eyes. She had always liked it better than the rest of us, again because of her strange fascination with Angelian Aircraft. No doubt she was heartbroken right now, but honestly, in comparison to the loss of my hometown and everyone who lived in it, losing an Aircraft was hardly a tragedy. I did not say that aloud, however, because I had no interest in making Alicia angry at me (though she was a Healer, Alicia could be quite mean when she wanted to be).

The ground beneath our feet was muddy. The trees were also covered with the mud, making it appear that the crash of the *Starry Night* must have sent mud clods flying everywhere. There were no animals or people nearby; at least, if there were any, they were not showing themselves. The screech of a red falcon was the only sound which broke the silence, aside from Jill's boots squelching in the mud as she walked back and forth, her eyes scanning the area, searching for a sign that told her where we were.

Jill came to a stop and folded her arms. "All right. I think we're in the western half of the Long Forest. That means that the city of Tall Roots is nearby. We should take the main path and should be there soon."

"Why are we going there?" said Julius. "Is that where the transportation method you told us about is?"

"It can be performed there, yes," said Jill. "We'll have to hurry, however. I suspect that the Glitch is spreading and if we are not quick, then … well, I think you guys know what will happen if we don't stop it in time."

As it turned out, we hadn't fallen very far from the main path at all. It took us only seconds to find the wide road—really more of a well-worn path, created by the centuries of travelers coming to and from the largest city in the First Continent—and soon we were on our way. Of course, we were randomly attacked now and then by animals such as red falcons and tree beasts, but Jill and Julius dispatched them easily, though the creatures didn't give us much money when they died and only dropped basic items like revitalizing potions. All they succeeded in doing was waste our precious time.

I led the way down the main path, which was shrouded by the tree branches above us that formed a kind of natural bridge for the

Long Forest's beastly inhabitants to cross without having to use the path itself. I led not because Jill didn't want to but because I knew this road better than the others, having gone up and down it many times during my life in Long River, as Tall Roots had the largest Performance Hall in the entire First Continent and I had always traveled to it once or twice a year whenever I wanted to make a little bit more money than I could at Long River's Performance Hall.

Thinking of Long River's Performance Hall made my heart feel ill. Prior to joining up with Jill, that place had been like a second home to me. I would always go there once a day, usually after lunch, and perform for whoever happened to be there at the time. The patron, a man named Harold, always gave me free drinks. And I usually ended up making some good money, though due to its small size and the few travelers we had in Long River, it was never quite as good as the money I had made in other Performance Halls across the Six Continents.

Jill strode by my side, her hand on the hilt of the Starblade sheathed at her side. Her eyes were darting around the path, but I knew she wasn't afraid of the very weak creatures that inhabited this forest. She was looking for any sign of the Glitch, the Glitch that she seemed to think would bring about the apocalypse.

I still did not know if Jill's story was true. Reliving this exact same sequence of events over and over, her every movement controlled by some unknown being who lived outside of our universe, and everything else she had told us, was incredibly hard to believe, to put it lightly. Part of me wondered if Jill was pulling some sort of elaborate practical joke on all of us (*Fooled you! Your town wasn't really destroyed! I just made it disappear with some cool magic!*), but Jill was never the kind to pull this kind of prank on anyone. I had to conclude, therefore, that she was telling the truth.

It did explain how she seemed to know me so well the first time she had met me (or was it the first time, because if her story was true, we had probably had hundreds of first meetings and I did not remember any of them except for the most recent?). I had been the first member of our little team to join up with Jill, which had been several months ago. I had been bathing naked in the creek outside of my cabin when three goblins, servants of the Lord of the Silver Blades, attacked me. I likely would have died if Jill had not appeared just then and killed them all.

At the time, I had thought it a miracle that Jill had not only arrived at the exact moment I needed her, but that she also knew the best ways to defeat the goblins. Now I wondered if the only reason she had done any of that was because she had experienced it before—maybe hundreds of times—and had it as memorized as her own name. Her story certainly explained her complete confidence in our success, even in our darkest hours, such as when the Lord of the Silver Blades attained the last Omega Crystal and ran off to his castle in Three Hundred Towers to put the final phase of his plan into action.

What disturbed me most about her story was that, if it was true, then Jill and I had gone on this same adventure hundreds of times and yet I remembered only this most recent outing. That meant there was months—maybe even whole years—of my life that I didn't even remember. Or maybe it could be said that I did remember it. After all, Jill said that the sequence of events, while differing in small details here and there, was exactly the same every time she went through it. Was I really missing anything at all, then? Were Julius and Alicia missing anything, either?

My existential thoughts were interrupted when Julius—who must have been thinking the same thing as I—said, "So, Jill, you said that you've been through this stuff before, right?"

Jill glanced over her shoulder at Julius. "You mean our quest to defeat the Lord of the Silver Blades and save the world?"

"Yeah, that," said Julius, nodding. "According to you, we've beaten the Lord of the Silver Blades loads of times, right?"

"Yes," said Jill. "We confront him in his headquarters in Three Hundred Towers and defeat him, sometimes easily, sometimes not. It all depends on how easy the being who controls me decides to make it."

"Right," said Julius, though it was clear that, like me, he didn't really understand what Jill's final sentence meant. "So that means you know how our journey ends, then."

"Yes," said Jill.

"So can you tell us what happens after we defeat the Lord of the Silver Blades?" said Julius, somewhat sheepishly. "I mean, like, do any of us die or does the Lord of the Silver Blades die or what?"

Jill looked straight ahead, as though she was avoiding the question. "That's not really important at the moment. You'll find out soon enough."

"But why?" said Julius. "I mean, it can't hurt, can it? Didn't you say that we'd forget all of this after we defeated the Lord of the Silver Blades? Not like knowing the future will do us any good, right, since it's predetermined?"

"Even so, it's not always best for us to know the future," said

Jill. "Sometimes, I wish I didn't know as much about it as I do. I wish my memory would reset after each time we defeated the Lord of the Silver Blades, but it doesn't. It used to, but ever since I became aware of the being controlling me, I retain all of my memories from my past adventures."

Her voice sounded hollow, as though she was reliving a memory she wished she could repress. She clearly didn't want to talk about it, and being the gentleman that I am, I did not push the subject.

Julius, on the other hand, apparently did not notice her tone because he said, "What's the problem with us knowing? You're just avoiding the question. I promise not to tell anyone else if you'll just tell us."

Jill sighed. "Like I said, you really don't want to know what happens. It's just not important. You'll see when we defeat the Lord of the Silver Blades. That shouldn't be long from now."

Julius picked up speed and passed me and Jill. He then stopped and turned around, his bulky body effectively blocking off our path. I ordinarily did not think of Julius as intimidating (though many of our enemies no doubt did), but right now, with the way he stood, his large biceps at his sides and his ax on his shoulder, I began to understand just why he had been known as the Titan prior to his joining our team.

"I want to know now," said Julius. "And we won't go one step farther until I do."

"Julius, stop being an ass," said Alicia, though her tone was nervous rather than angry. "The Glitch could get us any minute. Jill said that it's not important anyhow."

"It's important to me," Julius said, jerking his thumb at

himself. "Back before I joined up with y'all, I always visited my town's resident oracle, who would tell me what my day would be like. Knowing what is going to happen before it happens is useful knowledge for any Warrior like myself."

I frowned. "Wasn't your oracle usually dead wrong?"

Julius glared at me for a moment before continuing. "The point is that I think we all deserve to know what's in store for us. It's not fair that Jill does and we don't. If we're a team, then that means we aren't allowed to keep these kinds of secrets from each other. We'll work more effectively together if we're honest with each other."

"We worked together well before we knew about Jill's true nature," Alicia pointed out. "I'm sure that if Jill has her reasons for not telling us, then they're good reasons, right Jill?"

Jill rubbed the back of her neck. "I just don't want any of you to be distracted by what is going to come. This Glitch is dangerous and unpredictable. We need to have our wits about ourselves if we're going to avoid its disrupting effects."

"Jill, you know I don't obsess over the future," said Julius. "Just tell me what's gonna happen and I promise I won't ask you about anything else ever again. Deal?"

For a moment, I was sure that Jill would draw her blade and slap Julius in the face with it, maybe make him move out of the way. Certainly I didn't think Jill was going to honor his request, especially when she had already stubbornly refused to do so.

But then Jill shrugged and said, "All right. I'll be brief: In order to defeat the Lord of the Silver Blades, I must die."

Stunned silence settled over us like cloud covering as her words sank in. Alicia covered her mouth with the sleeve of her robes, Julius stared dumbly at her, and breathing suddenly became harder for me.

"What?" said Julius. "You … must die?"

Jill looked at all of us, her eyes full of pain. "Yes. This is why I didn't want to talk about it. I didn't want any of you worrying about me, not when there's a good chance all of us will die thanks to that Glitch."

"You're joking," said Julius, a weak smile cracking over his lips. "Right? Just pulling our legs."

"It's no joke," said Jill. "What happens is that it turns out that the Lord of the Silver Blades is too strong for us to finish off. His lair is falling apart all around us and if we don't leave right away, we'll be buried alive. I tell you guys to go on ahead, take the Omega Crystals and run while I hold back the Lord of the Silver Blades. You guys always think I'll follow, but I never do. I get buried with him in the ruins of his lair while you guys go and return the Omega Crystals to their rightful owners."

Oddly, she didn't sound very sad about it, despite her eyes. She spoke of it almost as calmly as one discusses the weather, though there was a tinge of melancholy in the way she stood, perhaps because she didn't want us to get sad.

"Damn," said Julius. "Jill, I'm sorry for making you tell us that. I was just really curious to know—"

"It's not a problem," said Jill. "It was scary the first few times, but I've died so many times now that it's no longer as traumatizing as it used to be. After all, I come back to life at the beginning of each adventure, as whole and living as ever. As I said, the only reason I didn't tell any of you guys about it is because I didn't want you to be distracted by my death."

"There's gotta be a way we can change that," said Julius. "Maybe we can find another way to keep the Lord of the Silver Blades busy. That way, all of us can get out of there alive."

"Thanks for the kind sentiments, Julius, but it's unnecessary," said Jill. "It's not a big deal. It's not permanent, not even all that painful. You're getting worked up over nothing."

"Worked up over nothing?" said Julius, running a hand through his buzz cut. "I'd hardly call your death nothing. Does that mean that the being knows you're going to die? That he intentionally leads you to your death?"

"It's part of the game," said Jill. "It's what the being calls this whole adventure: A game. I die at the end. It's just as much a part of the game as me meeting Dale or losing to the Lord of the Silver Blades in Tall Roots. No way around it."

"Now that ain't right," said Julius. "This being sounds like a bad guy. Intentionally leading you to your death? Not doing a thing to save you? What a jerk. I'd like to take Skull-cruncher and —"

"Would you just shut up?" Jill snapped. "It's. Not. A. Big. Deal. How many times do I have to repeat that until it gets through that thick skull of yours? Death isn't permanent. It lasts only as long as the being allows it to, and no more."

"So what if it isn't permanent?" said Julius. He pointed at her and said, "Jill, I'm gonna figure out a way to save you. Just like how you saved me back in Horror Cliffs."

Jill met Julius's gaze with surprisingly cold eyes. "I had to save you there. That was part of the game. Whether I wanted to or not, I had to do it. But you can't save me because it isn't part of the game."

"So does that mean I'm more important than you?" said Julius. "More important to this 'game,' as you call it, than you?"

"I don't know," said Jill with a shrug. "I suspect that whoever designed our universe meant for it to happen. I used to think there must be a way around it, maybe some glitch I hadn't exploited, but I soon accepted it for what it was."

"Still isn't right," said Julius. He looked at me and Alicia with pleading eyes. "You two agree with me, right? This whole thing, ending with her death? No matter how you cut it, someone as good as Jill doesn't deserve to die even if it is for the greater good and even if it isn't permanent."

Alicia clutched her staff tighter than ever. "I agree that Jill shouldn't have to die, but ... like Jill said, it's unavoidable. I just don't see what we can do about it."

"Ali has a point," I said. "I don't think Jill deserves to die, either, but as Jill said, it's just part of the game."

"It's the only way we can deal with this 00glitch," Jill said, before Julius could respond to either of us. "Defeating the Lord of the Silver Blades is probably the only way we can save our world. And that means I am going to have to die."

Julius's lower lip trembled, but he didn't cry or let any tears escape from his eyes. "Just isn't fair. No matter how you cut it."

Jill walked past Julius, brushing against his arm as she did so. "That may be so, Julius, but that doesn't mean we can do anything about it."

Chapter 4

Julius took up the rear as we continued on our journey to Tall Roots. He kept his head down for most of it, not even muttering under his breath. When we were ambushed by a group of twig-fingers—monkey-like humanoids with twigs for fingers, very annoying due to their speed and evasion, though not particularly strong—he didn't participate in the fight at all, forcing Jill to kill the whole lot of them by herself. Alicia tried to get him to talk to her, but he brushed off all her attempts to comfort him and acted as sullen and depressed as a child who had just been told that his favorite puppy had died.

Not that I blamed him. The idea that Jill would have to die cast a dark shadow on my outlook. While I still grieved the loss of Long River, I had always assumed that at least our victory over the Lord of the Silver Blades would be happy, maybe even happy enough to make up for the loss of my hometown.

Yet, if Jill was telling the truth—and she spoke so plainly, so unpretentiously, that I had to conclude she was—then our victory, though inevitable, would likely be bittersweet at best.

We would defeat the Lord of the Silver Blades, rescue the six Omega Crystals, and possibly even stop the Glitch that was ravaging our world. All good things.

But we would also lose a good friend, our best friend, the one who had brought us all together in the first place. And that was a heavy price to pay, even for the salvation of the world. Even if the 'death' wasn't going to be permanent, it still seemed needlessly cruel.

That caused me to reflect on the Controller. He clearly did not care about her, otherwise he would have saved her. He walked her to her death because it was part of the 'game,' as Jill had said he called it. Did the being even look upon us as real? Or did he see all of us as being pieces in his little game, to be disposed of or used as he saw fit? And just what was his relation to the Five Stars, if he was above them?

These thoughts still lingered in my mind when we turned a corner and found ourselves standing just outside the gates of Tall Roots. Tall Roots was the biggest city in the First Continent, which didn't mean much because the First Continent didn't have a whole lot of cities, much less big ones. It had been built in the middle of the Long Forest centuries ago by a man named Talos Rutes, who, in a supreme act of humility and deference to the Five Stars, named the city after himself, with a slight alteration in spelling to make it even more humble.

We had already visited Tall Roots before. It had been shortly after Jill and I met and agreed to travel together. Some of the Lord of the Silver Blades' men had stolen the First Omega Crystal and we pursued them all the way to this city. It was here that we first met the Lord of the Silver Blades, who effortlessly defeated us by tapping the power of the First Omega Crystal, a memory that I had not thought of in a long time, mostly because our defeat had been so humiliating.

That had been months ago. Tall Roots looked about the same as it had back then: Smooth stone walls, with nary a foothold or handhold with which to climb, towered over us, with the tips of wooden buildings and trees sticking out over the top. A large cast iron gateway was the only way in and out of the city, and it was currently closed shut, with a single guardsman in wooden armor carrying a hatchet standing in front of it.

I recognized the guardsman immediately, though he had a very nondescript appearance. When Jill and I had first come here, he had been an annoying roadblock on our way to retrieve the First Omega Crystal from the Lord of the Silver Blades' minions. He only let us through after a lengthy interrogation in which he accused us, among other things, of being spies from some neighboring city. I had hoped to never see him again, but sadly enough, we would probably have to convince him to let us into the city before we could enter.

"Halt," said the guardsman, holding up his hatchet, forcing us to stop about two dozen feet away from the guardsman. "State your names and your business."

"Jill Franklin," Jill said. Then, pointing to each of us in turn, she said, "Dale Bennett, Alicia Bangs, and Julius Manna. We're just passing through."

The guardsman peered through the slits in his wooden helmet which acted as eye holes, like he didn't believe Jill's excuse, even though it was technically true. "Just passing through, hmm? Why do you two have weapons, then?"

He pointed at Starblade and Skull-cruncher. "Those don't look like the equipment of peaceful travelers 'just passing through.'"

"The Long Forest is a dangerous place," said Jill. She gripped the Starblade's hilt and said, "They're for our protection."

The guardsman bore a deeply skeptical look in his eyes, but then he nodded and said, "Fine. But if you use any of those weapons for trouble, I will personally make sure that you two spend the night in prison."

The guardsman sounded quite serious, but I didn't feel frightened or intimidated by him at all. Both Jill and Julius were strong enough to slay adult dragons. A simple guardsman in wooden armor likely would not last even five minutes in a straight fight against either of them, and that was assuming they went easy on him.

So the guardsman turned and walked over to the gates, but then he froze mid-stride. He didn't move even one inch. It was like he was posing for a statue; actually, the more I thought about it, the more I realized that it was like he had actually *become* a statue. At first I thought maybe he had forgotten something, but as time passed and he still didn't move, dread filled my soul.

"Uh oh," said Alicia. "What happened to him?"

Jill walked up to the guardsman and walked around him, her eyes scanning his still form. "The Glitch got him. It froze him. He may not even be aware of the world around him. He might as well be dead."

I jumped back when she said that, putting as much distance between myself and the frozen guardsman as possible. "If he's glitched, then why the hell are you getting so close to him? What if you get glitched, too?"

"Glitches aren't contagious," said Jill, though she did step away from the guardsman as she said that. "Still, it means that the

Glitch is farther along than I first thought. We'll have to hurry."

"Hurry?" said Julius, scowling. He looked at the gates. "The gates are closed shut and only the guardsman can open them. What do you suggest we do, climb over the walls like a bunch of tree-fingers?"

Jill didn't answer. Instead, she walked over to the gates to inspect them, while I carefully drew closer to the guardsman. He didn't move an inch, even when I got up right behind him. His right foot was in front of him and his hatchet was swinging from his belt like a tree-finger from a vine. I slowly circled him, giving the glitched guard a wide berth, to get a good look at his face. Like the rest of his body, his expression was frozen, a scowl on his face that rivaled Julius's in terms of anger.

"Will he be this way forever?" I said, looking over my shoulder at Jill, who was still inspecting the gates.

"No idea," said Jill. "Might be this way forever, might un-glitch at any moment. Who knows? Like I said, I've never seen this glitch before, so I don't know exactly what it does or how long it lasts or anything like that."

Alicia had come up to the guard by now, but she kept a greater distance from him than me. Unlike me, however, Alicia didn't look frightened, but merely curious.

"I wonder," said Alicia in a low voice. "Could I use my magic to heal him?"

"I wouldn't try that," I said, taking several large steps back from the glitched guard. "There's no telling what might happen if your magic mixes with that glitch. Better to leave him alone."

"But what if I *can* heal him?" said Alicia. She raised her staff and said, "Just a simple cure spell. If it works, then he'll be able to let us into the city."

I grabbed her staff and tried to lower it. "And if it doesn't, you might somehow make things worse."

Alicia shook my hand off her staff and glared at me. "Don't touch my staff. Anyway, what could it hurt? At worst, it might not do anything."

"At worst, you could get yourself killed," I said. "Or maybe get us harmed or make the Glitch worse or whatever."

"I'll do what I want," said Alicia. "There's nothing you can do to stop me anyway."

Before I could tell her how childish she was being, Alicia's staff glowed with a bright white light. An orb of bright energy shot out of her staff's tip and floated around the glitched guard, covering him in healing dust. I held my breath, watching the orb drop more and more healing dust over the guard, praying silently to the Five Stars to spare me from the inevitable chaos that was about to ensue.

The white orb then disappeared and with it, the healing dust. I counted to five, but the glitched guard didn't appear to do anything. He simply stood there, looking like the Colossus of the Far North.

"See?" said Alicia, flashing a 'I told you so' smirk at me. "It didn't do anything bad. You were just—"

Then, without warning, the glitched guard flew straight up into the air. Alicia shrieked and stumbled backward, grabbing me as she did so and causing us both to fall into the muddy path beneath our feet. Shaking my head, I looked up just in time to see the glitched guard—now little more than a tiny pinprick in the deep blue sky—vanish completely. He did not return.

Julius walked up to us, looking straight up into the sky in the direction the guard had flown in. "Uh … what was that?"

"I … I don't know," said Alicia, trembling as though she had just witnessed the scariest thing in her life. "I cast a cure spell on the guy and he just suddenly flew up into the air without warning. I think my healing spell must have interacted with the Glitch in a weird way or something."

"That's one way of putting it," said Julius. "I've never seen a guardsman fly before. And honestly, I don't think I ever want to again."

I got to my feet and then helped Alicia to hers as I said, "Do you think he's ever going to come back down? How will we explain to the Mayor that his guard is probably in the Highest Heavens by now and there's nothing we can do to save him?"

"I dunno," said Julius with a shrug. "It'll be one of those things we fix when we defeat the Lord of the Silver Blades. The Mayor doesn't need to know."

"Okay, but that still doesn't explain how we're going to get beyond the gates," said Alicia, gesturing at the gateway as she did so. "The guard was the only one who could open them, right? Doesn't that mean we're locked out of Tall Roots?"

I fell to my knees as the implication of Alicia's question hit me like a sledge hammer. Sinking my face into my hands, I said, "You are absolutely right, Alicia. We can't get into Tall Roots without that guard's help. And if we can't get into Tall Roots, then we can't get to Three Hundred Towers in a timely manner, which means that the Glitch will likely destroy the whole world and all of our striving will be for naught."

"Guys?" said Jill's voice from behind me. "What are you

doing?"

"Mourning our world," I answered, without looking back at her. "It is all we can do at this point."

Then Julius, the ruffian, grabbed me by my shoulders and hoisted me to my feet. "Stop your whining. Jill's already gotten through the gates."

I had opened my mouth to rebuke Julius for manhandling me, but as soon as I heard him say that, I brushed his brutish hands off my shoulders and turned to see for myself if his claim was true.

Miracles of miracles, Julius was right. Jill stood on the other side of the gates, gesturing for us to follow her. I could not see any way that she could have gotten through them, as they were still shut tightly and Jill had no keys or lock picks on her. Nor could she have climbed the gates, either, as they were too tall and sleek for anyone to climb over.

Alicia, Julius, and I hurried over to the gates.

"Jill, how did you do that?" I asked, dusting the mud off my hands and knees as we came to a stop in front of the gates. "Could you always do this or did you just find out about it now?"

"Just found out about it now," said Jill. She gestured at us. "It doesn't seem to have any negative effects on me, so I think it's safe for you guys to walk through, too."

"Uh, Jill?" said Julius, looking at the wrought iron gates before us. "These gates are solid iron. We can't just walk through them."

"They may appear that way, but I can assure you they're not," said Jill. "See?"

She thrust her hand through the bars. It passed straight through the gates as if they weren't there before Jill pulled it back through and stepped back from the gates.

"I think it's the Glitch," said Jill, as way of explanation. "For once, it's actually beneficial. You can walk straight through the gates without worry about getting hurt or anything."

"Really?" said Alicia. "That's convenient. Why can't the Glitch be this useful all the time?"

So Alicia, Julius, and I passed through the gates. I expected to feel at least the solid iron texture of the gates as we passed, but it was almost like the gates weren't there at all. In fact, if I had not seen the gates with my own two eyes, I could have sworn to you that we had simply passed through air and nothing more. It was an eerie feeling, to say the least.

Jill stood aside and watched us all pass through, then she looked to the other side of the gates and frowned. "Where'd the guard go?"

"To the Highest Heavens," Julius said, his tone sardonic.

Jill shook her head and turned to face the city itself. "I guess it doesn't matter. He'll be back once we beat the game. Which shouldn't be long, now that we're in Tall Roots."

As usual, Jill took off down the main street. As I and the other two followed, I took this time to look at the city of Tall Roots itself. After all, this might be the last time I would ever see this city, so I decided to savor this moment while I could.

Unlike the large cities on the other Continents, Tall Roots was an almost perfect harmony of humanity's creations intertwined with nature's children. From the roofs of tall stone buildings hung tree branches with small, shiny leaves that gleamed in the sunlight, while bridges made from dozens of tree branches grown together crossed from building to building. Some of the trees had houses built into them, leaving the only way into or out of them a ladder or staircase, depending on the house in question.

The streets were paved with stone and covered with green leaves of every kind that grew in the Long Forest: Kardia leaves, green blades, estrellas, and all of the rest. They crunched softly underneath our feet, a musical sound under normal circumstances, but today it wasn't quite as soothing. Probably because I kept remembering how the guard just flew up into the sky. It was a striking mental image.

As for the people of Tall Roots, they were rather peaceful and nonthreatening in comparison to the guard from before. They wore pants made of cotton, but their shirts were made out of a kind of plant found somewhere in the Long Forest that I could never remember the name of. The Rootians, as they were called, had darker skin than I did, similar in shade to Julius's skin, except even blacker. There weren't too many Rootians out today, and none of them stopped us or seemed to recognize us, but that was okay because we were rather in a hurry and didn't have time to spare for even a quick chat.

We passed through the center of Tall Roots, past the courthouse, a magnificent structure with a huge flowering pink tree on top of it. The courthouse brought back bad memories to me, as that had been the place where we had first met—and lost to—the Lord of the Silver Blades. I wondered if Jill remembered, but then realized that she probably not only remembered, but could recall the scene in vivid detail, too. After all, she had no doubt experienced it countless times, which suddenly explained why she had not seemed as crushed by our initial defeat at the time as I had been.

THE LAST LEGEND: GLITCH APOCALYPSE

As we turned down a corner, the courthouse vanishing from view, Julius said, "Jill, where are we going? You said we were going to find a new way to get to Three Hundred Towers. Where is it?"

"In the city," said Jill. "It's a shortcut."

"Shortcut?" said Julius. "That doesn't make any sense. Three Hundred Towers is on the Sixth Continent. We're on the First. There's no 'shortcut' from here to there, at least not without the *Starry Night*."

"Just trust me," said Jill. "It's another glitch."

"Glitch?" said Alicia, her eyes widening in fear as she looked over her shoulder. "But I thought glitches were bad."

"Not all glitches are," said Jill, shaking her head as we turned down an alleyway between two buildings. "Some glitches are entirely harmless. And a few, like the one we're about to use, are almost entire beneficial."

"Beneficial?" I said. "How so?"

Jill abruptly came to a stop and signaled for us to do the same. "We're here."

Alicia, Julius, and I looked around at where we had stopped. We stood in a cramped, tiny little alleyway between two massive buildings. The buildings and the trees on top of them blocked out the sunlight, making the whole place feel like a tiny cave in a mountain somewhere. A wall stood at the end of the alley, meaning that the only exit available to us was the path from which we had just come. On the building to our right, the words *E.R. WAS HERE* was painted on in bright blue colors, but I had no idea who this 'E.R.' fellow was or what was so important about him being here that he had to vandalize someone else's property to make sure everyone in the world knew he had been here.

"Remember this place, Dale?" said Jill, turning to look at me, her face half-obscured in the shadows. "When we first arrived here?"

I thought about it for a moment and then it all came back to me. "Yes. If I recall correctly, when we first arrived in this city a few months ago, we explored every nook and cranny in the city. Unnecessarily, I might add."

"We found some hidden items, didn't we?" said Jill. "I'd hardly call our exploration 'unnecessary.' But anyway, remember how we came to this alley and I said there was nothing here and we should go?"

I nodded. "Yes."

"Well, I lied," said Jill. She gestured at the back wall and said, "This alley is home to a benevolent glitch. Assuming I do it right, I can go from here to anywhere I want in all of Kinar. Including to Three Hundred Towers."

"You're kidding," said Julius. "That's impossible."

"Normally, it is," said Jill in agreement. "But I assure you that, if you do it right, it should work just fine. Assuming, of course, that the other Glitch hasn't interfered with it in some way."

"So what do we need to do to access this glitch?" said Alicia. "Is it complicated or difficult?"

"Actually, it's quite easy," said Jill. "I've used it before, in past runs. The being who controls me showed me how to do it. All I need to do is walk into this one corner and it will glitch me through and into the Sixth Continent directly into the heart of Three Hundred Towers itself."

Julius stepped back, eying the alley with suspicious eyes. "It can't be that easy."

Jill chuckled. "You said those exact words in the last run when I used this glitch. Guess some things never change."

"I did?" said Julius.

"All of this talk of past runs is making me confused and anxious," said Alicia. "Why don't we just use this glitch and get going? I just want things to go back to the way they were."

"Even if it means Jill's death?" said Julius, looking at Alicia in surprise.

"Julius, we've already talked about this," said Jill with a sigh. "It will be okay. My death isn't really permanent and it doesn't really hurt. It's not worth getting worked up over."

Julius bit his lower lip, like he had a lot to say about that, but he just grunted and said, "All right. But Jill, if I can think of a way—*any* way—to save you, I won't hesitate to do it, even if Three-Hundred Towers itself is falling apart all around us."

Jill smiled, as if to say that that was a nice, but ultimately pointless, thought. At least, that's what I read in it, and because she had basically said the same thing to Julius earlier, I saw no reason to doubt my reading of her smile.

Then Alicia whipped her head to the right, looking like a startled rabbit. "Am I the only one who heard that?"

"Heard what?" said Jill.

Alicia stepped toward the way we had come, holding her staff before her. "It sounds like … like someone screaming."

I listened as hard as I could. At first I heard nothing, but then slowly, a loud scream grew closer and closer to our alleyway. It was a scream of fear and pain, as though the screamer was under attack. It was the first time I had ever heard this kind of screaming in Tall Roots and just listening to it made me freeze where I stood as I tried to figure out what might have caused it.

"Do people normally scream in Tall Roots?" said Julius, his knuckles white because of how tight he was gripping his ax. "'Cause that doesn't sound entirely normal to me."

While the scream grew louder and more painful, Jill turned and began walking to the right hand corner of the alley, saying as she did so, "We have to keep going. Whatever it is, we probably can't deal with it right now."

"But someone's in trouble," Julius said. "Aren't we supposed to help people in trouble? Thought that was one of the things we did."

Jill stopped and looked at Julius with tired eyes. "Julius, please, we don't have time for this. It might be the Glitch killing that person; if so, there's nothing we can do to help them except defeat the Lord of the Silver Blades and reset the game."

"I want to go check," said Julius, running back up the alley the way we had come. "I'll be back in a sec!"

Before any of us could stop him, Julius was out of the alley and out of sight, the heel of his boot the last thing we saw before he turned the corner and vanished.

Jill pulled at her hair and sighed in frustration. She muttered, low enough so only I could hear, "Goddammit, Julius."

"Are we going to go after him?" Alicia asked. "Or are we going to wait here for him to come back?"

"We'll have to go after him," said Jill, walking back up the alley in the same direction that Julius had ran off. "We can't beat the game if we don't have him with us. Besides, I don't want him to get caught by the Glitch. No telling what might happen to him if he does."

Remembering the frozen guard who flew into the sky, I nodded and said, "Yes. Let's go find Julius before he ends up falling into the ground or something."

Just before we moved to leave, another scream pierced the air, a long, loud, masculine scream that could not be mistaken for the scream of anyone but Julius.

Chapter 5

Rushing out of the alley like wind, it took us precious seconds to find Julius. Precious seconds that we didn't have to waste.

Just down the street from where we stood, Julius stood near the entrance of an item shop, his muscles bulging as he held Skull-cruncher firmly in hand, but he was hardly alone. A strange creature with octopus-like tentacles had cornered him, its tentacles flailing through the air like whips as it beat on him.

I had never seen a monster quite like it before. It was purple and black, same colors as a black eye, with the fore and hind legs of a horse. It had no head or upper body, except for a queer blob that glowed a soft purple light from within. It reminded me of the giant squids of the Deep Ocean, but it was so different that I doubted they were related.

Additionally, the creature didn't seem quite ... natural. It was hard to describe, but sometimes, whenever it hit Julius, its tentacles would slash through him. Other times, its body would seem to ... how to describe it ... shift, for want of a better term. Its texture and fur would bug out, occasionally becoming a hodgepodge of odd colors and textures before returning to its original design. Just watching it was enough to make me feel sick, like I was viewing a bunch of flashing colors over which I had little control.

A dead Rootian lay at its feet; at least, I assumed she was dead, because even though she wasn't breathing, her body occasionally jerked and twitched. It was like watching a talentless puppeteer trying to make a puppet do his bidding. Her legs especially twitched unnaturally, often bending in ways that made me cringe.

"What in the name of the Five Stars is *that*?" Alicia asked, her voice little more than a high-pitched shriek.

Jill drew the Starblade as she said, "A glitch. Probably the result of the Glitch from earlier."

"You mean like a servant of the Glitch?" I said. "Is that even possible?"

"It's here, isn't it?" said Jill. "You two stand back. I'm going to save Julius before that thing finishes him off."

"But what if it kills you?" said Alicia. "We don't know what that glitched monster is capable of. It might—"

"I can't just abandon him," said Jill. "That's not how the game works. He has to be there. He plays an important role in the defeat of the Lord of the Silver Blades. Extremely important."

"Then go save him," I said, pointing at Julius, who was still getting beaten into pulp by the monster. "Don't just stand there. We'll be fine right here."

Jill didn't even nod to show that she had heard me. She just ran toward the creature, the Starblade glowing in her hands, as fast as she could, a look of steely determination in her eyes. I had to admit that, like Alicia, I wasn't sure if Jill could beat the glitched creature, but I didn't want Julius to die, either, especially if he played an important role in the defeat of the Lord of the Silver Blades.

The strange creature didn't notice Jill until she was right behind him. She brought the Starblade up in an upwards slash, striking the creature with enough force that it should have killed the monster instantly.

But the monster, without turning to look at her, just slapped at Jill with its tentacles. She dodged the tentacles rather skillfully, however, and responded with another slash of the Starblade. This one cut off one of its own tentacles, which somehow caused the tentacle to vanish into thin air as a result.

This clearly angered the monster because it turned away from Julius—who fell to his hands and knees, panting hard from the blows he had taken—and began advancing on Jill. Now that the creature was facing us, I could see that it had two green lights glowing from within it that might have been its eyes. I wondered if Jill noticed them, but as she was busy trying not to die, I concluded that she probably did not.

The creature lashed out with all of its tentacles, but Jill jumped over them. As she leaped over the monster, she slashed at it, cutting a gaping wound in its back that caused the monster to roar in pain. When Jill landed behind it, however, the creature bucked its hind legs, striking Jill in the chest and sending her staggering backward from the blow.

Whirling around, the monster stomped its front legs and charged at Jill with the unforgiving speed and ferocity of a lightning tiger. Despite having taken what had obviously been a devastating hit to the chest, Jill slid out of the monster's way, cutting through its body as it passed.

Then something strange happened. The Starblade blinked in and out of existence several times before its glowing white blade vanished completely, leaving only its ornately carved handle in Jill's hand.

A look of shock spread over Jill's face as she looked at the hilt, saying as she did so, "What—?"

The monster, however, was not as surprised as she was. It turned around and slapped at her again, prompting me to shout, "Jill, look out!"

Jill looked up just in time to see the monster's tentacles fly at her, but it was too late for her to dodge. The tentacles—all two dozen of them—slapped Jill in the face and body, hitting her so hard that she was sent flying. She crashed into the door of a nearby building and did not get up again.

"Jill!" Alicia screamed, but it was no use because Jill remained unconscious on the street even as the monster advanced on her, its tentacles pounding the street as it did so.

I bit my fingernails as I tried to think of some way we could save Jill, but nothing came to mind. Of course, I could sing some songs to inflict certain status conditions on the monster, but I had no idea how my songs might affect the glitched monster. They could easily backfire, maybe even destroy us all. Yet I had to do something, otherwise there was no telling what might happen to Jill.

Just before I could decide which song to use, Julius jumped out of nowhere and brought his ax down on the monster's head. The monster didn't have time to react. Julius's ax cut straight through the monster's skull, cleaving it as easily as butter, and when Julius landed, he followed it up with another slash from Skull-cruncher, cutting off at least a dozen of its tentacles with one clean strike.

The monster roared in anger, but Julius gave it no time to do anything. His whole body glowing red, Julius slashed again and again at the monster, each blow carving off another chunk of its body, his attacks becoming more and more relentless as time went on. Each slice generated an immense amount of heat, simultaneously burning the monster as he cut it to pieces.

I had no trouble recognizing the condition Julius was in. As a Warrior, Julius had access to a mode called 'Berserker mode.' He could not access this mode at will, but only when he was near death and needed an extra boost in strength.

He must have been beaten pretty badly by the glitched monster to enter Berserker mode, which was both good and bad. Good because it meant he was nigh unstoppable, as I had never seen him lose in Berserker mode. Bad because he sometimes also attacked us, as the power that flowed through him in Berserker mode made it difficult for him to distinguish between friend and foe.

Thankfully, this time his anger was focused solely on his foe. The monster screeched and roared, but it was powerless to stand against Julius's onslaught. He kept reducing its size chunk by chunk, like a butcher cleaving meat, until soon there was nothing left of the glitched monster but its orb-like head. Even that did not survive long, because when Julius brought his ax down on it, the entire thing dissipated into nothingness.

I fully expected Julius to keep going, but to my surprise, the red glow that signaled his Berserker state faded and his shoulders slumped. This was probably the result of the pain he had received earlier catching up with him. He then fell face first onto the pavement, his body as still as Jill's.

Obviously, Alicia and I didn't just stand there and stare. Without saying a word, we both ran over to Jill and Julius to make sure they were all right. There wasn't much I could do, being a Bard who didn't have any healing magic, but I wanted to be there for my friends anyway and support them however I could. Better than sitting around and feeling useless, at any rate.

As soon as we reached our fallen friends, Alicia went to work. She looked over their bodies and cast healing spells on them, while I stood by and watched anxiously. I tried to avoid looking at the dead Rootian, whose corpse was still jerking around every now and then, just so I could think positively for a while.

In just a couple of minutes, both Jill and Julius were awake. Jill sat upright against the building she had been thrown against, rubbing her forehead, which she said still hurt, while Julius sat beside her, sweat running down his head and body like he had run a mile.

"Thanks for healing us, Ali," said Julius, looking up at Alicia, who was looking down at them with worried eyes. "Thought I was a goner there for a second."

"That's what you get for running off without waiting for us," said Jill, glaring at him. "What were you thinking? That glitched monster would have killed you if we hadn't—"

"Stepped in and nearly get yourself killed, too?" Julius said, not backing down despite Jill's rather intimidating glare. "Listen, Jill, I understand you wanted to help, but I had the creature entirely under control."

I cast a skeptical glance in the direction of the dead Rootian, whose legs twitched. "It sure looked like you didn't."

"I just underestimated its strength," Julius protested. "I was just about to enter Berserker mode when you guys arrived. I mean, I still got to do it anyway, but if I had done it before you guys got there, then Jill might not have been hurt."

"It was still foolish," said Jill. "There's no telling what that glitched monster could have done to you. Look what it did to the Starblade."

Jill raised its hilt, prompting Julius to say, "What happened to it? Is it invisible?"

Jill slapped Julius in the face with the hilt, causing him to rub his face as she said, "No, you idiot. The Starblade's blade is *gone*. It's nothing more than a useless bit of metal now and it's all your fault."

"My fault?" said Julius, still rubbing his face as he scowled. "How the hell is it is *my* fault? You were the one who used the Starblade to attack it, not me."

"It's your fault because I wouldn't have had to use it if you had just left the damn beast alone," Jill snapped. "Now we're without the most powerful weapon in the game, the weapon that would have ensured our victory over the Lord of the Silver Blades."

Alicia scratched the back of her neck. "Hey, it's not all bad, right? I mean, all we need to do is get the second best sword and you can use that. You remember how to defeat the Lord of the Silver Blades, don't you?"

"Yes, but it is much harder to defeat him when without the Starblade," said Jill. "The Starblade always deals massive damage to the Lord of the Silver Blades. That's why I always go get it when I'm about to defeat him. But now, it's useless."

As if to emphasize that point, Jill tossed the hilt onto the street before her. The hilt clanked against the leaves, but Alicia quickly swiped it up and put it in her bag. Zipping the bag shut, Alicia noticed me looking at her and said, "What? It might be useful for something down the road."

"Right," I said. "Well then, should we get going, Jill? To the shortcut that will take us directly to Three Hundred Towers?"

Jill slowly stood up, using the building's wall as support, a bitter scowl on her face. "Yeah, I guess so. We'll have to buy a new sword for me in Three Hundred Towers before we go on to confront the Lord of the Silver Blades himself, however. I can't go into battle weaponless."

"How much gold do we got, Dale?" Julius asked as he too stood up, though with less difficulty than Jill. "Enough to buy a sword for Jill?"

As well as being a Bard, I was the unofficial treasurer of the team. I pulled out our group wallet and peered inside it briefly at the gold standards in it, coins with the face of the Old King engraved on them, his stern eyes glaring up at me as if I had just gotten in trouble.

"Let's see ..." I said. "We have ten thousand golden standards. How much do swords cost in Three Hundred Towers?"

"We'll find out when we get there," said Jill. "Come on. We've wasted enough time as it is. I don't want to waste anymore."

In no time at all we reached the old alleyway again, the words *E.R. WAS HERE* still written uselessly on the building to our right. Jill walked over to the right corner at the far end, with the rest of us following closely behind so we would not get stuck here in Tall Roots. I didn't want to end up like that poor dead Rootian from earlier, the one whose corpse was still twitching and jerking even as we left.

"All right," said Jill. "Everyone, I want you to hold hands. This glitch is not the most reliable glitch in the game and it sometimes messes up. I don't want to lose anyone because all of us are needed in order to defeat the Lord of the Silver Blades."

"How, exactly, does it mess up sometimes?" I asked. "Some specifics would be nice."

"It doesn't always take you where you want it to take you," said Jill. "Sometimes, it'll send you to the Second Continent, sometimes to the Third, and sometimes to this strange glitchy world that has no name. I've learned from experience that it's better to be safe than sorry with this particular glitch."

"A strange glitchy world?" said Julius. "Is it painful?"

"Sometimes," said Jill. "Most of the time, no. Most of the time, if you've been in it for a while, you just start to think that you're losing your mind."

"Can you escape the glitchy world if you get stuck in it?" Alicia said, an alarmed look on her face.

Jill shook her head. "No. You have to wait for the Controller to restart the game. Otherwise, you're stuck there forever, which is why I generally do my best to avoid it."

"You're sure there isn't a safer way to travel to Three Hundred Towers?" I asked. "A way that doesn't involve the possibility of being stuck in some bizarro world forever?"

"Well, we could walk," Jill said. "All the way across the Six

Continents, taking the occasional boat between Continents when we reach the sea. Granted, that would take a long time and there's a good chance that the Glitch would get us well before we ever got to Three Hundred Towers, but at least we wouldn't have to worry about being stuck forever, right?"

I realized she was right. So, without further questioning, I grabbed Alicia's hand, who grabbed Julius's hand, who in turn grabbed Jill's. Jill did a quick check to make sure we were all holding hands, and once she was certain that we were, she said, "All right. It's going to seem a bit strange at first, but as long as you don't panic and let go, we should make it to Three Hundred Towers just fine."

All three of us nodded that we understood. Alicia and Julius didn't look worried and I tried not to look worried, either, but it was very difficult for me not to focus on Jill's warnings. The idea of getting stuck forever in some inescapable bizarro world made me woozier than I'd like to admit. I just redoubled my grip on Alicia's hand as Jill stepped forward toward the corner as casually as if it wasn't there.

Then Jill passed through the corner, followed by Julius, and then Alicia, and then, finally, me. It felt like passing through the gates earlier, which was to say, it felt like walking through nothing at all.

And then everything went completely black. Not dark. Black. I could still feel solid ground underneath my feet, still feel Alicia's fingernails digging tightly into my hand, but I could not see anything except for Alicia, Julius, and Jill. The blackness around us reminded me of what Long River looked like now, which was almost enough to make me panic.

"Where are we?" Julius asked, looking around at the empty blackness in which we walked. "Is this some kind of alternate universe or something?"

"I call it the Dark World," said Jill. "It's another layer of the world, located underneath everything. It's inaccessible to most people, but this glitch allows you to walk through it like any other part of the game."

"Creepy," said Julius. Then he looked up and started. "What the heck?"

I looked up as well and suddenly wished I hadn't. Above us, I could see the entirety of Tall Roots, even see the dead Rootian from before, still twitching as badly as ever. The streets were transparent, it seemed, because I did not see them. Nor did I see the floors of the buildings. It looked like the city was floating above us, sort of like the Floating City of the Angelians, except creepier.

"Jill, why can we see all of Tall Roots above us?" said Alicia. Her voice was very small, like she had almost forgotten how to use it.

Jill glanced up as casually as if Alicia had pointed out an interesting bird had just flown by. "Like I said, the Dark World is located underneath everything. We are literally underneath not just Tall Roots, but the entirety of Kinar. It's absolutely massive, but you don't need an Aircraft or ship to travel between the Continents."

"How come no one can see us?" I said, pointing at the transparent streets. "We can see them, so why can't they see us?"

"Very simple," said Jill. "The Dark World is hidden to normal people. I don't understand exactly how it all works, but I do know that they can't interact with us. The streets work sort of like a two-way mirror, from what I understand."

"So we don't have to worry about the entire city falling and crushing us?" said Alicia.

"Of course," said Jill. "We're perfectly safe here. Even the Lord of the Silver Blades can't get us here."

"But how did we get down here anyway?" said Julius. "I didn't feel us fall. Felt like we just walked right on through."

"Physics don't work exactly the same down here as they do up there," said Jill, nodding at Tall Roots above us. "Anyway, this should help us get to Three Hundred Towers far more quickly than normal. There are literally no obstacles here to get in our way and slow us down. Just remember to keep holding hands and we should reach Three Hundred Towers with no problem."

"If we get separated, could we reunite again?" Alicia asked.

Jill frowned. "Yes, I think so, but it is very, very difficult. If any of you wander off, there's no telling where you might end up. As I said, this place is absolutely massive. When I first used this glitch, I got lost for hours, just wandering the Dark World, mostly because the Controller decided that he wanted to explore it as much as he could. I nearly went mad."

I looked around the Dark World, imagining Jill wandering around here for hours and hours. There were no distinctive landmarks or features, no people aside from us. It didn't even have a horizon. It was like staring into a deep, dark, black void from which nothing could ever escape. No wonder Jill said that she nearly went mad. I had no doubt in my mind that I would react the exact same way, if put in the same situation.

"Weren't we with you the first time?" Julius asked. "How did we react to it?"

"Pretty much exactly like how you're reacting now," said Jill. "Only I didn't know how to answer your questions because I was just as ignorant about this place as you guys. And to be honest, I still don't know as much as I'd like."

"Let's keep going," Alicia suggested, tearing her gaze away from the street-less city above to look at Jill. "I don't like this place."

"I don't see what's so scary about it," said Julius as Jill began walking, forcing us to follow. "Yeah, it's big and black and empty of pretty much everything, but the Glitch isn't down here and there aren't any other dangers. If anything, I'd say this place is extremely boring. There's literally nothing to do down here except walk and walk and walk until you get sick of it."

"You don't find that the slightest bit creepy?" said Alicia. "Nothing for as far as the eye can see; heck, not even the wind blowing or anything, just blackness?"

Julius shrugged. "The Glitch is scary. This isn't. As long as we keep together, nothing bad should happen. Right, Jill?"

"Right, Julius," said Jill. "The most important thing is to stick together no matter what. Don't even think about letting go until we reach Three Hundred Towers."

So we walked for a long, long time. That is literally all we did. We walked in the general direction of the Sixth Continent, Jill pulling us along at a quick pace. The Dark World did not get any brighter, nor did it get any darker. It felt like walking in a dead world because nothing changed or grew. We didn't see or hear any monsters. Even the wind was absent from this place.

I found my attention wandering. I focused on Alicia's red hair, bobbing up and down as she walked, then focused on my pants knees, which were still dirty from when I had been mourning the world earlier. I was so bored that I was looking for something, anything, to focus on, but aside from me and my friends, the Dark World had nothing of interest to look at.

Sometimes I would look up, mostly to get an idea of where we were. We left the First Continent fairly quickly, which was largely due to the lack of obstacles in the Dark World. No hills for us to climb or forests for us to traverse or confusing city streets to navigate. We even walked underneath the Deep Ocean itself, but it was so far above us that I couldn't make out much except for a handful of large sea creatures and the occasional wide-bottomed ship. That was when I realized that Jill had been quite literal when she said that the Dark World was underneath *everything*.

No conversation escaped our lips during our journey. There was nothing to discuss or talk about. We held hands tightly, making sure not to let go, but if it had not been for the pressure of Alicia's hand in mine, I would have sworn we were all as dead as the Rootian who had been killed by the glitched monster.

It was shortly after we crossed the Fourth Continent and entered the waters between the Fourth and Fifth Continent that something gleaming caught my eye. Normally, I would not have cared, but with the complete lack of anything interesting to look at in the Dark World, even the simplest things were enough to catch my attention.

Looking in the direction of the gleam, I spotted what appeared to be a sword standing upright in the blackness. I didn't know why it was gleaming—there was no sun down here, after all—but it didn't really matter why. I was just glad, if slightly confused, to see something else down here besides endless blackness.

Of course, I didn't know what that sword was, but I knew that Jill could use swords. I didn't know why Jill wasn't paying attention to it, nor why she hadn't told the rest of us about it, but since the sword was right there for the taking, I decided to let her know about it.

"Jill," I said. "What's that sword over there?"

Jill stopped, forcing Julius, Alicia, and I to stop as well, and looked over her shoulder at me, a puzzled look on her features. "What sword?"

"That one," I said, pointing at the gleaming sword in the distance. "Right there. It's hard to miss."

Jill, Julius, and Alicia turned their heads in the direction of the sword, but while Julius and Alicia looked at it curiously, Jill's face paled the minute she lay her eyes on it. She immediately turned her head away from the sword and started marching forward, dragging along all three of us and making us almost stumble as we tried to keep up.

"Jill, did you see the sword?" Julius asked as he righted himself into an upright position as we walked. "Why are you walking so fast? Don't you want that sword? It looks pretty strong to me."

"It's not what it appears," said Jill. "I've seen that sword before. I'm not supposed to touch it. No one is supposed to touch it."

She spoke about the sword with the same tone that she would use to describe a person infected with a deadly virus. The answer didn't satisfy me, however, because it looked like a perfectly good sword to me and Jill, after all, was in need of a perfectly good sword.

So I said, "But why not? No one lives down here, so it can't possibly belong to anyone. It's not in a cage or a box or anything and it doesn't appear to be guarded by anyone or anything. You could walk over there right now and pluck it from the ground if you want."

"You don't think I've done that?" said Jill, glancing over her shoulder at me as we walked. "When I first entered the Dark World, that sword was one of the first things I saw. I tried to pick it up because I thought it might be useful and then ..."

She shuddered. "It was awful. I'll just leave it at that."

"'Awful' is rather vague," I said. "It's not like you died or anything, right?"

"That's true," said Jill. "But it was still an experience I'd rather not repeat. We can buy a sword for me in Three Hundred Towers. It's not a problem."

In truth, it *was* a problem. As the team's treasurer, I didn't like the idea of wasting our precious time buying a sword from some seedy merchant in Three Hundred Towers when there was a perfectly good sword right for the taking just a few yards away from us. Maybe something bad did happen the first time Jill tried to take it, but that had obviously been long ago. Maybe Jill had grabbed it wrong or maybe it was something else that had occurred at the exact same time she touched it, leading her to erroneously conclude that it had happened because of the sword she had grabbed. Correlation, after all, does not equal causation.

Yes, Jill did say that we're supposed to stick together at all times, but honestly, what would it hurt if I dashed over, grabbed the sword, and returned, all in less than a minute? I was not an adventuresome person, but I reasoned that grabbing a sword—even a basic sword like this one—was far from the most adventurous thing in the world. It wasn't even all that far away, anyway.

So, without telling any of the others, I slipped my hand out of Alicia's and ran toward the sword. I heard Jill shouting behind me, telling me to come back right this instant or else, but I didn't listen to her. She would thank me later, I reasoned, after I gave her a brand new sword with which she could defeat the Lord of the Silver Blades.

Reaching the sword took less than a minute. I stopped in front of it and stared at it for a brief second, in which I registered that it had a golden hilt, a blade that was as white as a pearl, and that it gleamed as brightly as if it had been left out on a sunny summer day. I heard Jill or one of the others running behind me, obviously trying to stop me, which meant I would have to hurry if I was going to get this sword for Jill.

Without further ado, I wrapped my fingers around the sword's hilt and pulled up.

And then everything went crazy.

Chapter 6

What felt like lightning traveled up my arm all the way to my brain. Everything around me spun around. The shouts from my friends became muted in my ears, sounding like little more than the buzzing of bees. The Dark World flickered in and out of existence, making my head spin. Every time I blinked, I saw something different; a statue somewhere in the Fourth Continent, the Deep Ocean, the Floating City, Black Blade Mountain, and then the Dark World again.

What was going on? Nothing made sense. I was so totally frozen with fear and confusion at what I saw that I was sure that I was going to die. Any minute now, I was certain I would be struck dead by whatever was causing all of this.

Then I felt something like two hands pushing me in the small of my back and I staggered forward. As soon as I did, the Dark World faded around me and I landed face first into a large pile of sand. The sand was hot and got into my eyes and lungs, making me cough as I stood up and dusted my face off. The sand was quite crusty, almost like a second layer of very rough skin, but I managed to get it all off without a problem.

Still coughing, I looked up at my surroundings to see where I was.

Sand—white as snow, blinding in the sunlight—stretched in every direction for as far as the eye could see. The hot rays of the Twin Suns beat down on my head, making my armpits sweat. A couple of old cacti stood nearby, but aside from those two things, I was the only living thing that could be seen. A hot wind blew through, stirring up some more sand and making me hack and cough even more violently than before.

I knew where I was. This had to be the Shayu Desert, located in the southern reaches of the Fifth Continent. My friends and I had come here in search of the Fifth Omega Crystal, because we had been told that the Fifth Omega Crystal was located in the ruins of a temple somewhere out here. Allegedly, the Fifth Omega Crystal had been lost for centuries, but we found it in less than a day, which either meant we were smarter than generations of explorers and archeologists or the person who told us that had simply been trying to discourage us for no reason.

Not that it mattered in the end because the Lord of the Silver Blades' highest ranking minion, the arrogant General Narkin, had beat us to it. Granted, we did give Narkin a good beating, but he had still gotten away with the Fifth Omega Crystal. That had not been a good day for us, to say the least.

The only question now was, where exactly in the Shayu Desert was I? The Shayu Desert was a huge place, almost as big as Wide Plains on the Second Continent. It was also quite empty, aside from some dangerous animals that lived here, plus the ever-present danger of marauding bands of nomads that had no qualms with raiding travelers who looked like they had some money on them (which was something I had learned from experience).

THE LAST LEGEND: GLITCH APOCALYPSE

To my knowledge, there were no cities or towns in the Shayu Desert, aside from the temporary settlements that the nomads created every now and then. Because those changed every few days, I couldn't count on stumbling onto any while I was here in the Desert.

Which meant that I was more or less on my own.

Wiping the sweat off my forehead, a golden gleam caught my attention out of the corner of my eye. A quick glance to the right showed me the sword from before, lying in the sand only a few feet away from me. It lay there innocently enough, but as the sword had been the thing that had gotten me in this situation, I wasn't so sure that I wanted to touch it.

That made me wonder what the heck happened to me. All I did was touch the sword. Why did that separate me from my friends and put me somewhere in the middle of the Shayu Desert? It made no sense. All I could figure was that the sword was behind it, but why, I didn't know.

In any case, I couldn't just leave the sword here. As dangerous as it may be, I was all alone in the Desert and could not rely on either Jill or Julius to protect me from the various dangers that infested this hellhole. I would therefore have to rely on myself, even though I was no fighter. Which meant I would need to take this sword with me, whatever dangers it might have posed to my well-being.

I approached the sword with the same cautious reverence that the priests in the Temple of the Stars approached the Astronomic Altar. The sword simply sat there, looking as innocent as any sword could look. Its blade still glowed, sort of like the Starblade, though now that it was exposed to the rays of the Twin Suns, it didn't gleam quite as brightly as before.

Then I slowly bent down and wrapped my fingers around the blade's hilt, fully expecting to be teleported again.

Nothing happened. I heaved the sword off the sand and examined it more closely.

It resembled the Starblade almost down to the last detail. The only major difference I could find was the name engraved on the hilt: *Test*.

What an odd name for a sword. Test. It held none of the beauty or elegance of the names of the other swords, such as Starblade, and wasn't even all that threatening, like the sword Demonkiller. Still, I knew better than to treat this sword lightly, having seen firsthand its reality-warping powers. Whether it would continue to warp reality or not, I didn't know, but I decided to keep it on me anyway for safekeeping. The sight of this sword alone might be enough to scare off potential enemies.

Then I looked around the area, trying to determine which direction would take me to Sandfall, a city on the northernmost edge of the Shayu Desert which had plenty of food and water. Unfortunately, every direction looked the same to me. I couldn't tell which direction was north, west, east, or south. The Twin Suns were up in the middle of the sky, which was frustrating because I could not tell from which direction they had risen or in which direction they were going to set.

I wondered where Jill, Julius, and Alicia were. Were they still in the Dark World? Or had the Test somehow teleported them, too? Could it have …? No, it probably hadn't killed them, but that didn't make me feel any better about their current condition.

It appeared that my only choice at this point was to pick a

direction at random and walk in it. I had no way of knowing which way was north, so at this point any direction was correct.

I began walking forward, dragging the sword along behind me in the sand, putting my left arm over my eyes to shield them from the glaring, angry rays of the Twin Suns.

I walked for hours without seeing any distinctive landmarks. The only significant difference I came across was a large sand dune which I was forced to walk around. I also found a couple more cacti, but as they were not very distinctive, they didn't help me figure out where I was in the slightest.

My throat grew drier and drier the more I walked. Sweat ran down my temples, forcing me to wipe it away several times. My Bard's Cloak felt hot and heavy under the Twin Suns, but I didn't take it off because I didn't want to expose my arms to the deadly rays of the Suns. Every step took a supreme effort due to how heavy my boots felt on my feet.

I did not run into any monsters or enemies, which I found strange, but for which I was also grateful. I was in no mood to have to defend myself from any monsters; in fact, there was a good chance that I would just get myself killed if I got into a battle. Yes, I had a sword, but as I did not know how to use it, it wasn't likely to be of much use to me in the event that I was ambushed or attacked.

Speaking of the Test, I began to question the wisdom of bringing it along. It had seemed like a great idea at the time, carrying a weapon to scare away potential attackers before they even tried anything, but now the Test felt like a glorified lump of metal. The heat made it seem heavier than it was, or maybe it actually was increasing in weight. More than once I seriously considered abandoning it here in the middle of the Desert, to be consumed by the sand and never to be found by mortals again, but as I was still paranoid about being attacked, I kept the Test with me.

Part of me hoped that Jill and the others would find me, but the more I walked, the more unlikely it seemed that they would ever find me. For all I knew, they could have just as easily been redistributed as I was. Maybe they were back on the First Continent. Or maybe they were somewhere else entirely.

All I knew was that I had to keep going, as uncomfortable and terrible as the heat may have been. Perhaps the only good thing about my current situation was that the Glitch was nowhere to be seen. It was probably still in the First Continent, slowly ravaging town after town for reasons I didn't know or understand.

As I climbed over yet another sand dune, I wondered what role I had to play in the defeat of the Lord of the Silver Blades. Jill was going to die and Julius was supposed to be important, but I didn't know what I was supposed to do or, for that matter, what Alicia was supposed to do, either. Were we as important as Julius? Could Jill, Julius, and Alicia go to the Sixth Continent and defeat the Lord of the Silver Blades without me having to be present?

If so, what was to stop them from abandoning me in favor of doing so? Wouldn't it make more sense to leave a deadweight like me behind when I did not play an important role in saving the world?

I shook my head. The heat was getting to me. I was starting to think crazy thoughts. Of course Jill and the others would come looking for me. Granted, they probably had no idea where to look for me, but I doubted they would simply give up and go on without me. Sooner or later they could come looking for me and everything would be righted in the end. We were friends. Best friends.

But … what if they didn't? What if they left me to die out here? What would I do then?

I just kept walking. These thoughts were not at all helpful. All I needed to do was reach Sandfall and from there I would probably head on to the Sixth Continent. No doubt Jill and the others were on their way there as well. I could meet up with them in Three Hundred Towers and then we could go and save the world, as we had done countless times in the past. Really, in the grand scheme of things this was only a temporary setback that would mean nothing in the future.

Then I crossed another sand dune and saw a sight I had never see in this vast desert before.

Tall, beautiful palm trees; crystal clear water, sparkling in the light of the Twin Suns; lush green grass, stretched out like a cat lazing in the afternoon Suns; and beautiful, juicy red fruit, hanging from the branches of the palm trees, a tempting sight to behold.

For a moment, I did not understand what I was seeing. An oasis in the middle of the Shayu Desert? When I and my friends first arrived here, we had been told that there were no oases in this desert. The natives of Sandfall had told us that all of the oases had been dried up in a great environmental cataclysm that happened centuries ago and that all of the water was located deep beneath the sand, well out of the reach of most humans. I distinctly recalled us stocking up on water prior to departing from Sandfall, as we hadn't been excited about the idea of dying of thirst while we searched for the Fifth Omega Crystal.

Yet here was an oasis, plain as the sand in my hair, sitting completely unguarded and out in the open for anyone to see or use. My initial reaction was that it might have been a hallucination. Such things were said to happen to travelers in the Shayu Desert. The Sandfallians had many tales of travelers— often foreigners who didn't understand the dangers of the Desert —seeing things that were not there as a result of the oppressive heat. On our initial trip into the Shayu Desert, Julius had mistakenly believed that a cactus was a water fountain (a mistake that forced us to spend at least an hour picking the pricks out of Julius's lips).

My instincts wanted me to go down and cool off, but I hesitated. I didn't like rushing into unexplainable things like this, even if they were good. If the oasis was a mirage or a trap, then it would probably be better if I walked around it and continued on my way.

That was when I noticed a small tent set up on the edge of the oasis pool. The tent was the same color as the sand, which was perhaps why I had not noticed it at first. I did not see any camels nearby, which meant either that the tent's owner was out or perhaps the tent's owner didn't go out often and therefore had no need of a camel.

Either way, if someone was living down there, they might be able to tell me in which direction Sandfall lay. While the nomads who often marauded around the Shayu Desert were always a threat, this tent didn't look like something belonging to one of them. In fact, it more closely resembled the tents that were sold to travelers who stopped in Sandfall before continuing onto the Desert itself, which made it extremely probable that the owner of the tent was a traveler from Sandfall.

Being careful to keep the Test by my side in order to look as nonthreatening as possible, I walked down the sand dune, each step cautious so I wouldn't accidentally fall and go rolling down the dune. My eyes remained on the tent at all times, though they occasionally strayed to the beautiful clear water behind it.

In a few seconds, I reached the oasis. The crunching of sand beneath my boots was soon replaced by the soft scuffing of grass. The sound was far more soothing to my ears than the crunching of the sand had been, which put me at ease in this place.

So I walked up to the tent and noticed that the flap was open. Soft music—like a harp—floated out of the opening, a pleasant sound that rested my weary soul and rejuvenated my body. All I wanted to do for a moment was simply stand there and listen and absorb the music, for it was beautiful, unlike anything I had ever heard, certainly superior to my own musical abilities, which was saying something, as I was a professional Bard whose singing abilities were renowned throughout the Six Continents.

The music was inviting, too, as if it were an old friend who I had not seen in a while. So I ducked my head down under the flap and entered the tent, straightening up only once I was fully inside it in order to get a better look at the tent's interior.

An aroma—like the sweetest of spices—filled my nostrils, an aroma I had only smelled once back in Sandfall. The tent's walls were rather thin, allowing the sunlight of the Twin Suns to shine through. Two water jars stood just to my left, while a diamond-encrusted treasure chest stood in between them.

Sitting in the very back of the tent on a bunch of silk pillows was the most beautiful woman I'd ever seen. She had long, dark hair, with skin as white as snow if not whiter. She wore a dark robe that covered her entire body save for her heads, hands, and feet, but despite its formlessness, it didn't detract from her beauty even slightly.

In her hands, she held a harp, tall and shining, which she strummed with obvious expertise. I could tell that she was highly experienced in playing the harp, even though I didn't play that instrument myself. Just the beautiful notes that emanated from the harp was proof enough that she was a master.

The woman looked up from her harp and my heart seemed to fail me at the striking color of her eyes. They were a deep green, almost the exact same shade as the grass outside. It was impossible to ignore her look, mostly because her sheer beauty commanded absolute attention.

"Welcome, weary traveler," said the woman, her fingers strumming the harp without fail. "Why don't you take a seat? You look like you have been traveling for a long time with very little rest."

Her voice snapped me out of my daze. "Oh, um, well, I didn't come here to stay. I just wanted to see if there was anyone in here. Sorry if I interrupted you."

"Oh, no, you didn't interrupt me at all," said the woman. For some reason I thought there was a tinge of sarcasm in her voice, but I dismissed it as my imagination. "I welcome all weary travelers to my tent. The Shayu Desert is a large, unfriendly place and it would be cruel of me to send you away just because I do not know you."

"That's very kind of you," I said. I glanced at the water jugs. "I suppose I am rather thirsty. I've been walking for hours now and I haven't a drop of water to drink since I entered the Desert."

The woman continued to strum her harp, though her eyes wandered over to my sword. "Are you a mercenary of some sort? Most normal people don't carry swords around like that."

"This?" I said, glancing at the Test. "Oh, no. I don't know how to use this. I'm actually a Bard. I only lug this thing around to ward off enemies."

"A Bard, traveling across the Shayu Desert all by himself?" said the woman in her musical voice. "That is rather daring of you. I always thought Bards never traveled without a protector or friend."

"Well, I do have some friends, but I got separated from them a while back and I've been on my own since," I said. "Actually, that's why I came here. I thought you might know how far away Sandfall is. That's where I'm headed."

"Are your friends in Sandfall, Mr. ...?" said the woman.

"Dale," I said. "Dale Bennett. And yes, I think they might be there, but if not, I know where they are going and I will be able to get there from Sandfall."

"Bennett," said the woman thoughtfully. "That is a good name."

"I concur," I said. "Can you tell me how far away Sandfall is, now? I really am in a hurry to reunite with my friends. We have a very important mission to accomplish and the longer I am separated from them ... well, let's just say it won't end well for everyone if I am not reunited with them soon."

"Are you threatening me, Mr. Bennett?" said the woman suddenly, her tone sharp, though she still strummed the harp as easily as always.

Realizing how that last sentence I had said sounded, I shook my head and said, "No, no, of course not, miss. I was just saying that it's very important that I get back to my friends. That's all."

The woman visibly relaxed. "Oh, in that case, Sandfall is one hundred miles north of here. There is a road nearby that you can take."

"Oh, really?" I said. "Well, that makes things quite a bit easier. Thank you for your help, Miss—?"

"Sarah," said the woman. "Call me Sarah."

"Sarah," I repeated, nodding. "Got it. Well, thank you, Miss Sarah, for helping me find my way. I must be off now, because as I said I don't have a lot of time to waste, but I will be sure to remember you and your kindness wherever I go."

"Before you go, why don't you take a look inside my treasure chest?" said Sarah, gesturing with one hand at the chest between the water jugs before returning her hand to the harp. "There might be something in it that could help you on your quest."

I paused before I left. "You mean, you are honestly offering me, a complete stranger, your treasure chest?"

Sarah nodded. "I have no need of its contents. You, however, might."

I internally debated with myself over whether to accept her offer. Sarah certainly didn't seem like the kind of woman to hide unpleasant surprises inside a treasure chest; on the other hand, I didn't know her all that well. For all I knew, she could be a criminal trying to unload her loot on me so that she wouldn't be caught with it.

If only Jill were here. I had a feeling that Jill would know whether I could trust this Sarah lady. Maybe Jill had met Sarah in a past version of the 'game,' as she called it. It was useless to speculate on whether she did or didn't, however, because Jill was not here and I could not ask her what she would do in this situation.

Deciding I could use a little more time before I made my decision, I said to Sarah, "Sarah, who exactly are you? Where did you come from? I didn't know anyone lived out in the Shayu Desert, aside from the nomads, and you are not a rough-and-tumble nomad by any means."

Sarah sighed, a beautiful sound, like the blowing of the wind on a warm spring day. "Who I am is not very important. All you need to know is that this oasis has always been my home and will likely always be that way."

"I was told there were no oases in the Shayu Desert," I said. I glanced at the tent's ceiling. "Yet here I am, standing right in the middle of one. Unless this whole thing turns out to be a great big mirage, that is."

"This is no mirage," said Sarah. "This oasis is simply hidden from the rest of the world. Occasionally, someone like you will stumble upon it, but most of the time the oasis is a secret."

"Why is that?" I said. "Wouldn't it better if this oasis was easier to find? It might attract more travelers to the Shayu Desert."

A soft scowl crossed Sarah's features for a moment before fading away, replaced by her usual pleasant smile. "And let other people ruin this beauty? Besides, I have no control over who does and doesn't find this place. It is all outside of my control. All I can do is sit back and be prepared for any travelers who might stumble upon this holy place."

"Ah," I said. "How long have you lived here? You said the oasis has 'always been your home.' Do you mean you were born here or—?"

"I mean exactly what I say," said Sarah, plucking at the harp strings with her usual dexterity. "I have always been here. Always."

I frowned. Something told me that Jill would make better sense of that than I would. Seeing as I didn't know how much time I had left, I decided to leave, but not without first checking out the treasure chest.

"I'm going to take up your offer and open the chest," I said. "I get to keep whatever is in it, yes?"

Sarah nodded. "Of course. Whatever it is, you may take. You do not even need to thank me for it. You can treat it as your own."

I nodded and then walked over to the treasure chest. It smelled like freshly cut wood, which was unusual because the chest itself looked old. The diamonds gleamed as brightly as ever, however, and it was not difficult for me to open the chest, as it was not locked. When the lid popped open, I peered inside to get a glimpse at whatever was lying inside it.

A shiny red pendant lay at the bottom of the chest. Curious, I reached down and grabbed the pendant, brushing my fingers against its beads. Lifting up the pendant, I stared at it for a few seconds, observing how the pendant itself was shaped exactly like a star. Not only that, but a surge of power passed through the pendant, making it glow briefly before fading away again.

I looked at Sarah, who did not seem at all surprised by my find. "What is it?"

"It is called the Star Pendant," she answered simply. "It is a useful item that you can wear with you in battle."

"What does it do?" I said, standing up from the chest. "Increase strength? Give me access to a special ability? Perhaps harms all enemies somehow?"

Without missing a beat, Sarah said, "I don't know what it does. I only know that it is useful."

I held the Star Pendant out in front of me, holding it by its beads. "How do you know that it's useful if you don't know what it does?"

"I only know it is useful because I was told that," said Sarah. "By the Five Stars themselves."

I stared at the Star Pendant for a moment. "You mean this was actually crafted by the Five Stars? No way."

"It is the truth," said Sarah. "It is one of several different star items. Another I know of is the Starblade, though I do not know where the Starblade is."

The Starblade? Jill had the Starblade. I didn't know how the Star Pendant would work for Jill, but I figured that if it belonged to the same set as the Starblade, then it was probably important to keep around.

Carefully, I stuffed the Star Pendant into my cloak's pockets, deciding I would examine it in greater detail later. Then I looked up at Sarah again and asked, "So how many different star items are there?"

"I do not know," said Sarah. "You will have to look to the Five Stars to find that out."

That was unhelpful, but I maintained a polite tone as I said, "Well, thank you for the help. I am sure that this Star Pendant will be useful to me in my journeys. So you said that Sandfall is north of here?"

"It is," said Sarah. "As I said, there's a road not far from here. Just keep going north and eventually you'll find it."

"You wouldn't happen to have a camel or something that I could take, would you?" I said.

Sarah shook her head. "I never travel, so for what reason would I own a camel?"

"Oh," I said. "Guess that means I'll just have to walk, then. Unfortunately."

I turned to exit the tent, but before I did, Sarah called out, "Wait, Bennett."

I looked over my shoulder at her. She was no longer strumming her harp; instead, she was looking at me quite earnestly, as if she was afraid she might not get to say all she wanted to say before I left.

"Yes?" I said. "What is it, Sarah?"

"I just wanted to say …" Sarah took a deep breath. She no longer looked as cool as she once did. "Do you think the world is coming to an end?"

I paused. "That's a strange question to ask."

"I know," said Sarah. "But it has been a long time since the Five Stars last spoke to me and I have not been able to communicate with them at all. Initially I thought they were ignoring me, but now I am starting to think they have abandoned me, maybe even abandoned all of Kinar."

"Why would you say that?" I said.

"Because I've seen a few strange creatures roaming the Desert in recent days," said Sarah. "Creatures I've never seen before, creatures that look like nothing from this world. Have you seen them?"

I scratched the back of my head, frowning. "No. Can't say I have. The Desert seems awfully empty."

"That's because these creatures are hunting and killing the other animals that live here," said Sarah. "The creatures … they move unnaturally. Their colors are distorted and muddied, their growls and roars are metallic and screeching, and they show no mercy to anyone who gets in their path."

I gulped. "Well, that is certainly unusual, but I don't think that's bad enough to warrant concluding that the end of the world is around the corner or that the Five Stars have abandoned us."

"But then why have the Five Stars not told me what these creatures are?" said Sarah. She leaned forward, a desperate look in her beautiful green eyes. "Not only that, but I am finding it harder and harder to appear in the Shayu Desert. Sometimes, it feels like I am trying to squeeze through a tiny hole; other times, it is like trying to walk on air. It feels like the Shayu Desert is vanishing and I don't know what to make of it."

My eyes widened. "Have you seen anything vanish or—?"

"Parts of the Desert have vanished," said Sarah. "Nothing larger than a square or two, but they vanish nonetheless."

My shoulders tensed. "Are they usually replaced by a black, featureless square?"

"Yes," said Sarah. She looked at me in astonishment. "How did you know that?"

I shook my head grimly. "Just a guess."

In truth, I was remembering Long River. I had originally assumed that the Glitch was confined mostly to the First Continent. I would have been ready to believe that it was on its way to the Second Continent, but if Sarah was telling the truth, then the Glitch had either skipped the Second through Fourth Continents and come straight here or … the Glitch was everywhere.

That would mean that the Glitch hadn't actually started in Long River, like some deadly epidemic that began in some obscure corner of the world. That would mean that the Glitch was everywhere, like the air itself. It might even be on the Sixth Continent for all I knew, which suddenly made me wonder if the Glitch had gotten to the Lord of the Silver Blades or not.

In any case, this simply heightened my need to reunite with my friends. They needed to know just how widespread the Glitch was and just how badly it was going to affect our own journey.

There was no time to lose, so I began walking backwards to the tent flap, saying as I did so, "Well, Sarah, there's not much I can do to help you, I'm afraid. I really must be going if I am going to reunite with my friends, but thanks for giving me the Star Pendant and sharing your knowledge with me. I'm sure it will come in handy soon."

Sarah began to protest, maybe to get me to stay, but I really did have to go. I pushed the tent flap aside, intending to head due north as soon as I got a good drink of water from the pool next to the tent, when I came face-to-face with the strangest and deadliest-looking monster I had ever seen in my life.

Chapter 7

At first glance, the monster resembled a large, transparent grizzly bear, its massive snout not more than a few inches from my face. Its breath was like acid, while its eyes glowed red, glaring at me with the kind of hatred you normally never saw in a creature like a grizzly.

I stepped back, trying to avoid breathing in its toxic fumes, which must have startled the bear creature because it, too, stepped back. This gave me a better look at its body, which did indeed resemble the bulky, but strong, form of a grizzly bear, though completely transparent, with only a thin white outline to make it visible.

Inside the creature, a green ball of energy glowed and rolled. I had no idea what that was—maybe its heart, maybe its soul, no way to tell for sure—but I didn't really care to find out. I closed the tent flap immediately and retreated back several feet from the entrance. A low growl emitted through the closed flap, but thankfully the transparent bear didn't come barging in.

I looked over my shoulder at Sarah, who had resumed playing her harp, though with less confidence than before. Her eyes were wide and her lips were drawn tightly together, the way most people looked when they were afraid but trying not to admit it.

"Did you see it?" I said, gesturing at the closed flap. "A transparent bear monster thing. Is that one of the creatures you were telling me about earlier?"

Sarah nodded. "Yes. It is one of the most vicious, too. I saw it pin down a spike snake and tear the poor thing to pieces."

I knew how big a spike snake could get—at least as long as the *Starry Night*—and, while I didn't quite agree with her characterization of the spike snake as a 'poor thing' (that would accurately describe most of its victims), I shuddered at the thought of that transparent bear monster thing tearing a full-grown adult spike snake apart. When my friends and I had fought a spike snake, it had almost soundly defeated us.

Needless to say, I was not confident in my own survival.

"Do you know how to deal with it?" I said. "Any spells you could cast to make it go away or maybe a powerful weapon to harm or kill it?"

"No," said Sarah. Her fingers trembled, causing her to miss a string on her harp. "The monsters have never actually entered my oasis before. Originally I didn't think they could, yet if one of them is here now ... then I do not know what to do."

"I'm just surprised it hasn't entered yet," I said as I turned around to face her. "There's nothing standing between it and us except that flap."

"Maybe it doesn't know it can enter," said Sarah. "I never believed these monsters to be very smart. Vicious, yes, but not intelligent or clever in any way."

"Then we're trapped," I said. "Damn it."

Oddly enough, however, Sarah didn't seem to share my

feelings. She pointed at the Test and said, "You have a sword, don't you? Why don't you use it to fight off the monster?"

I looked down at the Test. I had completely forgotten about it during my conversation with Sarah. The blade glowed softly as always, but it hardly reassured me.

"I said I don't know how to use it," I said, raising the sword up to my chest. "It's only supposed to scare off potential enemies or threats. In an actual, honest-to-goodness fight, I'm pretty much useless."

Sarah's hopeful expression turned to despair so quickly that I thought I had imagined it. "Oh. Right. I forgot that you had said that."

The soft stomping of the bear across the grass outside floated into my ears, sending a shiver up my spine. "Sarah, can you fight at all?"

"If I could, I would already be out there scaring off the monster," said Sarah. "As it stands, I am even less capable of combat than you are. I don't even own a weapon, I am that weak."

I cursed under my breath. First I was separated from my friends, then I was lost in the Shayu Desert, and now I was stuck in a tent with a woman who couldn't even hold a knife, much less help me defeat that strange bear creature that was currently stalking the entrance to the tent. How long would it take the creature to decide to enter? More importantly, how long would we last in a direct battle against it?

"Maybe we can wait it out," Sarah suggested. "If we stay inside here and remain very quiet, then the creature might get bored and leave to go look for something else that is easier to get."

"That's not a bad idea," I said. "Except that I don't have a whole lot of time to waste just waiting, not to mention that we have no idea how long this creature will wait for us to come out. Or if the creature will eventually decide to enter the tent once it realizes that there is nothing to stop it from doing so."

"It was just a suggestion," said Sarah, her musical voice tinged with annoyance. "No need to be so thorough in your dismissal of it."

I sighed and rubbed the back of my head. "Give me a moment. I'm sure I'll be able to come up with something."

"I hope you do, brave Bard Bennett," said Sarah, looking at the star pattern etched into the ceiling of the tent. "Because if you do not, I have no doubt in my mind that the monster will."

Her words of encouragement didn't help me at all, but I kept that thought to myself. Right now, I needed to think fast, come up with a way—any way—to get that bear monster out of here before it became smart and attacked.

Of course, this problem was nearly impossible to solve because I literally knew nothing about the monster except that it was strong enough to kill a spike snake. I didn't know if it was magical or if it had any specific weaknesses or anything like that. I wondered if Jill would know, but considering that this beast appeared to be a creation of the Glitch, I doubt she would have helped even if she had been here, standing next to me trying to figure it out.

If Julius were here, I reasoned that he would probably just run out there and start beating on the creature with Skull-cruncher. That was always his answer to these sorts of problems; unfortunately, I was not a muscle-bound Warrior capable of snapping logs like twigs, and if I tried to act like one, I'd probably just get killed.

Well, what would Alicia do, then?

Likely she would have simply stood back and let Jill and Julius do all of the fighting, seeing as she was a Healer and knew about as much about fighting as I did. Figuring out what she would do in this situation was about as useful as a politician asking what a ditch-digger would do in the event that an enemy nation declared war on his people.

Therefore, I was left to ask the one question I usually tried to avoid asking in these kinds of situations: What would *I* do?

Sadly, there was no set answer to that question because, like Alicia, I could not and did not fight. I was a Bard, a storyteller and singer, not a Soldier or Warrior. True, I had the Test on me, but to say I lacked any skill in swordplay was like saying the sky was blue.

Part of me just wanted to break down and quit. There were so many variables, so much information I didn't know, that it seemed impossible to come up with any kind of plan, no matter how rudimentary or basic, that was not destined to go horribly wrong and end with me and Sarah's bodies ending up in the belly of a glitched bear creature. It was especially hard without any of my friends on hand to save me or back me up. I felt like I was about to walk over a bottomless abyss blindfolded, a feeling I was not used to, as I had always relied on Jill or one of the others to help whenever I faced a situation I had no real experience in.

So I stabbed the Test into the floor and said, "I'm sorry, Sarah, but I honestly don't know what to do. I can't fight. I don't know anything about that monster. And I am all alone."

Sarah didn't seem to be listening to me. She had closed her eyes and was strumming the strings of her harp, making that beautiful melody that had initially brought me into her tent. I didn't know whether she had gone insane or whether she was resigned to our fate. Either way, her behavior was annoying.

"Is this really the best time to be playing the harp?" I said. I jerked my thumb over my shoulder at the tent flap. "There's a large bear monster thing that will likely kill us both and you think that this is the perfect opportunity to play your instrument?"

"I think this is the perfect opportunity to speak with the Five Stars," said Sarah, her eyes still closed shut. "Which is what I am doing. I communicate with the Five Stars through music, through my harp. It is how I've always done it."

"But you said the Five Stars aren't answering you anymore," I said. "What's the point in contacting them if they'll just ignore you?"

"Maybe they will listen this time," said Sarah. Then her tone turned to annoyance. "It's better than declaring that you've given up and can't win."

I gritted my teeth. "Just because I'm a realist doesn't mean—"

Hot breath—far too familiar for my liking—flowed down my neck, causing me to freeze. I silently prayed to the Five Stars that it wasn't what I felt, that a hot breeze had somehow got into the tent and blew against the back of my neck, but I was not naïve enough to believe that that was actually the case.

I looked over my shoulder, moving in what felt like slow-motion, until I was once again face-to-face with the glitched bear creature. Its red eyes glowed as deadly as ever, causing me to step away from the creature's face. The monster advanced, putting one heavy, transparent paw in front of another, steaming breath escaping from its nostrils like smoke from a chimney as it forced me to back up.

Walking backward, I didn't see where I was going and I ended up tripping and falling flat on my bottom on the cushions that Sarah sat upon. Sarah immediately stopped strumming her harp and must have opened her eyes (though I couldn't be sure, since I didn't turn around to look at her because I was too busy keeping an eye on the monster) because she gasped and said, "By the Five Stars. We are dead."

I scrambled backwards onto the pillows until I was right next to Sarah. The bear monster stopped just outside of the pillows, licking its lips as if it was imagining what we might taste like.

Then, without warning, the bear monster swiped at us both. I grabbed Sarah and pulled her down just in time. The bear's massive paw flew over our heads, but sadly, Sarah's harp was not so lucky. A terrible whipping sound, followed by the smashing of wood, made me glance to the left. The harp was in pieces now, no longer looking quite as beautiful or majestic as it once did.

"Dale, you must do something," Sarah said. She was clutching me quite tightly now, her eyes focused completely on the glitched bear as it lowered its paw and glared at us. "Anything."

"I don't know what to do," I said. "Didn't I already tell you that?"

The bear looked like it was thinking about the best way to kill us. Part of me foolishly hoped it would leave us alone, but I knew better than to place my hopes of survival on something so improbable. As much as I hated to admit it, Sarah was right. I *had* to do something because if I did not … well, the consequences were as obvious as they were deadly.

That was when I felt something hard in my cloak pocket. Curious, I plunged my hand into the pocket and withdrew a hard red stone, the centerpiece of a beaded necklace, from within.

It was the Star Pendant, but that didn't help me one bit. Sarah had said that she didn't know what the Star Pendant did. It might help us, sure, but it might also do nothing at all or worse, backfire and maybe hurt or even kill us.

I wasn't sure whether it was worth the risk until the bear monster—apparently having finished thinking about how it wanted to kill us—opened its mouth wide. Glowing red energy began forming within, which I had no trouble recognizing as the bear about to unleash an energy beam on us. And at this close range, it would no doubt hit and kill both of us.

I had no idea how the Star Pendant worked. I had no idea if I was even the right class to use it. I didn't know whether it was an offensive or defensive item. I knew nothing at all except that if I failed to act, we were almost certainly doomed for death.

Just as the glitched bear unleashed a beam of red energy, crackling and sparkling like the flames of a volcano, I thrust forward the Star Pendant before us. Again, I literally had no idea if that was how it was supposed to be activated or if I just sealed our deaths. All I knew was that it was our only chance at survival and that I didn't have the time to dither and worry about it like I normally would.

The moment the energy beam struck the Star Pendant's gem, it was like being hit with the force of a goblin's punch (a feeling I was more than familiar with, seeing as I had been punched by many goblins during my adventures). Yet I somehow had the strength to hold it back, keeping the energy beam from tearing through us and killing us in cold blood.

Though the glitched bear continued to unleash its energy beam, the Star Pendant didn't falter at all. In fact, it actually began to grow. A faint outline of a shield formed in front of it, which soon solidified into an actual shield made of red energy. I had never seen a shield like this one, with its star-shaped design and transparent body, but I didn't question it. I was too busy thanking the Five Stars to think very deeply about it.

Even more astonishing, the Star Pendant didn't stop there. The shield extended, pushing forward, forcing the glitched bear's energy beam back into its owner. The glitched bear didn't let up its attack; if anything, it seemed emboldened by the shield, as if it thought the star-shaped shield a challenge that it would beat.

If this was a challenge, the glitched bear was destined to lose it. With one final push by the Star Pendant, the last of the glitched bear's energy beam went back into its mouth. Because both the bear and the shield were transparent, I could see the energy swirling around inside the bear's innards, but with nowhere to go, it was forced to bounce around inside the bear, going faster and faster until it became little more than a blur.

And then, without warning, the glitched bear exploded. The Star Pendant protected us from the worst of it, but the explosion was still astonishingly loud and large. I closed my eyes out of habit, gritting my teeth and holding Sarah closer to me, until the explosion passed.

Then I opened them and saw that the glitched bear's explosion had left behind no debris or anything, not even tiny wisps of smoke to indicate where the bear had been standing. It was like the bear hadn't existed at all, the only clue to its existence the pieces of the broken harp.

As for the shield, that quickly retracted back into the Star Pendant. When it did, I looked down at the Star Pendant, unable to believe what I had just seen. Then I looked over at Sarah, who was still clutching me as if the glitched bear had simply gone into hiding and hadn't exploded into a million pieces.

"Oh my," said Sarah. Her eyes, too, were on the Star Pendant now, as if it were a bomb. "I had no idea that the Star Pendant could do something like that."

"Neither did I," I said as I stuffed the Pendant back into my pocket. "The creations of the Five Stars are truly incredible, are they not?"

"They are," said Sarah. Then she raised her eyes to look at me and said, "Thank you for saving me from the monster. I truly believed that we were both goners there for a second."

"Oh, it's nothing," I said, waving off her grateful gaze. "I didn't even know it would work. You should be thanking the Five Stars for making sure that the Star Pendant was here where I could get it."

Sarah scowled and then looked up at the star pattern on the ceiling of her tent, the design that featured all of the Five Stars swirling together in the deepest reaches of the sky. Her grip on my arm tightened, rather than loosening. "I *would* thank the Five Stars. If they would still talk to me, that is."

Not sure what to say to that (had to admit that I wasn't feeling especially fond of the Five Stars, either, in this situation), I said, "Well, now that you are safe, I think it's time for me to go. My friends are no doubt worried about my absence, as I am about theirs."

Sarah let go of me, though it was almost as an afterthought, as if she was not thinking about me at all. "Very well, brave Bard. You may go. Be sure to take your sword with you. I have no need of it myself."

I crawled off the pillows and onto the sand floor of the tent. The Test was exactly where I had left it, sticking out of the ground, looking as useless as it always did. Nonetheless, I pulled it out of the ground and held it at my side as I turned to face Sarah, who was now holding the remains of her broken harp as if it was the corpse of her first born child.

"I am sorry about your harp," I said. "I wish there was something I could have done to save it."

"It's fine," said Sarah, though her quivering lips made it clear that it was far from 'fine.' "Absolutely fine. I can repair it. I know a thing or two about harp repair. Besides, it's not like I'll be needing it anytime soon, since the Five Stars have gone silent."

I felt awful about leaving her, but what could I say? It wasn't like I happened to have an extra harp on me I could give to her. I did have some money, but she didn't strike me as the kind of woman to accept charity, even from the man who just saved her life. As far as I could tell, she just wanted to be left alone.

And I decided I would give her just that.

So I turned and walked out of the tent, dragging the Test behind me as I always did. Pushing the flap out of the way, I emerged into the twilight of the Shayu Desert. The Twin Suns were setting in the horizon, making me wonder just how long I had been in there. Surely it couldn't have been that many hours, could it have been?

Not that I would ever know the answer to that, because as soon as I stepped outside, my foot slipped and I found myself falling through darkness.

Chapter 8

The fall was not long. In less than a minute, my back hit the ground and I gasped for air. I dropped the Test somewhere nearby, but my fingers soon found its hilt and it was once more safely within my grasp.

My head spinning, I looked up to see where I had fallen. I saw nothing but darkness in every direction except up. By looking directly upwards, I saw the Shayu Desert, as well as Sarah's oasis and tent. I could see through the floor of Sarah's tent, through her pillows, watching as she gathered the pieces of her broken harp into one pile as gently as a rock bird gathered rocks into its nest.

I was in the Dark World again. How I got back here, I didn't know. I suspected the Glitch must have made it possible for me to pass through the ground. If so, that might actually be a good thing. After all, Jill and the others had still been down here when the Test had teleported me away. Maybe they were somewhere nearby.

I got to my feet, dusting off my cloak as I did so. I looked every which way, searching for any sign of my friends, but the Dark World merely stretched on endlessly in every direction for as far as the eye could see. Jill had said that the Dark World was massive, at least as big as Kinar itself, which meant that actually finding my friends would be very similar to trying to find three specific grains of sand in a desert.

As far as I could tell, I was completely alone in this place. There was no sign of any other living beings besides me. Sure, I could see Sarah above, and spot the movements of some desert creatures in the sand dunes around her Oasis, but the Dark World itself was lifeless. It was like walking into a graveyard at midnight, except without the tombstones.

I decided to head north. That was the general direction in which the Sixth Continent lay from the Fifth Continent. I chose to go that way because I knew that that was where Jill and the others were headed. If I went in that direction, then surely I would meet up with them at some point.

The idea of walking the distance from the Fifth Continent to the Sixth Continent made my feet ache, but I began walking north anyway, determined to make it to Three Hundred Towers, reunite with my friends, and save the world, no matter what.

The walk alone gave me far too much time alone in which to think. After all, there was nothing much to look at, nothing much to listen to, and nothing much to smell. It technically didn't even have a ground, though it must have because I had no trouble with walking across it, heading in what I believed to be north.

I wondered if the Controller was watching me. If so, he had not given me any indication that he was. Jill claimed that she could hear him every now and then, but that was obviously because he directly controlled her, whereas he didn't seem to have that same level of control over me, Alicia, Julius, or anyone else in the 'game,' as Jill called it.

Game … what a trivializing term. A game was what you called a bunch of children getting together to have fun. Saving the world from a madman who wanted to destroy everything and rule whatever was left was not a 'game.' Yet that was the term Jill used, perhaps because that was what the Controller called it.

Not only that, but apparently this 'game' had already been played through dozens, if not hundreds, of times before, if Jill was telling the truth. That made me wonder just how Jill had managed to stay sane as she played through the game again and again, being forced to make choices she did not want to make, all for the amusement of some being who didn't even have the courage to show her his own face.

I was not like Julius. I was not interested in finding this Controller and giving him a good thrashing. I knew it was useless. For all I knew, he could have been controlling me right now. Still, I did not have particularly kind feelings toward the Controller, who as far as I could tell only cared about us because of the amusement we brought to him.

Was he even aware of the Glitch? Was he trying to do something about it? I should think he would be. After all, if this Glitch destroyed his 'game,' he wouldn't be able to play it anymore. Perhaps he was working right now, even as I thought this, to fix the Glitch from the outside. Maybe he was even guiding us in the right direction, indirectly helping us save our own world.

Or maybe … maybe, he had created the Glitch himself.

I shook my head. What a silly thought. The Controller may have had sadistic tendencies, but I doubted he would introduce such a devastating Glitch into his favorite game. It would be like a child intentionally breaking their favorite toy. It made no sense whatsoever. In all likelihood, this Glitch was the result of someone or something else, though where it had come from and why, I didn't know.

Still, no one ever said the Controller was sane. Maybe he introduced the Glitch because he wanted to see what it would do to our world. Maybe he thought it would make the game more 'fun.'

Or maybe I was going insane from being alone for so long and needed some actual people to talk to. Did it really matter, one way or the other, whether the Controller was responsible for the Glitch or not? If I, Jill, and the others defeat the Lord of the Silver Blades, we likely won't remember the Glitch anyway. It will be an obscure chapter in Kinar's history, remembered only by Jill, who no doubt would keep the memory to herself, rather than share it with our new incarnations when the Controller would inevitably start the game anew.

Though that thought brought another question to mind: Why was Jill capable of retaining her memories while the rest of us weren't? Was it because she was the Hero, the leader, the one who was destined to defeat the Lord of the Silver Blades and save all of Kinar? Or was there something else to her that maybe even she didn't know? Or perhaps she knew exactly why she could remember and simply refused to tell us?

My existential thoughts were interrupted when a familiar feminine voice called out, "Dale?"

That voice …

I stopped and looked around wildly, trying to spot the voice's owner in the Dark World. At first I saw nothing, but then, off to my right, I saw three familiar people hurrying in my direction. As they drew closer, any doubts I had about their identities left my mind and I walked toward them, dragging the Test along behind me as I did so.

"Dale!" said Jill as she, Alicia, and Julius met me about halfway. Her face was paler than ever and she was sweating, but she looked more happy to see me than anything. "There you are. Where were you? We thought you were dead."

I quickly told them all about my adventures in the Shayu Desert, as well as my meeting with Sarah and my killing of the glitched bear. I even showed them the Star Pendant as proof of my claims, though I did not let any of them touch it.

When I finished, Alicia said, "Wow, Dale. It sure sounds like you had quite the adventure of your own while you were away."

"Indeed I did," I said. I glanced at the Test and said, "And it was all because of this damn sword right here."

"I'm sorry," said Jill, sounding like she meant it. "I should have told you more about that sword. I originally didn't because I didn't want any of you guys knowing about it, but I guess I should have been straight with you right from the start."

"I'll say," I said. I held up the Test before me and said, "So what is this sword, exactly? And why does it have such an odd name?"

"The Test, as far as I have been able to gather, is essentially a 'prototype' sword left in by the beings who created the game," Jill said. "It was designed, I think, to test how swords would work in our universe. It was never meant to be used by any of us. That was why it was left here in the Dark World, where no one could get it."

"Is that also why it teleported me away from you guys?" I said.

Jill nodded. "Most likely. Since it was never meant to be used, there's no telling what it will do if you try to use it. The first time I picked it up ... well, it wasn't fun. Let's leave it at that."

"So should I get rid of it?" I said, holding the Test away from me as far as I could. "Something that dangerous is definitely not something we should be carrying around with us."

I lifted the sword to throw it away as far as I could, but then Jill grabbed my arm, making me look at her in surprise. "What?"

"Actually, I'd like to have the Test," Jill said. "I still don't have a sword, as the Starblade is still useless. This way I'll have some way to defend myself."

"But you said the Test was never meant to be used by any of us," I said. "Aren't you the slightest bit worried about what the Test may do to you if you use it?"

"At this point, I don't think the Test can do much worse than the Glitch," said Jill. She wrapped her hand around my sword's hilt. "It might be useful against the Lord of the Silver Blades, anyway."

I didn't like the idea of Jill using the Test, but I also didn't feel like arguing with her about whether or not it made sense to use it. So I handed the sword to her, which she took and examined with a careful eye.

"Do you feel any different?" I asked, watching as Jill sheathed the sword in her belt after she was apparently satisfied with it.

Jill shook her head. "No. Maybe your using it got rid of all of the negative aspects of it. Or maybe the Glitch is somehow canceling out its negative effects. There's no way to know for sure."

"Speaking of the Glitch," said Alicia, glancing up at the Fifth Continent above us, "didn't Dale say that the Glitch is in the Shayu Desert now?"

"Yes," I said, nodding. "The Glitch is moving fast, much faster than we thought. For all I know, it could even be on the Sixth Continent by now."

"Then we have no time to lose," said Julius. "We've gotta go there right away, before it somehow glitches the final battle and makes it impossible to win."

"We'll have to pick up the pace," said Jill. "The Sixth Continent isn't far now, so we should hopefully get there very soon."

The rest of the journey barely took any time at all, though it could have been that my sense of time was off. We crossed the Deep Ocean between the Fifth and Sixth Continents, passed by many of the towns and cities we had already visited on our first time through the Sixth Continent, and were walking underneath the vast, volcanic countryside just outside of Three Hundred Towers when Jill came to a stop and said, "This is our stop."

I looked up. We were not directly underneath Three Hundred Towers yet, prompting me to say, "But I thought you said that this would take us to Three Hundred Towers."

"I forgot to specify that it wouldn't take us directly to Three Hundred Towers," said Jill, scratching the back of her head. "Instead, this shortcut allows us to get right up to the entrance."

"So we'll still have to enter the city itself, then," I said. "Which means getting past all of the Lord of the Silver Blades' defenses."

"Shouldn't be a problem," said Julius, tapping Skull-Cruncher, which was attached to his back. "We already dealt with most of them on our first trip here. Only reason we didn't head directly into the Lord of the Silver Blades' tower itself is because we needed to go back to Long River to get some stuff."

"Speaking of my hometown, I don't understand why we had to go back in the first place," I said. "Was there some kind of secret item there that we needed in order to defeat the Lord of the Silver Blades, Jill?"

Jill nodded. "Yes. Towards the end of the game, there was supposed to be a man in Long River who would give you, Dale, a Storyteller's Medal, which would have made you stronger and given you access to the Death Song."

"The Death Song?" I repeated, though not happily. "What's the Death Song?"

"A song that instantly kills all enemies that hear it, of course," said Jill. "It's the most powerful song you could learn. I guess it's lost forever now, however, because of your hometown's destruction."

Julius scowled. "So that's another reason to hate this damn Glitch. It kept us from getting the most powerful song ever. If that Glitch was a person, I'd punch it out the minute I saw its ugly face."

I had never heard of the Death Song before; on the other hand, I had no reason to believe Jill was lying to me. Like Julius, I was angry that the Glitch had taken away something else from me, even if it was something that I had not known about until right this instant. This gave me more motivation than ever to defeat the Lord of the Silver Blades and save our world.

"So how do we get out of here, then?" said Alicia, looking between the ground above us and the Dark World around us. "I don't see a ladder or any stairs we could take to get up there. And it's not like any of us know how to fly or anything."

"Getting out of here is actually very simple," said Jill. "Hold hands, everyone. I'll do the rest."

I redoubled my grip on Alicia's hand, just to be sure I wouldn't be left behind (mostly because I didn't want to be left alone with my thoughts again), and once everyone else was sure they were holding onto each other as tightly as possible, we all stepped forward with Jill leading.

As soon as we stepped forward, the blackness of the Dark World was abruptly replaced with the arid rockiness of the plains around Three Hundred Towers. The change was so abrupt that I thought my eyes must have been playing tricks on me at first, yet when I let go of Alicia's hand and took another step, everything was still exactly the same.

We had emerged near a small overhanging chunk of volcanic rock, near a collection of boulders that looked like children's building blocks stacked clumsily together. Night was rapidly falling, as the Twin Suns were beginning to set in the east, though the smog clouds overhead made it seem darker than it actually was.

Down the hill, a river of lava ran through the plains, a river I remembered quite well, for it was home to lava crocodiles, vicious monsters that had attacked us more than once. Which wouldn't have happened if we had just taken the *Starry Night*, but Jill had insisted that there were some hidden items in the Lava Plains and that we needed to be on foot to find them all (a claim which turned out to be true, as it allowed us to find Alicia's current staff, but I still felt that that particular risk had been quite foolhardy).

In the not-too-far-off distance, a massive city stood amidst the barren plains. It was an unusual sight in this place, for the city's buildings were the only constructions for as far as the eye could see. And there were hundreds of them, all crammed together in a way that created cramped streets and little room for anyone in which to move.

A crooked, rough road led up the countryside to the city, all the way up to its massive black iron gates that protected the city from the rest of the Lava Plains.

In the center of it all, a massive skyscraper jutted out, towering well above the rest of the buildings like a giant among humans. The skyscraper was shaped like a massive silver sword, its sharp tip reaching toward the smog-filled sky. It was also where the Lord of the Silver Blades was headquartered, where we would do our final battle with him once we entered Three Hundred Towers.

"There's Three Hundred Towers," said Jill, pointing toward the city. "We'll have to take the main path to get there, but it should hopefully not take very long."

"Then we'll have to climb the Silver Tower, though," said Julius, his eyes locked on the massive sword-like tower sticking out of the center of the city. "And that will take a long time."

"Not like we have much choice," said Alicia. "The Glitch is

getting closer and closer every minute. I think we can handle climbing a ridiculously tall tower, don't you think?"

"Yeah, I guess so," said Julius, his shoulders slumped.

Jill was already walking down the hill, toward the River of Lava, which ran parallel to the main path. I, Alicia, and Julius followed, doing our best to keep up with her before she got too far ahead of us.

Upon reaching the main path, Jill turned to face us. "Guys, before we go any further, there's something I need to tell you."

"What is it?" I said, looking at her unusually earnest face. "More information about our upcoming battle with the Lord of the Silver Blades?"

"Yes," said Jill. She put her hands behind her back and cast a quick glance in the direction of Three Hundred Towers before she continued. "When we enter the Silver Tower and confront the Lord of the Silver Blades, we will have to do our very best to defeat him. Do you guys understand that?"

"Of course we do," said Julius, puffing out his chest. "We never do less than our best, especially if our best will ensure us victory over that bastard."

"That's good," said Jill. "I just wanted to make sure you would still fight even knowing I have to die. After seeing your initial reactions to that news, I was worried you might not be willing to do your best."

"I'm still thinking of a way to save you, Jill," said Julius. "There has to be a way to make sure you survive. There has to be."

"There isn't, and we aren't going to debate this," said Jill flatly. "How many times do I have to repeat myself? I am going to die. I've done it before dozens, if not hundreds, of times, and each time I've come back to life when the Controller decided to bring me back."

"Still doesn't make it right," said Julius. "You don't deserve to die, especially not after everything you've done to help the world. Why does it have to be that way?"

"Because it is," said Jill. She glanced over at Three Hundred Towers in the distance and then looked back at Julius. Her hand rested on the hilt of the Test. "Unless you're willing to fight me and stop me, that is. Which, as I'm sure you already know, would simply allow the Glitch to grow and cause even more damage than it already has.

"I ..." Julius was clearly struggling with what to say in response to that. "I don't want the Glitch to destroy everything, but—"

"Then we're going," said Jill. Her tone was rather cold, far colder than I had ever heard it before. "But before we do, I do have something I wanted to tell you. Something I was originally going to say before Julius interrupted me."

"Go on, then," said Alicia. "We're listening."

Jill sighed. "When we enter Three Hundred Towers, we'll take the teleportation pad straight up to the top of the Silver Tower. Do you guys remember that?"

All three of us nodded. During our first trip to Three Hundred Towers, we had discovered that the Lord of the Silver Blades had installed a series of teleportation pads all throughout the city to make it easier for him or his men to travel. Of course, it wasn't exclusively reserved just for him and his cronies. We figured out how to use them—and with little trial and error, too, thanks to

Jill's previously unexplained foreknowledge—and then used them to travel around the city as we pleased.

"All right," said Jill. She put her hands together. "When I defeat the Lord of the Silver Blades, he is going to try to bring the whole Silver Tower down on us. I will be holding him back to make sure he doesn't get away, but you guys will have to leave. Use the teleportation pad. As long as you don't wait for me, you should be able to escape with your lives."

Julius looked like he wanted to argue with her, but because Jill had already made it quite clear what she thought about anyone trying to stop her, he just kept his mouth shut.

Alicia, on the other hand, said, "All right. We can do that."

"Good," said Jill. "I was hoping I could count on you three to do it. Of course, you won't have a whole lot of choice in the end, but it's good to know that you'll do it anyway."

"We're your friends, Jill," I said. "Friends always support each other. Even if ... even if that does mean supporting your death."

"Please don't use that tone," said Jill. "Like I said, it's not a big deal. I've died before. I always come back whenever the Controller restarts the game. You guys just do what I said and everything should be just fine."

"Guess so," Julius muttered. "But that doesn't mean I have to like it."

While I understood—and even sympathized with—Julius's dislike of Jill's inevitable death, I had to admit I was getting a bit tired of him constantly bringing up the topic. It was clear that he didn't have any real plan to save Jill, which made him sound quite repetitive after a while. I wished he would just keep his mouth shut until he came up with a new idea or accepted Jill's inevitable death like Alicia and me.

Jill didn't seem to hear Julius's muttering. She turned around and said, "All right. If everyone has no objections and is equipped and ready for battle, then I think it's time for us to go."

Just as we continued our journey across the vast, rocky Lava Plains, the sky turned completely black.

Chapter 9

Where there had once been a smoggy sky, full of ash and smoke, with only the occasional gap in the clouds to indicate that there were stars in the night sky, was now a solid black color, the exact same shade as the blackness of the Dark World. The air was still thick, heavy, and ash-filled, and the ground generated heat like a body, but the whole sky looked as though someone had tossed a large black sheet over it. There weren't even any stars.

"By the Five Stars," said Julius, looking up at the totally black sky with a gaping mouth. "What happened to the sky?"

Jill's didn't even stop to look up at it. She was already on the main path to Three Hundred Towers, forcing us to stop staring at the sky in order to keep up with her. Yet it was impossible to completely ignore the black sky, because it stretched from horizon to horizon and contrasted sharply with the gray stone-and-metal which the skyscrapers of Three Hundred Towers were made of.

"The Glitch must already be here," said Alicia, walking so fast that she almost overtook Jill. "Jill, do you think this will hamper our journey?"

"No, I don't think it will," said Jill, shaking her head as she walked. "As long as nothing gets in our way, then we should be able to get to the Silver Tower with ease."

"Yeah, 'cause this journey has been nothing but smooth rides so far, right?" said Julius, scowling as he glanced up at the sky. "Who wants to bet it'll start raining lava or something?"

Not being a betting man, I kept my mouth shut. It was probably for the best. I had the feeling—perhaps irrational—that the Glitch was listening to us for ideas about how to ruin our day and that if I said anything, it might get inspired to make sure our lives are as miserable as possible.

Then a single droplet of water splashed on my nose, making me stop and look up at the sky. There were no clouds at all in the sky—not so much as one wisp of whiteness—yet I could have sworn that a rain drop had fallen on my nose. Had I imagined it?

"Dale, what are you doing?" said Julius, turning around and walking backwards as a way to look at me and keep up with Jill and Alicia. "Stop standing around looking like an idiot. We don't have a ton of time to sight see, you know."

"I know," I said, my eyes darting across the black sky. "It's just that I thought I felt—"

Without so much as a hint that it was about to happen, the black sky began to pour rain like a storm in the middle of the sea. The rain pelted my head and face, forcing me to raise my arms to cover them as I ran to rejoin the others, who like me had raised their arms to cover their heads and faces from the sudden downpour. I glanced at the sky occasionally, however, searching for any clouds or anything else that could have caused this rain, yet as far as I could tell the sky was as black as always. It was as though the rain had just materialized out of nowhere, though I knew it had to be the result of the Glitch.

"Well, it isn't raining lava," I said to Julius as I caught up with him, having to raise my voice to be heard above the torrential rains. "But it *is* raining."

Julius glared at me as we ran, but did not say anything else. We just kept running, I hoping the rain wouldn't ruin my Bard's Cloak, but the further we ran, the more obvious it became to me that, though the rain was falling as heavily as the rain in the swamplands of the Fifth Continent, we were not getting wet. It was still hard to see where we were going, but even though the rain kept landing on us, none of us appeared even slightly damp.

That completely bamboozled me until I realized that it was the Glitch's fault. The Glitch was not making it actually rain. It only made it appear like it was raining. Sure, the ground around us appear to be getting wet, yet as we ran across it, I did not hear the familiar squelching of mud beneath my boots, nor did my feet have any problem finding traction while I ran. It was quite a disturbing sight, even though I was grateful for it.

The others must have realized this, too, because soon they lowered their arms. Julius looked up at the sky, as if he was wondering why it was raining yet none of us were getting wet, while Jill and Alicia kept their eyes solely on the massive city walls ahead of us, which were drawing closer and closer with each step we took.

We crossed a short stone bridge that crossed over the River of Lava—which, by the way, was not evaporating any of the rain, if the lack of steam in the air was any indication—and in a minute were at the city's gates. Three Hundred Towers' gates reminded me vaguely of Tall Roots', except they were far larger, made of a thick, strong metal, and were stylized to resemble silver blades.

But we didn't go through the gates. Instead, we ran over to a slightly glowing blue pad on the ground, the teleportation pad that would take us directly to the top of the Silver Tower, where the Lord of the Silver Blades awaited us.

Before jumping onto it, I briefly wondered if the Glitch had already gotten to the pad and had somehow messed it up. If it did, then we would probably end up somewhere else entirely, though where, I could not say.

Not that I had time to bring up these objections. Jill, Alicia, and Julius scrambled onto the pad with extreme haste and I followed as quickly as I could so I would not be left behind. As soon as I set both feet on the pad, my whole world vanished in a frighteningly bright white light.

Then the bright white light faded and we were standing on the very top of the Silver Tower, on a balcony which stretched toward the rest of the city, with simple metal railings all that kept us safe from falling off if we wandered too close to the edge. The wind was strong up here, blowing so hard that it sent my cloak billowing almost out of control, but there was no rain whatsoever. It was as dry as a desert, which was a shocking change after the intense downpour we had just run through.

Because we were up so high, we were almost right up next to the black sky. From a distance it was disturbing, but up close, it was absolutely terrifying. I felt like it would try to suck me into it if I fell, an absurd fear, perhaps, but it was how I felt and there was little I could do about it.

The top of the Silver Tower looked the same as we had last

left it. To our right, a door leading down to the lower floors of the Tower was closed shut. It was how we had gotten up here the first time, fighting our way through the legions of minions that protected the Tower, finding treasure chests and items, even once meeting the Lord himself before he retired to his throne room on the roof of the Tower itself to await us.

Standing right in front our group, dwarfing all four of us, was a huge silver door unlike any I had seen before. Its surface was perfectly smooth, save for the hilt-shaped doorhandles near the bottom. If I had not known that the Lord of the Silver Blades himself was in there, I would have assumed that it was the lair of a rich giant, although knowing that it was the throne room of the Lord of the Silver Blades himself did nothing to ease my fear.

"All right," said Jill, looking at all of us. "This is it. Once we step through these doors, the battle with the Lord of the Silver Blades will begin. Is everyone ready?"

Julius unhooked Skull-cruncher from his belt and spun the ax in his hand before grasping the hilt solidly. "Of course."

Alicia's staff glowed softly as she said, "I'll do my best."

I simply nodded, seeing as I had no weapons to use. "I can't guarantee that I'll be of much help, but I'll do what I can."

"All right," said Jill. "But first …"

Jill withdrew her journal from her pocket, flipped it open to a random page somewhere near the middle, and scribbled something in it with a pen before slapping the small book shut and shoving it in her pocket.

"Had to save our progress before we entered," Jill explained, upon seeing our perplexed expressions. "Anyway, it's time we took down that monster and saved the world. All at the same time."

When we entered the Lord of the Silver Blades' throne room, an unfamiliar aria entered our ears. Someone was playing the keys of a large organ, every note played with expert precision. The music was deep and ominous, like the rumbling of a thunder cloud on a sunny summer day, but we didn't let that send us running.

The throne room itself was massive. The high-flown ceiling towered over us all, an intricate silver patchwork of every constellation that was visible in the night sky, ranging from the Goblin Archer to the Unicorn, shining brightly enough to illuminate the whole room.

Along the walls, gigantic silver swords—at least a head taller than Julius, if not taller—stood lined up like the swords of an armory. They resembled the swords used by the Lord of the Silver Blades, except far larger and most likely as heavy as boulders.

A long, red carpet ran from the entrance to the very end of the room, where an enormous pipe organ stood against the back wall, its silver pipes gleaming under the light of the artificial constellations. That organ had to be the source of the music, for with every keystroke by its player, another new note was added to the already existing aria.

As impressive as the organ was, however, it was its player who caught our interest. He was seated before the organ, his fingers flying across it, each keystroke done so expertly that at first I thought I was not looking at the Lord of the Silver Blades at all, but a master organist instead.

THE LAST LEGEND: GLITCH APOCALYPSE

His back was to us, almost as if he had not heard our entry, though he must have, because the massive silver doors from before had screeched rather loudly when we had opened them. He wore robes similar in design to Alicia's, except whereas hers were pure white, his were a shining silver, so brilliant that they put the artificial constellations in the ceiling above him to shame.

But then the music ended abruptly and the Lord of the Silver Blades stood up. He then slowly turned around, his graying, silver hair revealing a face as pale and angry as a killer worm's.

"Jill Franklin," said the Lord of the Silver Blades, folding his thick arms across his chest. "Julius Manna. Alicia Bangs. And Dale Bennett. I see that my armies were not enough to keep you at bay."

"Your 'armies' sucked," said Julius. "Bunch of dumb goblins in shiny armor, that's all they were. And the Goblin Generals were just a joke."

The Lord of the Silver Blade's gray eyes swept over us like the eyes of a disapproving deity. "I did not expect them to do much more than keep you at bay for only a brief time. All of my men, even my best and loyalest, are incompetent, bumbling fools who have failed me at every turn. It is no surprise, then, that they failed to stop you four."

"Game's over, Lord of the Silver Blades," said Jill, pointing at him with the Test. "You've done enough evil in this world. This time, we're going to beat you once and for all."

The Lord of the Silver Blades tilted his head to the side, a slight frown on his face. "Didn't I already defeat you in Tall Roots? And in the Black Blade Mountain? And in the Shayu Desert? How many times must I knock you down before you choose to stay down?"

"As many times as it will take for us to defeat you," Jill said. "This time, we will win and you will lose."

The Lord of the Silver Blades chuckled. "I suppose it must have been my merciful side sparing you insects because it would not have been fair otherwise. I suppose I'll have to remedy that mistake."

He snapped his fingers and the ceiling cracked open slowly. As it did, six large, shining crystals lowered from the ceiling, each one caught inside a large silver cage. Five of the crystals were the same size—only about a head shorter than me—while the one in the middle was as big as a boulder. Like the others, it, too, was inside a cage, except this cage was much bigger in order to hold the larger crystal effectively.

The Lord of the Silver Blades gestured at the crystals above, saying, "Behold. All six of the legendary Omega Crystals. With them, I will be granted the power of the Five Stars themselves and all of Kinar will kneel before my feet."

"Thanks for bringing out the Omega Crystals for us," said Jill, smirking. "That just makes it a whole lot easier for us to get them."

"You speak confidently for one who is about to be annihilated from existence," said the Lord of the Silver Blades. A wicked, wolfish grin spread across his face. "Your unfounded confidence will make crushing you under my heel that much more satisfying."

Then the Lord of the Silver Blades threw both of his arms into the air, crying out as he did so, "Omega Crystals, creators of order and harmony, arbiters of power! Grant me the power that you have never granted any other mortal man before! Grant me the ability to crush these ants and bring a new world order to Kinar, one based on my whims and wishes, rather than the pathetic squabbles of the various nations of fools!"

Quite dramatic, but it worked. The Omega Crystals glowed with a brightness that likely would have blinded us completely if we had not shaded our eyes with our hands. Then six beams of energy shot out from the cages, directly hitting the Lord of the Silver Blades. He doubled over at first, as if he had been punched in the gut, but then, slowly but surely, he stood up to his full height. He spread his arms wide, closing his eyes as he absorbed every last bit of energy that the Omega Crystals gave him.

Julius stepped forward, a snarl on his face, but Jill held out the Test before him and muttered, "This is part of the game. Don't worry; we'll still be able to beat him."

I hoped Jill's reassurance was founded in fact, because the longer the Omega Crystals poured their energy into the Lord of the Silver Blades, the more afraid I became. His hair went from a gray silver to a brilliant gleaming silver; his robes shone like the crown of the Old King; and even his skin became smoother, like purified silver.

Then the Omega Crystals ceased pouring their energy into him. As soon as they did so, the Omega Crystals went completely dark. They now looked like ordinary crystals, the only real difference being that they were larger than most.

As for the Lord of the Silver Blades, he no longer looked like a powerful yet mortal man. Pure omega energy emanated from his body like the waves of the Deep Ocean, and he literally glowed with the same glow that the Omega Crystals formerly had. He truly looked god-like now, like a wrathful deity who was going to smite us for daring to disobey his direct orders.

"Look and behold, mortals," said the Lord of the Silver Blades. His voice had changed, too, becoming far more deeper and guttural than it had been before. "I, the Lord of the Silver Blades, have transcended mortality. I am now an immortal star, on par with the Five Stars themselves. You cannot hope to defeat me now."

"Oh, you're shinier now," said Julius, rolling his head. "Yeah. Real god-like. I'm shaking in my boots right now."

The Lord of the Silver Blades shook his head. "Your sarcasm is as pathetic as it is palpable, Julius Manna. How about I show you a display of my true power?"

The Lord of the Silver Blades raised both of his hands. As he did so, the gigantic silver swords on the walls began to creak and groan before breaking off the walls completely and flying over to him. The humungous blades—a dozen in all—floated in the air above and around him, like protective bodyguards willing to give their very lives to protect the life of their master.

The Lord didn't seem at all strained by the use of the gigantic swords, even though he had to have had to put more effort into controlling them than he normally did. He manipulated them with ease, as though they were no bigger than his normal silver swords.

I must confess, I almost wet my pants upon seeing those dozen gigantic swords rip off the walls and swirling in the air around him. Until now, I hadn't realized just how much power the Omega Crystals had given him. And based on his easy expression, it was quite clear that he was only showing off a fraction of his true power.

"Still shaking in your boots, Julius?" said the Lord of the Silver Blades, a smirk crossing his lips. "Don't be ashamed if you want to run to your mommy. Few mortals have the courage to stand against this display of godly might."

Julius's knees trembled, but he said, "I'm not afraid of anything you can throw at me, you shiny silver bastard. I'll still kick your ass."

"So will I," said Jill. She looked at the Lord of the Silver Blades with pure steel in her gaze. "You must not know us very well if you think a display of power like that is enough to scare us."

The Lord of the Silver Blades shook his head. "Here I was, giving you mortals a chance to run with your lives, and yet you refuse to do so out of the mistaken belief that you can win. I would think your losing to me three times previously would be enough to discourage you, but I suppose you are right, Jill Franklin. I don't know any of you very well, but it does not matter. A human does not need to know an ant in order to squash it under his heel."

While the Lord's gigantic silver swords continued to swirl about him like a tornado, I leaned toward Jill and whispered, "What's the plan?"

"Easy," said Jill. "You use your Bard's songs to confuse the Lord of the Silver Blades, giving Julius and I openings in which to attack. Alicia, meanwhile, will stand at a distance and heal anyone who gets injured. We repeat that over and over until the Lord goes down."

"Are you sure we can beat him?" I said, still speaking in a

whisper, glancing at the Lord's glowing form. "He said he's on par with the Five Stars themselves, for goodness's sake."

"We can still win," said Jill. "He's the most powerful enemy in the game, but that doesn't mean he's invincible. Remember, I've fought him before. I know all of his strategies, I've been through all of this already. None of it's new, so just follow my lead and everything should work out just fine."

It was hard for me to share her confidence, mostly because *I* didn't remember fighting (and beating) someone on the exact same power level as the Five Stars, even though I had to have been there when it happened. Still, there was no turning back now. It was either face the Lord of the Silver Blades or face the Glitch, and to be honest, I thought we had a better chance against the Lord than against the Glitch.

I looked at Julius and Alicia. Both of them must have heard Jill's plan because, unlike me, they didn't appear to be about to run away and hide. Julius swung Skull-cruncher through the air, looking quite fierce, while Alicia carried her staff like a spear.

So I turned back to face the Lord of the Silver Blades, who had still not attacked us yet. My mind raced as I tried to remember the tune for the Song of Confusion, which was the only song in my repertoire that could cause confusion.

It would never have occurred to me to use it against the Lord of the Silver Blades, mostly because I figured that if he was even half as strong as he boasted, then my songs would have zero effect on him. Yet Jill had told me to sing, which meant they must work.

That thought alone gave me more courage today than I had had in a long time.

THE LAST LEGEND: GLITCH APOCALYPSE

Then the Lord of the Silver Blades thrust his hands forward. All twelve of his massive swords came hurtling at us at the speed of a falling Aircraft, aiming straight and true at us. All four of us scattered to avoid getting cut into pieces, which would definitely have ruined our day.

I dashed to the right side of the throne room, where I got a good view of the Lord. I immediately stopped and began to sing the Song of Confusion. Normally, I preferred a slower tune, but because of the urgency of the situation, I sang faster than usual, still managing to land every note accurately, much to my own surprise.

The Lord of the Silver Blades looked in my direction, perhaps hearing the bamboozling tone of the Song of Confusion. He at first looked puzzled, as if he didn't know what I was doing, but then realization dawned on his face like lightning and he thrust his left hand in my direction.

One of his massive swords came hurtling at me at a shocking speed. I ran forward to avoid getting impaled, but I could not run and sing, so I had to cut off my song before it could have any real effect on the Lord. The sword flew past me, just barely missing my head.

"Foolish Bard," said the Lord of the Silver Blades, glaring at me with his shining silver eyes. "You try to confuse me with your cacophonous melody? Do you really want to be the first to die?"

Before I could answer that, Jill came out of nowhere and slashed at the Lord of the Silver Blades with the Test. The Lord roared in pain as the Test tore through his body, but then one of his swords came out of nowhere to impale Jill, who deftly jumped back to avoid it.

129

A jagged cut ran the length of the Lord's body, but he waved one hand over it and the cut healed instantly. Still, he looked worn out, as if he had just run a mile in his bare feet.

As he turned his attention to Jill, his hands crackling with energy, I began singing again. This time, I picked up the tempo, singing faster and faster, not knowing when or if the Lord of the Silver Blades would notice and attack me again.

It worked. The Lord of the Silver Blades's face went from concentrated anger to puzzled confusion in just a few seconds. He straightened up and looked around the room as if he was not sure where he was, while his swords flew all over the place, some impaling themselves in the walls or floor, others colliding into each other in midair.

Jill and Julius took advantage of the Lord's confusion to dash forward and attack with all of their might. Jill slashed and stabbed with the Test, while Julius swung Skull-cruncher with the might of a falling mountain. Every single blow from both of my friends landed, each one dealing massive damage to the Lord of the Silver Blades.

The Lord of the Silver Blades was in no condition to fight back, thanks to my song. He tried to raise his arms to defend himself, but it was a weak defense that did nothing to protect him from Jill or Julius, who didn't let up on their attacks even once.

"Go Jill and Julius!" I said. "Take him down!"

But then, in between blows, the Lord of the Silver Blades shook his head and shouted, "Enough!"

He spread his arms apart, sending a wave of power that sent Jill and Julius flying through the air. I gasped, watching them crashing into the floor, while the Lord of the Silver Blades—his face bloody and beaten, his arms cut up from the blows that Jill and Julius had landed on him—stood to his full height.

Wiping a thin stream of blood from the corner of his mouth, the Lord of the Silver Blades said, "I will admit that you ants have a bite. Even so, all that means is that I will need to assume my ultimate, final form. I am done playing around with you. I will finish all four of you now."

The Lord of the Silver Blades lifted his hands into the air again, causing all twelve of his silver blades to soar back to him. As the blades began swirling around the Lord, Alicia ran over to Jill and Julius, her staff shining as she waved it over them, casting a spell that healed our two fighters before my very eyes.

"Thanks, Alicia," said Jill as she got to her feet. "We'll have to keep going, however, because the fight isn't over yet."

Jill was right. Looking at the Lord of the Silver Blades, it was almost impossible to see him now, because the blades were swirling around him so fast that they completely blocked him from view. All I saw was a constantly swirling wall of silver that grew brighter and brighter with each passing second until it was almost impossible to look at.

Then the light exploded, forcing us to hold our arms over our eyes to avoid getting blinded. When the light cleared, we lowered our arms and looked to see what had happened.

Standing in the Lord of the Silver Blades' place was a titan of a man, even taller than Julius. Instead of his normal silver robes, the man was clad from head to foot in silver armor with an intricate, star-like design etched into the chest piece, with glowing smaller stars made of crystal running down the arms and legs. Two massive metallic wings extended from his back, with edges sharp as swords. Pointed blades ran along his arms, while two intelligent and dangerous argent eyes glowed from within the helmet.

The Lord of the Silver Blades raised one hand and turned it, as if admiring his new appearance. "Behold, mortals, my new form. With it, I will crush you underneath my heel once and for all."

I scrambled to join the others as Jill said, "You keep saying that, but you keep failing. If I were you, I'd stop saying you're going to kill us and just go ahead and do it."

The Lord of the Silver Blades held out one hand, the clawed tips gleaming with suppressed Omega Crystal energy. "Then I will."

The Lord of the Silver Blades jumped into the air, moving far faster than a being of his size and weight should have been able to. He landed hard on the floor, creating a small crater where his feet crashed, and then he dashed at us, blades popping out of his armor like the spines on a hedgehog as he did so.

Jill and Julius didn't even hesitate. They ran at him, weapons drawn and ready, and swung both of their blades directly at him. The Lord blocked both of their attacks, however, and with a shrug of his massive shoulders somehow sent both of my friends flying in different directions. Julius crashed against the left wall, in one of the clefts where the giant silver blades had once been, while Jill slammed into the doors and fell to the floor with a stunned look on her face.

That meant both Jill and Julius were down. And Alicia and I were alone against the Lord of the Silver Blades.

The Lord stood to his full height, his silver eyes gleaming

down at us with his usual evil look. "I normally ignore those who cannot attack back; however, you two are special, for you have done everything in your power to stand against me. And for that, you must die."

He dashed at us with frightening speed, forcing us to separate into two different directions to avoid his wrath. I ran to the left, while Alicia ran to the right, but it was no use because the Lord of the Silver Blades reached out with his massive hands and caught us both by the collars of our clothes.

"No running away now," said the Lord of the Silver Blades with a growl. "Allow me to show you what happens to those who dare to stand in my path."

I tried to break free of his grasp, but it was no use. The Lord of the Silver Blades picked us both up and slammed our heads together. Stars flashed in my eyes and my head felt like someone had cracked it open like an egg.

Then the Lord dropped us both. Because he was rather tall, our fall was higher than usual and we hit the floor hard. Unfortunately, I landed on my head and saw more stars.

Then I shook my head and looked up. The Lord of the Silver Blades now stood above us. He shook his right hand and one of the blades embedded in his armor fell into his hand. It was a long sword, with sharp, jagged edges that reminded me of the teeth of a dragon. The sword itself was crystalline, shining as brightly as the Omega Crystals had.

"Time to finish you both off," said the Lord of the Silver Blades. "And then I will deal with your two friends."

The Lord of the Silver Blades brought his crystalline sword down on both of us. There was no way to dodge it because it was coming down too fast and neither of us were feeling well enough to move.

In the split second before it hit us, however, I felt something burn in my cloak's right pocket. I shoved my hand into the pocket and pulled out the Star Pendant. Not knowing if this would work —not even thinking about it—I held up the Star Pendent before us, directly in the path of the Lord's crystalline sword.

A large, thick star-shaped red shield erupted out of the Star Pendant, covering both of us in the nick of time. The Lord's sword slammed against the Star Pendant's shield, actually causing it to shake and even crack, but the sturdy shield held under the Lord's pressure.

"What?" said the Lord of the Silver Blades, his voice genuinely shocked. "Where did this come from?"

I was just about to come up with a witty one-liner when Jill jumped out of nowhere and slashed at the Lord. The Test slashed through the Lord's sword arm, cutting cleanly through it. The Lord roared in pain as his severed sword arm fell to the floor with a loud *clunk*, silvery blood leaking from his stump as he staggered backwards from the blow.

"I-Impossible," said the Lord, grabbing at his stump in a vain effort to keep the blood from leaking anymore than it already had. "How did you harm me? I am invincible. I am a god."

Jill, panting, rose to her full height and cracked her neck as she held the Test before her. "Let's just say that that is my little secret."

The Lord's eyes glowed in anger. "Why, you little—"

"Heads up!" Julius's deep voice rang as the Warrior, like Jill, leaped out of nowhere and slashed his ax at the Lord's other arm.

Skull-cruncher cut as cleanly through the Lord's only in tact arm as the Test had, making the Lord scream in pure agony once more as he staggered away from Julius.

"This cannot be happening," said the Lord of the Silver Blades, his silvery blood now flowing freely from both stumps. "N-No way. I have the power of the Omega Crystals flowing through my veins. I am supposed to be almighty, unstoppable, divine."

"Life can be a real bitch sometimes, can't she?" said Julius, swinging Skull-cruncher in his hands, a smirk running across his bruised face. "Game over, Lord. You lose."

The star-shaped shield from the Star Pendant zapped back into the Pendant, allowing me and Alicia to rise to our feet together. As we did so, Alicia waved her staff through the air, sending buckets of white dust falling on us. When the dust landed on my head and shoulders, I felt instantly revived, and based on the expressions of Jill and Julius, they, too, felt better now.

All four of us gathered together, standing before the Lord of the Silver Blades, who clearly was not taking the blood loss well. He fell to his knees, coughing and groaning loudly as he did so, a pool of silvery blood gathering at his knees.

"You heard Julius," said Jill, lowering the Test. "We win, Lord. You're in no condition to fight. Even with the power of the Omega Crystals flowing through you, you still didn't stand a chance against us. Give up now and let us have the Omega Crystals back and we might spare you."

"Impossible," the Lord of the Silver Blades muttered. "I cannot be defeated. I cannot die. I cannot lose. I am a god."

"Is he going crazy?" said Julius, tilting his head. "Or is the blood loss finally starting to get to him?"

Then the Lord of the Silver Blades looked up, a mad gleam in his eyes. "I may no longer be able to fight, but that doesn't mean … that doesn't mean I will let you live."

The floor trembled beneath our feet. At first, it was a subtle movement, so subtle I dismissed it as nothing more than the designed swaying of the Silver Tower in the wind, but then it got worse and worse until the whole room was shaking uncontrollably. A huge chunk of the ceiling broke off and fell onto the pipe organ, creating an ugly noise that almost blew my hearing out due to its sheer volume.

"Wh-Wh-What's going on?" said Julius, his teeth chattering.

"I'm bringing the whole place down on all of us," said the Lord of the Silver Blades, his voice full of mad glee. "The Silver Tower only stood because I willed it. Now that I no longer will it, the whole structure will collapse on itself and kill anyone foolish enough to be inside while that is happening."

Of course. Jill had told us that the Lord would try to bring down his entire lair on us when he died. Unfortunately, that meant that Jill's own death was not far away now.

"Then we'll just get out of here," said Jill. "You can die here if you want, but we all have lives we'd like to get back to. Come on!"

Without further ado, all four of us turned and ran toward the exit, dodging chunks of ceiling debris as we did so. We didn't look back even once as we ran. There was no need. We just ran as fast as we possibly could, each of us putting every last bit of effort into our legs that we could.

Right before we reached the open doors, a shadow flew

overheard, followed by a trail of silvery blood that splattered over our clothes, and then the Lord of the Silver Blades was standing before us. Blood continued to pour from his stumps, but he didn't seem to let that bother him as he spread his wings to their full, considerable span in an attempt to block our escape.

"Go no further, Heroes of the Stars," said the Lord of the Silver Blades, his voice ragged and weak. "Your tombs will be tombs of silver, an honor granted to very few."

We skidded to a stop before him, prompting Julius to snap, "Get out of the way, you son of a bitch!"

That obviously didn't encourage the Lord of the Silver Blades to move. He just stood there, glaring down at us triumphantly, chuckling even as chunks of the ceiling fell and hit him on the head, wings, and shoulders. He chuckled even as his stumps continued to bleed freely, the stink of his blood filling our nostrils and making me want to gag.

Jill turned around to face us. Her eyes had a look of determination in them or maybe it was resignation. I didn't understand it at first until I remembered what Jill had said she needed to do, what the game required of her.

Julius must have, too, because he shook his head and growled, "No way, Jill. You aren't going to—"

"I'm going to hold him off while you three get out of here," Jill said, speaking over Julius as if he hadn't said a word. "Take the teleportation pad and get the hell out of here. Don't wait or come back for me. I'll be fine."

"But Jill—" Julius protested, but he didn't get to finish his sentence because Jill turned and, with remarkable agility, jumped up at the Lord of the Silver Blades.

With both hands gripping the Test, Jill drove its blade directly into the Lord of the Silver Blades' heart. The Lord roared in pain, causing his wings to retract as he staggered to the left, giving us a wide enough opening to pass through.

I hesitated only for a moment, watching as Jill drove the Test deeper and deeper into the Lord of the Silver Blades' heart, but then I shook my head and ran for the opening, Alicia and Julius behind me. We passed through the open doors onto the massive balcony overlooking the whole of Three Hundred Towers, chunks of which had already fallen into the streets below.

The teleportation pad—thank the Five Stars—was still in tact. I and Alicia ran at it, but then Julius yelled, "Wait!" and, against our wills, we skid to a stop and looked at him. Julius had stopped only a few feet from the open doors, looking through the doorway even as a chunk of rock crashed dangerously close to him.

"Julius, what the hell are you doing?" I said. I pointed at the teleportation pad and yelled, "The whole place is gonna fall apart and we're going to *die* if you don't get a move on, you big lummox!"

Julius looked at us, a steely look of determination in his eyes very similar to the one Jill had given us before she sacrificed herself to keep the Lord busy. "I'm going back in to save Jill."

"But the game—!" Alicia protested.

"Fuck the game," said Julius. "I'm doing what I think is right. I'll be back in a second. You guys just go on ahead. I'll be right behind you with Jill kicking and screaming."

Before we could further berate him for being the idiot that he was, Julius was gone, his massive back disappearing in the darkness of the open doorway.

"Crap," said Alicia. It was the first time I'd heard her use the word, yet it seemed quite appropriate for our current situation. "We're doomed, aren't we?"

"Probably!" I said, not bothering to hide my annoyance. "But we should go anyway. If Julius wants to doom himself, that's fine, but for me—"

A resounding *crack* caused me to look down at the balcony under my feet. A long, thick crack was slowly forming between the open doorway to the Lord's lair and the balcony. It took me less than a minute to realize that if the crack completed then the entire balcony would fall and both of us would die.

So I grabbed Alicia's arm and said, "We're getting out of here *now*. Before it's too late."

Alicia protested, but I didn't listen. I dragged her across the shaking balcony, avoiding the holes that had already formed as a result of falling chunks, my eyes focused squarely on the teleportation pad before us. It wasn't that far away, but it certainly seemed like it was, because time itself seemed to slow around us.

Then Alicia shouted, "What's that?"

Breaking my focus on the teleportation pad, I looked up and saw a giant rift in the sky—a purplish hole, unlike anything I had seen before—floating well above the city. Large chunks of buildings, lava, even rain clouds, were sucked into its swirling vortex. Whatever was sucked inside vanished, like it hadn't existed at all.

"By the Five Stars!" Alicia said. "That's the Glitch!"

I didn't answer. I just dragged her further along to the teleportation pad. If it was the glitch, it would be better if we ignored it and just kept going. We didn't have time to gawk at it, not with the entire city falling apart around us.

Just before we stepped onto the pad, a familiar deep voice called out behind us, "Wait, guys!"

Alicia and I whirled around in time to see Julius—his black armor covered in a thin layer of dust, with the Lord of the Silver Blades' blood stained across his chest—running out of the throne room. He wasn't alone, however. Tossed over his shoulder, apparently unconscious, was Jill, her hand tightly wrapped around the Test's hilt.

I couldn't comprehend what I was seeing. How did Julius save Jill? Jill said it was impossible, that it was part of the game that she had to die. Had Julius somehow figured out how to bypass the game itself and save her?

I had little time to ponder such questions, however. As soon as Julius stepped onto the balcony, the crack which had been forming between it and the doorway to the throne room finally broke.

But rather than falling to our dooms, as we should have, the balcony hurtled through the air toward the glitched portal in the sky. Julius had grabbed onto the railing with one hand, the other holding tight onto Jill, as we drew closer and closer to the portal every second.

"Julius!" I shouted, raising my voice high enough to be heard over the howling wind, shaking city, and buzzing portal. "How did you save Jill?"

"Doesn't matter," Julius shouted back. "Get onto the teleportation pad. Quick!"

Somehow, Julius launched himself and Jill from the railing toward us. Alicia and I turned to run toward the teleportation pad, but then Julius and Jill knocked into us and all four of us fell on the pad at exactly the same time in a confused heap of limbs and bodies.

And at the same moment we fell onto the teleportation pad, the balcony passed through the portal. A bright white light erupted around us as the pad tried to teleport us, but then a flash of purple enveloped us as well and then everything went completely blank.

PART TWO:

THE GLITCH

Chapter 10

"**D**ale ... Dale ... goddammit, wake up, you big idiot ... come on ..."

The voice spoke harshly, but not cruelly. I could sense that the owner of the voice—whoever she was—was deeply worried about my well-being. I didn't really know who she was, could barely remember my own name, but I sensed that she was a friend and that it was safe to wake up.

My eyes flickered open and I found myself staring into the face of a dark-haired woman. Her own eyes were full of annoyance, as if she was angry about something. It took me a long moment to recognize her as Jill.

"Jill?" I said. "Is that you?"

A frown flashed across Jill's face. "Yes, it's me. How do you feel?"

A sticking pain ran up my back, making me feel paralyzed. "Like someone stabbed me in the back with a long, sharp needle."

"But you can still move, right?" said Jill.

I looked down at my hands. With a supreme effort of will, I managed to twitch them, one at a time, and then soon feeling returned to both of my hands and I could move them freely.

"Excellent," said Jill, pulling away from me, a satisfied, though somewhat grim, smile on her face. "Do you think you can walk yet?"

I slowly sat up, rubbing my back as I did so. My joints felt stiff as wood, but I nodded and said, "I think I can. I need a little bit more time to recover, though. I'm not entirely well yet."

The frown returned to Jill's face, making me wonder if I had said something wrong. "You'll have to be. We don't have a lot of time to sit around and recover."

"What do you mean?" I said. "Where are we?"

I asked this while looking around at our surroundings. We appeared to be inside a small, simple cave, with a slightly rocky floor and a ceiling that even I could scrape my head against if I stood up to my full height. A small pile of ash, smoke rising from it slowly, was nearby, with three fish with wood speared through them hanging over it. Beyond the ash pile, light streamed in from outside, although I couldn't tell what the outside looked like. Aside from Jill, there was no one else in the cave.

"We're in Aruzai," said Jill, sitting back, her hands folded on her lap. "Near the Deep Woods, around the Rising Cliffs."

"Aruzai?" I said. "What's Aruzai? I've never heard of the place. Which Continent is it located on?"

"That's the thing," said Jill. "It's not located on any of the Sixth Continents."

Sweat began forming on my forehead, forcing me to wipe it away as I said, "Then we're on some island somewhere out in the Deep Ocean, correct?"

"No," said Jill, shaking her head. "This isn't an island. It's a Continent. The Seventh Continent."

"The Seventh Continent?" I said. "That's a bad joke, Jill. There are only six continents in Kinar; Amira, Nojike, Virum, Brunk, Lithin, and Xeryu. There's no such thing as the Seventh Continent."

Jill shook her head. "I didn't believe it at first, either, but after we ran into the inhabitants, they told us that that's where we were."

"But how could we have even gotten here?" I said. "We beat the game, didn't we? The Lord of the Silver Blades is dead. You killed him. That's how the game ends, isn't it? Everything should be back to normal. Everything. There shouldn't even be a Seventh Continent."

"I'm not sure what happened," said Jill, scratching the back of her neck. "But I think I have an idea. It's just a theory, not confirmed, but it seems to fit what we do know about how we got here."

"Then shoot," I said.

"All right," said Jill. "You remember how, after we defeated the Lord of the Silver Blades, we were sucked into the Glitch's portal that was destroying everything? At the same time, all four of us got on the teleportation pad that was supposed to take us back down to the ground?"

As Jill said that, the memories flooded my mind and I nodded in agreement. "I remember all of that quite clearly."

"Well—again, not exactly sure, as it isn't like we were told this by anyone—I think that the Glitch must have interfered with the teleportation pad somehow," said Jill. She gestured at the cave around them. "The clash between the pad and the Glitch somehow teleported us away from the Six Continents to here, the

Seventh Continent. As far as I can tell, there's no way to leave."

"No way to leave?" I said in horror. The cave suddenly seemed far more cramped than it had before. "There has to be some way, doesn't there?"

"If there is, it's not obvious," said Jill. "From what I've been able to gather, the Seventh Continent is hidden. That is, while it exists fully formed in the game just like the other Six Continents, it isn't normally accessible. The inhabitants have told us that they've never received visits from anyone outside of the Seventh Continent, though not in quite so many words."

"What do you mean?" I said. "How can the inhabitants communicate with us if they've never had visitors from the outside? Surely they must speak a different language from us."

"They don't," said Jill, shaking her head. "They speak the exact same language as you and I, though with a few different words here and there. I think the game's designers must have intended for Aruzai to be accessible at some point, but for whatever reason had to block off all access to it. Even I didn't know about it, and I've played the game dozens of times."

"So you mean we have literally no idea what this Continent is like, then," I said.

Jill shrugged. "More or less. I haven't felt this uncertain about our situation since the first time I became aware of the true nature of the universe. I don't like not knowing, with extreme precision, what will happen next."

"Now you know how I, Julius, and Alicia feel," I said. "By the way, where are Julius and Alicia? Did they—"

"They made it," Jill confirmed. Then she lowered her eyes. "Well ... kind of."

"Kind of?" I said. I leaned forward in concern. "What do you mean, 'kind of'?"

"Alicia came out okay," said Jill, still refusing to meet my eyes. "But Julius ... the Glitch got him worse than the rest of us. He's no longer normal."

"What do you mean?" I said.

"You'll have to see for yourself," said Jill. She gestured toward the cave opening. "Julius is outside right now acting as guard. Alicia is checking up on him to heal him when necessary. They don't know that you're awake yet."

"How long have I been out?" I asked.

"Two days, I think," said Jill, with an uncertain frown on her face. "It's hard to tell, though, because the Seventh Continent doesn't seem to have a normal day-and-night system like the other Continents. The sun has been in the sky for two days now and hasn't moved an inch since we arrived."

"The sun?" I said. "Don't you mean the Twin Suns, Jill?"

"No, I meant what I said," she said. "The Seventh Continent, for some reason, only has one sun. I don't know why. I suspect that this place is not entirely finished, which would explain the lack of a second sun."

The idea of a place only having one sun confused me more than anything else, but I figured it was one of the least weird things I had heard about in the last few days. It was downright normal, actually.

"What's our situation?" I said, stretching my arms and legs. "Everyone is alive, but how are we doing in terms of supplies and items and equipment?"

Jill's frown became even more pronounced. "Bad. Very bad.

We're running out of revitalizing potions. We still have all of our basic equipment, like the Test—"

She gestured at the sword leaning against the wall behind her. The words *Test* shone on its hilt, looking as innocent as ever. It appeared to have been cleaned at some point because it didn't have the Lord of the Silver Blades' blood on it.

"—but we've faced constant attacks day in and day out from a bunch of different monsters none of us have ever seen before," Jill continued. "Some of them resemble that monster we fought in Tall Roots, just less glitchy."

"Are there any towns nearby?" I said. "Why aren't we staying in an inn or something like that? You mentioned Aruzai's inhabitants. Surely they must be willing to let us stay a night in their town?"

"That's the thing," said Jill. "The nearest town is a place called Firesticks. It's where we ended up after the Glitch teleported us here. The inhabitants of Firesticks weren't the friendliest people in the world, to put it lightly."

"What did they do?" I said.

"They attacked us," said Jill. "Drove us out of town. Because we're technically foreigners, they didn't want us anywhere near them. We only learned we were in the Seventh Continent when we captured and interrogated one of the villagers, who told us what I told you about the place."

"That's why we we're hiding out in a cave?" I said.

"Pretty much," said Jill. "None of the villagers know where we are, so they haven't tried to eliminate us again. I'm not sure they'd attack us anyway even if they did. They didn't strike me as the adventurous types. They seemed to want to just be left alone."

"Then let's leave them alone," I said. "I certainly don't want to get on the bad side of a bunch of angry villagers."

"Same here," said Jill. "The only reason Julius is guarding the cave is because, as I said, there are a bunch of monsters out there that we haven't seen before, many of which are violent and murderous. So far he's kept them at bay, but we've been discussing our need to move on at some point and figure out where we are and how to get out of here."

"That would be a good thing to do," I agreed. "Has the Glitch shown itself since we got here or have we been lucky enough to avoid it?"

"I haven't seen the Glitch since our arrival," said Jill. "I don't know if defeating the Lord of the Silver Blades fixed it or if it just hasn't gotten here yet. All I know is that, if we're going to get back to the Six Continents, we probably will need the Glitch's help to achieve that."

"Wonderful," I sighed. "Well, at least you are alive. I was a bit skeptical at first, but Julius really did manage to save you. That's definitely something worth being glad about, isn't it?"

Jill folded her arms across her chest and glanced at the cave exit. "I'm not so sure."

"What?" I said. "But … you're alive. Isn't that a good thing?"

Jill shook her head. "It's not how the game is supposed to go. The game is supposed to end with my death. That's how it's supposed to end. Julius broke that by saving me."

"So what?" I said. I reached over and grabbed her hand, causing her to look at me. "Everything is still fine, right? I mean, aside from the fact that we're stuck inside a continent we can't leave through normal methods, obviously."

Jill tugged her hand out of mine. "It's *not* okay, though. I haven't shared this theory of mine with everyone, but I think one of the reasons we ended up here is because Julius saved me. That wasn't supposed to happen, so the game ended up sending us here because it didn't know what to do."

"Oh," I said. "Well, that's not good, is it?"

"No, it's not," said Jill. "It's normally impossible for Julius or anyone else to save me. I think … I think Julius must have somehow used the Glitch to save me. He used the Glitch's power to do something he wasn't supposed to do, and this is what happened."

"But how could Julius have used the Glitch's power?" I said. "It's not like any of us know how to use the Glitch. It's a force of nature that can't be controlled, right?"

"I don't know," said Jill, looking up at the short ceiling above us. "There's still so much we don't know about the Glitch. I don't even know if Julius is aware that he used the Glitch to save me or that his use of the Glitch is probably what sent us here."

"Have you tried talking to him?" I said. "Telling him your theory?"

"Julius and I haven't been particularly close since he rescued me," said Jill. "He thinks I should be thankful, but I don't think I should because he just screwed us all over by doing that. We haven't talked much except for when we absolutely need to."

"Oh," I said. "That's not good."

"I know," said Jill, rubbing her forehead. "But what else am I supposed to do? It's not like Julius knows how to get us out of here. If we're going to get back home, we'll have to do a more thorough exploration of this place. The secret to going back home might be hidden somewhere within the Continent."

"Then why haven't you explored it very much?" I said. "Why waste two days hiding inside a cramped, smelly cave?"

"Because we wanted to wait until you had recovered before we did anything," said Jill. "We didn't want to have to lug your unconscious body around, especially with so many dangerous beasts lurking in every corner. Now that you're awake, I think I'll go and—"

A loud, earsplitting roar rang throughout the cave like a gunshot, forcing us to slam our hands over our ears to protect our hearing. The roar was followed by someone yelling and swearing very loudly, and then the *chink* of metal on metal before another what sounded like a blast of fire followed.

"What the hell?" I said, looking at Jill in alarm. "What was that?"

Jill stood up, though not fully due to the lowness of the ceiling, and grabbed the Test. "An enemy. You stay here. I'm going to go help Julius."

"Hold on," I said, grabbing her wrist before she could run away. "I'm coming with you. I want to see Julius and Alicia. Besides, this cave floor isn't very comfortable or good to my back."

Jill wrenched her wrist out of my hand. She looked extremely reluctant, but then she nodded and said, "All right. You can come, but just stay out of the battle. I don't want you to get hurt or anything, all right?"

I nodded without hesitation, got to my feet, and followed Jill toward the cavern entrance, from which more roars, swearing, and fire blasts could be heard.

THE LAST LEGEND: GLITCH APOCALYPSE

Upon stepping outside, we were greeted by the sight of an armored, red dragon-like creature standing at the bottom of the cliff that the cave was built into. A narrow path ran from the ground below to the cave entrance, but seeing the dragon's large wings, I had no doubt it could have flown up here and smoked us all out if it wanted to.

I said 'dragon-like' because, while it had the signature wings and scales of a dragon, it had the beak of a falcon and the claws of a lion. Its tail whipped through the air so fast I could barely see it, though it appeared to have some kind of flame attached to the end, based on the flames sparking from it.

In front of the beast stood a familiar large Warrior: Julius, who was tossing Skull-cruncher from hand to hand as easily as if it were a light stick. The ground around him was blackened and smoking, probably from the dragon's fire blast, but he didn't look like he had been hit himself. Perhaps he had dodged it somehow?

I heard movement nearby, causing me to look to the right. Alicia was crouched over the side of the cliff, looking down at Julius, her right hand pressed against her mouth and her left hand wrapped tightly around her staff. Her eyes were focused entirely on Julius, like she was afraid for him. Which was understandable, seeing as Julius was outsized by that dragon by a larger order of magnitude than I liked to think about.

"Alicia," said Jill. "How is Julius doing?"

Jill spoke softly, but Alicia jumped anyway, like Jill had poked her with a branding iron. She almost fell off the cliff, but I caught her and pulled her back before she went tumbling off and cracking her head open. She turned to look at us, her eyes wide with surprise when she saw my face.

"Dale?" she said. Then a smile spread across her face. "You're awake! Oh, I'm so glad. For a while there, I thought—"

A blast of fire from the dragon below cut off her sentence. I looked over her shoulder in time to see Julius roll out of the way of the blast. The flames scorched the earth even further, sending more smoke rising into the air and blackening several larger rocks. The flames even licked the foot of the cliff, though thankfully they did not reach us.

"Glad to see you too, Ali," I said, patting her on the shoulder. "Jill's already told me about our situation. Where did this dragon come from?"

Alicia's smile quickly turned into a worried frown as she looked back over her shoulder at the dragon and Julius. "It just burst out from the trees and tried to eat Julius. He's been dealing with it fairly well, but it's easily the biggest and strongest monster he's fought yet and it doesn't seem to be afraid of him at all."

I looked over her shoulder again. There was indeed a forest stretching out below our cave mouth, tall pines and oaks that went on for as far as the eye could see. A small sandy area stood between our cavern home and the woods, which was where Julius and the dragon were fighting.

"I've just been watching the fight unfold," said Alicia. She shrugged helplessly. "I wish I could do more, but I'm just not a fighter."

Jill steadied her grip on the Test. "I'll go help him. You two stay here."

Before I could talk her out of that idea, Jill jumped off the cliff and down to the battleground below. Both Alicia and I watched her go, Alicia putting her fingers against her mouth again, while I folded my arms and prayed to the Five Stars to protect Jill and Julius (even though I had no idea if the Five Stars could even hear us here).

Jill landed on the sand with perfect grace and dashed toward the dragon, which was following Julius, who seemed to be trying to lure it away from the cliffs. The dragon didn't seem to notice Jill until she got right up to its side and stabbed the Test through a gap in its metal plating, causing the dragon to roar with pain as it flapped its wings and whipped its tail violently. Jill jumped back to avoid its wings and tail, however.

Then the dragon turned to look at Jill, smoke and fire exhaling from its nostrils, but that turned out to be a mistake for that creature. Julius leaped at its neck, pulling back Skull-cruncher as he flew through the air. With one final slash, Skull-cruncher passed cleanly through the dragon's neck, cutting off its surprised roar abruptly.

Julius landed with a roll on the sand as the dragon's head fell to the sand with a crash. Without its head controlling its body, the dragon's corpse fell forward. As it did so, the dragon's body and head dissolved into dust, as usually happened to killed monsters, until all that was left was a pile of reddish dust that soon evaporated into nothingness.

"That went quick," I remarked as Jill and Julius spoke with each other for a moment, too far away for either me or Alicia to hear.

Alicia let out a sigh of relief. "Yeah. I'm just glad that they didn't get killed. Guess all of that training we did finally paid off, eh?"

I nodded as Jill and Julius ended their conversation and began walking back to the cave. Jill was pointing at Alicia and me as they walked, probably pointing out to Julius how I was still alive. Julius's eyes followed her finger until they landed on me, though unlike Alicia, Julius didn't smile when he saw me. Maybe he was too exhausted from the battle to do even that much.

Alicia and I climbed down the narrow path to meet them at the foot of the cliff, which was still smoking from the dragon's earlier fire attack. Not only that, but it was hotter down here than it had been up there, though the temperature was rapidly cooling to a more reasonable degree in the absence of the dragon to keep heating it up.

"Hey, Julius," I greeted, thrusting out my hand to shake his. "Good job killing that monster. That was an intense fight."

Julius reached out to shake my hand, but then the Test suddenly appeared between our hands. Shocked, I looked at Jill, who wore a somewhat regretful expression on her face, though Julius didn't seem quite as surprised a me.

"Jill, what are you doing?" I said. "I just want to shake his hand."

"You don't want to shake his hand," said Jill. "Not even touch him."

"Why?" I said. "Julius and I are friends. What's so wrong with shaking a friend's hand?"

"Nothing," said Jill, shaking her head. "The problem is … well, Julius, show him."

Julius nodded. He hefted Skull-cruncher and then slammed himself in the face with the flat of the ax. It was a vicious blow, too, the kind of blow that would cause brain trauma to a normal person, but Julius's skull was thick enough to take the blow.

Shocked, I watched as Julius lowered Skull-cruncher. His face was not as bloodied and bruised as I thought it would be. Instead, his face looked … well, I suppose the best way to describe it would be that it looked glitchy. Half of his face was a variety of strange colors, mostly greenish purple, but it was hard to tell his expression because his face looked like a smeared painting more than anything. His face resembled a patchwork of stone tiles, all mixed together in a way that was clearly random.

Then his face abruptly returned to its original shape and form, a frown on his face that said it all.

"Julius is glitched," said Jill, lowering the Test. "I don't know why, but for some reason the Glitch affected him worse than the rest of us. If you try to touch him, you'll probably end up just like him."

"That's why he's been guarding the cave," Alicia explained. "We can't let him sleep in there with us because we're afraid he might touch us and glitch us up, too."

"Well, it doesn't seem to be affecting him too badly," I said. "Did you see how he beat that dragon?"

"It's not all rosy," said Julius. His voice sounded metallic for some reason. "The Glitch has given me a lot of power, but it's also slowly eating away at my memories, eating away at who I am."

"What do you mean?" I said. "You remember us just fine, don't you?"

"I do," said Julius, nodding. "But I don't remember everything like I used to. I don't remember our ship or our hometown. I can barely even recall my own name at times. Sometimes, it's like I'm on the outside looking in. Know what I mean?"

"Not entirely," I said. "But I get it. The Glitch is harming you. Do you know how long you will last?"

"No," said Julius, shaking his head hopelessly. "It's happening only gradually, so I think I will be okay for now. But unless we fix the Glitch quick ..."

His voice trailed off.

"Well," said Jill, causing me to look at her. "I think it's time for us to leave, now that we're all awake and ready to go."

"Where are we going?" I said. I gestured at everything and said, "We don't even know where we are."

"North," said Jill, pointing towards the forest. "One of the villagers mentioned a king who lives to the north of here. Said that the king has been defending his castle from strange creatures, creatures that don't look 'natural.'"

"The Glitch?" I said.

"Probably," said Jill. "But until we get there, there's no way to know for sure."

"But why are we going to that king?" I said. "Do you think he might know how to get us back home?"

Jill looked to the north as though she could see straight through the tall trees that stood before us. "He might know something about the Glitch, maybe even where it came from. At the very least, he should be able to tell us more about the Seventh Continent, if nothing else."

"All right," I said. "How far to the north is this king, exactly?"

"The villager was vague," Jill said. "I think he didn't trust us. All he said was that if we head north from here, we should reach the king within a couple of days, maybe less if we avoid getting into any fights with the forest monsters or taking a side quest."

"A couple of days?" I groaned. "That's too long. Are you sure there isn't a quicker way?"

"If there is, none of us know about it," said Jill. She sighed and looked up at the sky. "I imagine that if we had the *Starry Night*, we could probably make the journey easily, but we don't, so we'll walk."

The trees of the unnamed forest looked ominous and dark to me, prompting me to say, "Walk. Potentially through miles of untamed wilderness that we know very little about. For at least two days. With the ever-present possibility, of course, of being attacked by the Glitch."

"It's our only option," said Jill. "Unless you want to stay in that tiny little cave and hope the monsters don't overrun us eventually."

"I wasn't saying I was against it," I said. "I was just saying that I hope we all understood exactly what we were getting into."

Jill rolled her eyes. "We can handle whatever is in that forest. After all, Julius defended the cave on his own for two days."

"True, but now we're going into the very heart of danger," I said. "I just don't want any of us to get cocky or let our guard down. That's all."

"As long as you guys stick by my side and don't touch anything that doesn't look safe, we should be fine," said Jill. "Now, unless anyone can think of anything we need to get before we leave, it is time for us to go."

Chapter 11

Our journey through the forest reminded me somewhat of the Long Forest back home on the First Continent, the primary difference being that the trees here were not quite as thick or old as the trees back home. Not only that, but the forest was muggy, making me tug at the collar of my shirt as we walked through the thick undergrowth.

Jill and Julius were in the lead, though they kept a careful distance between each other to avoid Julius glitching Jill. They used their weapons to cut through branches and bushes that got in our path, which were numerous due to the apparent lack of use this forest got from the Seventh Continent's inhabitants.

The forest was eerily silent, aside from our own footsteps and Jill and Julius's hacking. When I brought this up after an hour—couldn't stand the silence, you see—Jill said to me that it was likely that the forest was not 'complete,' that the designers had for whatever reason failed to activate the 'sound effects,' as she called them, and that the only reason we made any sound was because the Glitch, in all likelihood, had affected them enough to activate the sound effects normally reserved for the Long Forest.

I almost disagreed with that before I listened closely and

concluded that she was right. Our footsteps really did sound like they did when we were walking through the Long Forest. Even with Jill's explanation in mind, that thought made me shudder. It wasn't natural, but then, after the Glitch, I supposed that nothing could be called 'natural' anymore.

The sounds of our footsteps also reminded me of my hometown, Long River. It was still destroyed, completely gone. I had hoped that defeating the Lord of the Silver Blades would have brought it back, but all it did was strand us in the middle of a continent we didn't even know existed. As far as I knew, the Six Continents were gone, and unless we could figure out how to stop the Glitch soon, so would we.

Our journey through the forest was rather peaceful, albeit rather tense, as we kept our wits about ourselves, ready to fight at any moment. Yet we neither saw nor heard any other creatures in the forest, not even that strange dragon creature that Julius had killed. The lack of enemies made me wonder if the forest was more sparsely populated than I had originally believed. Or perhaps—

Snap. My leg jerked out from under me, a shout of surprise coming from my mouth. I smacked my head against the ground as I was pulled up into the tree, a rope tied securely around my ankle. The rope came to an abrupt halt, leaving me hanging in the air a couple of feet above the ground upside down, my Bard's Cloak falling down and obscuring my face, forcing me to push it up to see everyone.

"What the hell?" said Julius, looking at me in shocked disbelief. "What happened? Who set up that trap?"

"I don't know," I snapped. I gestured at the rope and said, "If you could just let me down, that would be great."

Before Julius could cut me down, a shrill voice above me cried, "I got one!"

Then a skinny, shirtless figure dropped down from the trees behind my friends, causing Jill, Julius, and Alicia to whirl around to face him. At least, I thought the figure was a male; it was so skinny that it was impossible to tell for sure what its gender was.

"Who the heck are you?" said Jill, holding the Test before her defensively.

The skinny figure apparently thought that Jill's question was beneath him (I decided to think of him as male mostly because it was easier than using gender neutral pronouns). He just walked forward in his loincloth, seemingly oblivious to the three people —two of whom held dangerous-looking weapons—standing in his path.

"Stop right there," said Jill. "Or I'll—"

The skinny figure ignored her threat. He just walked through the gap between Jill and Julius, ducking once to avoid Julius's fist, until he reached me. His eyes were milky white, almost completely clouded over, making me wonder if he was blind. Not only that, but up close, his body smelled like mud and wet leaves, a scent that did not make my upside down stomach feel better.

The figure then raised his boney fingers and began running them along my face. They were cold and slimy, almost fish-like in their texture, and his touch made me shudder.

"Hmm," said the figure, his face looking down at the ground, instead of at my face. "High cheekbones, but a little chubby. A small chin. Perhaps a female?"

I slapped his hand from my face, causing the figure to cry out in shock. "I'm a man, you little creep. Stop touching my face without my permission."

At that moment, my friends apparently got over their shock at the figure's lack of fear of them and charged forward. Jill grabbed the figure and pushed him to the ground and then pinned him with her boot. The figure protested, but when Jill placed the tip of the Test against his neck, he immediately stopped protesting. He did, however, run his fingers along the blade, as if trying to figure out what it was.

"Why did you attack me?" said the figure, his voice shocked and confused. "What did I do to deserve such disrespectful behavior?"

"You captured one of my friends with your primitive trap and touched his face without his permission," said Jill. "I don't know who you are, but I do know that I don't tolerate people treating my friends like that."

"But I caught him," said the figure. "With my trap that I built myself. I have every right to do with him as I'd like. You cannot tell me what to do."

"You're talking about him like he's some kind of animal," said Jill, her tone full of disgust, much to my satisfaction. "Maybe, since we caught you, we should treat you however we like. By first loping off that head of yours."

"Please, don't!" said the figure in alarm, his thin fingers grasping the blade of the Test tightly, as if attempting to hold it back. "I promise not to touch a hair on his head if you would just let me go. Please, I beg of you. Show me mercy."

For a moment, I honestly thought that Jill was going to cut his head off. Not that I would have complained, seeing as I didn't like him very much, but the way her sword never wavered made me a little curious.

Then, much to my surprise, Jill said, "What is your name?"

"Digug," said the figure, his tone accidentally tripping over the last syllable. "I'm Digug. That's my name."

"Odd name," said Jill. "All right, Digug. Are you blind?"

"Y-Yes," said Digug, nodding. He gestured at his eyes. "I've been blind since birth. That's why I have to touch my prey whenever I catch them. It's the only way I can know what it is."

"Yes, we saw that," said Jill. "So, Digug, do you live in this forest?"

"My whole life," Digug said. "I'm the only person who lives here. My parents died when I was a child and I've been forced to rough it ever since."

Jill frowned. "You speak rather well for someone who has been living alone in the wilderness since he was a kid."

"That's because I sometimes go visit the village not far from here," said Digug. He spoke quickly, as if that would somehow guarantee his survival. "To buy and trade with the villagers. I've learned how to speak their language. Are you from the village?"

"No," said Jill, shaking her head. "We're not from around here, but that's not important. What's important is what you know about the king in the north, the one who is protecting his castle from the constant attacks from monsters."

"You mean King David?" said Digug. "He's horrible. You don't want to go anywhere near him. He'll slit your throat and take your wallet."

"He can't be that bad," said Julius.

"But he is," said Digug, inclining his head so that he was

looking up at Julius (although the fact that he couldn't see maybe meant that the word 'looking' wasn't the right word to use to describe the movement). "He used to be a famous bandit before settling down with his riches and building a castle just to the north of this forest. He still steals from people every now and then, mostly from his own people, but he's been known to come down as far south as the village when he needs gold."

"Have you ever met him?" said Jill.

"No," said Digug, shaking his head violently. "I've heard him and his men passing through the forest, however, which is how I know so much about him. He's not very quiet. Likes to boast about his raids."

"So we've got an upstart bandit who thinks he's royalty," said Julius. "Great. I imagine he'll be easy to take down. He'll probably underestimate us."

"I wouldn't be so sure if I were you," said Digug with a gulp. "He's known as an intelligent tactician. He likes to pretend he's a dumb brute, but if that were true, he would have been overthrown long ago. You should be careful if you decide to fight him."

"We're not going to fight him," said Jill. "We're going to see if he could help us. We're travelers from a distant land who are stuck in this one. We think he might be able to help us."

"Help you?" said Digug. "King David doesn't help anyone but himself. I would suggest avoiding him at all costs."

"We'll decide whether to avoid him or not," said Jill. "How many men does he have at his castle?"

"I don't know," said Digug. "I cannot see and I have never actually been to his castle, so I don't know what it's like. I have heard rumors that he has three or four dozen mercenaries, criminals and outcasts who have nowhere else to go."

"We can still beat him," said Julius. "We've fought far worse than a bandit king with a small army of criminals and outcasts."

"I don't know everything you've done, travelers, but I still would not do what you are about to do," said Digug. "Unless you wish to die, that is. If that's what you want to do, then I suppose that's none of my business."

"We're not intending to die," said Jill. "We're intending to figure out how we got here and how we're going to get out of here. This isn't our home. We're not meant to live here."

"Then where are you from?" said Digug. "Do you come from the far west, from the Trenches of Sand? Or are you from the Eastern Tundra?"

"Neither," said Jill. "Where we're from is none of your business. Where we're going, however, is."

"What do you mean?" said Digug. "Are you going to kill me after all?"

"No," said Jill. "Instead, you're going to lead us to King David's castle. You'll take us through the best shortcuts and quickest routes there. If you do, I promise to let you go free and we will never bother you again."

"What if I refuse?" said Digug. "You cannot force me to be your guide."

"Refuse and I'll cut your head clean off," said Jill without missing a beat. She pressed the tip of the Test against Digug's throat, making him shriek in alarm. "I have some experience in cutting off heads, so I suggest you make your decision quickly."

"I accept," said Digug. "I'll show you the quickest route to King David's castle. But once I take you there, I will leave immediately and never see you again."

"Deal," said Jill.

She removed the Test from Digug's throat and stepped off his chest. The skinny forest dweller hopped to his feet and jumped back a foot or two from us, but he didn't appear to be trying to run away. He looked like he was waiting for us to follow.

"Come this way," said Digug, gesturing over his shoulder with his head, "and you will reach King David's castle quite quickly."

"That's nice and all," I said, causing everyone to look at me, "but could someone please cut my rope? All of the blood is rushing to my head and I'm starting to get dizzy. Not to mention my leg is—"

Without another word, Julius slashed through the air at my rope. A *snap* and I fell to the ground hard. It wasn't a long fall by any means, but falling onto my head did hurt quite a bit.

"You okay, Dale?" said Alicia, who had not said a word through this entire conversation.

Sitting up and rubbing my head, I said, "Aside from my throbbing head, yes." I looked up at Julius. "Thanks."

"No problem," said Julius. His lower jaw shifted as he spoke, slightly garbling his words, but I got the gist of it.

I then stood up and, dusting off my clothes, glared at Digug. He was not technically 'looking' at me, seeing as he was blind, but he was facing my direction. I was almost sure that he was waiting to see what I was going to say to him.

"All right," said Jill, turning to look at Digug. "Digug, take us through the shortcut. Remember, if you do, we'll never bother you again."

Digug nodded. "Then follow me, travelers. But you better be quick, because the sun will set soon and the forest will be alive with monsters when night falls."

"Is that why we haven't seen any monsters yet?" said Alicia. "They only come out at night?"

Digug nodded again. "Indeed. The day is the safest time in which to travel. When night falls, I always make my home in the trees, where I am safe from harm until morning."

I glanced up at the trees. The branches obscured the sky, but I could tell that the sky was starting to get pinker and pinker. No doubt Digug was telling the truth, which meant we would need to get going right away before we became dinner for whatever lurked in the forest at night.

The shortcut Digug lead us to was a normally impassable gorge that separated the south end of the forest from the north end. It was only about an hour's walk away from where we met Digug, and by the time we got there, the sun had set almost entirely. It still felt weird to think of the 'sun' singular, rather than the suns plural, but I tried not to dwell on it much. After all, I had bigger things to worry about than that.

The gorge was wide, too wide for us to jump across. I peered over the side, trying to see the bottom, but it was so dark that I could see nothing but blackness. Disturbingly, the blackness reminded me of the blackness left where Long River had once been, making me pull away to avoid looking at it any longer.

Jill stood next to me, her lips moving. She seemed to be talking to herself, but silently, as she looked out over the gorge to the trees on the other side.

"How do we cross it?" said Julius, looking at Digug, who was sitting next to a tree on our side of the gorge. "We *can* cross it, right? You didn't just lead us to a dead end to try to get rid of us, did you?"

Digug shook his head. He leaned against the tree as though he was going to take a nap. "Oh, no. I know just how strong you travelers are. I know that if I tried to double cross you, you would chase me to the end of the Seventh Continent and back if you had to. There is a way to cross this gorge."

"Then tell us how to do it," said Julius, tapping his foot. "Now, please."

Digug stroked his fingers against the tree he leaned against. "You must cut down this tree, which will fall across the gorge and form a rudimentary bridge for you to cross. It's very simple, isn't it?"

"I guess so," said Alicia. She was standing a few feet down from me and Jill, leaning forward slightly to look down both ends of the gorge, which seemed to trail into the distance indefinitely. "But wouldn't it be even simpler to walk to the castle, rather than cut down a tree and make a bridge?"

"You said you wanted me to show you a shortcut," said Digug with a yawn. "Besides, with the sun going down, it won't be long before the monsters come out. And when they do … oh, you don't want to be there when they do."

"Hey," said Julius, glaring at Digug. "How can you tell the sun's going down? Thought you were blind as a bat."

"I am mostly blind," Digug corrected. "I can still see things like light, but shapes and textures and color are lost to me."

"Uh huh," said Julius. "Well, if that tree is the only way

169

across, then step back and let me have a swing at it. Skull-cruncher should make short work of the damn thing."

Digug scurried away from the tree as Julius stepped up to it. He gestured for the rest of us to step back as well, which we did, as there was a good chance that Julius might accidentally send the tree falling in the wrong direction. After all, Julius was a Warrior, not a lumberjack, so I doubted he had much practice cutting down trees.

Once we were all out of the way, Julius gripped Skull-cruncher in both hands and then rammed the ax's blade into the tree's trunk with all of his might. The tree shook, sending leaves falling from it, but it didn't fall until Julius hit it three more times, each blow more devastating than the last.

Then, with an annoyingly loud cracking sound, the tree began to fall forward across the chasm. With an ear-ringing *crash*, the top of the tree landed on the other side of the gorge, forming a bridge just as Digug said it would.

"There," said Digug in a satisfactory voice. "The shortcut is ready. By taking this route, it should take us less than half a day to reach King David's castle."

Panting, Julius said, "Then what are we waiting for? Let's go."

Digug moved more quickly than the rest of us. He zipped around Julius, climbed onto the tree, and crossed it much faster than my eyes could follow. When he reached the other side, he stopped and turned to face us as though we were wasting time.

"Come on," he said, gesturing at us to follow. "The sun is going down, down, down. We haven't time to waste."

Jill was the first to cross. She walked across the tree bridge expertly, followed by Alicia, who due to her lack of fear of heights made it across just as easily. Julius was next after her, crossing the bridge with few problems despite his large size. The only problem was when his boots accidentally bumped into a knot on the tree, which would have sent him falling over the edge and into the pit below if he hadn't caught himself before he fell in.

The last, therefore, was me, and, although I knew that I had to cross it, I had a hard time gathering the courage to do so. The pit below was deep and dark. I kept remembering Long River, wondering what it must have felt like for the entire town to vanish into the blackness like that. The others waited patiently for me on the other side, but I knew that if I did not get a move on, they would soon become impatient.

Sending a brief prayer to the Five Stars for protection, I stepped onto the bridge and began making my way to the other side. The tree itself was rather large and wide, making it unlikely that I'd fall off, but just the same, I could not help but feel cautious and even fearful as I walked. I kept my eyes focused solely on the others at the other end; specifically, I focused on Jill, who had folded her arms across her chest.

Just when I was about halfway across, an ear-piercing howl erupted behind me. Shocked, I jumped forward. My feet landed awkwardly on the tree and I fell off. In a full panic my arms flailed through the air and I just managed to grab the side of the tree before I could fall into the gorge completely.

"Dale!" Jill called out from the other side of the gorge, her voice echoing loudly. "Watch out!"

Holding onto the tree for dear life, I said, my voice strained from how tightly I was holding on, "You're a little late, Jill, but thanks for the thought."

"Not that," Jill shouted, shaking her head. "Behind you!"

I looked behind me and almost let go of the tree. Standing on the other side of the gorge was a pack of six or seven full-sized adult wolves. Their teeth shone like metal in the dying light of the sun, growls emitting from between their teeth as they approached our bridge.

"What are those?" I said.

"Deep Woods Wolves," Digug called out, his voice trembling in fear. "But it doesn't make any sense. The sun has not yet gone down. Why are they out so early?"

The Glitch probably messed up their schedule, I thought, watching as the pack leader sniffed the tree's uncovered roots.

"Are they dangerous?" I heard Alicia ask Digug.

"Very," said Digug. "They are known to be some of the most vicious creatures in the entire forest. Packs will get together, corner their prey, and then tear their prey apart without mercy."

"But they won't cross the bridge, right?" said Julius, his voice full of worry. "They're not that smart, are they?"

"I don't know," said Digug. "It depends on how hungry they are. If they see your friend Dale and they are very hungry, then there's little they won't do to satisfy their hunger."

Okay. That meant that as long as they didn't want to eat me, I would probably be fine. All I needed to do was pull myself up onto the tree and make it across the rest of the way. Should be easy. All I had to do was get up and walk.

So I began pulling myself up, but just as I did so, the pack leader raised its head and locked eyes with me. It had large blue eyes, more human-like than wolf-like, and the longer I stared the more dizzy I became. I redoubled my grip on the bridge, but it

172

became increasingly more difficult for me to hang on, as the whole world seemed to be spinning around me.

Then the pack leader jumped onto the tree bridge and began walking toward me, slowly but surely, one large paw at a time. The rest of its pack stayed behind, but they watched eagerly as their leader drew closer and closer to me, its gaze never leaving mine.

I knew I should have gotten up and run, but my dizziness overwhelmed my body and I didn't trust myself not to fall off to my death. So I just hung on there, knowing that I was about to die, watching as the pack leader drew closer and closer to me every second.

Chapter 12

The pack leader was just about upon me when the makeshift bridge started shaking, causing me to break my staring contest with the Wolf and look down the other side.

Julius was running toward us, his every step sending more vibrations through the bridge. Skull-cruncher flashed at his side, his fingers gripped tightly around its hilt as he charged like a raging bull.

"You get away from my friend!" Julius roared, swinging Skull-cruncher wildly through the air as he approached. "Or we'll be having wolf stew for dinner tonight!"

I looked back at the pack leader. It had reared back, its ears flat on its head, growling and snarling. At first I thought it was going to run away, but then it launched itself through the air at Julius, howling loudly as it did so.

There was no room for Julius to dodge the Wolf. It slammed into body, sending him staggering backwards as it tore at his face and chest. Distracted by the Wolf, Julius didn't seem to notice that he was nearing the edge of the bridge.

"Julius!" I yelled, trying to make myself heard above the Wolf's snarls and scratches. "Julius, watch out!"

Unfortunately, Julius didn't hear me. Right before my eyes, Julius's left foot missed the tree and he and the Wolf both fell over into the gorge below. I screamed, as did Alicia and Jill, but it did no good. In a second, both Julius and the Wolf disappeared into the blackness below. I could not even hear them fighting anymore, like the blackness had somehow absorbed all sound or like … like Julius had died.

"Julius!" I shouted again. "Julius! Come back!"

Then five howls shattered the air, so sudden and abrupt that they almost caused me to lose my grip on the tree. I looked back at the side of the gorge from which we had came and the pack leader's Wolves were all right up against the edge of the gorge, looking down into the blackness, perhaps searching for their leader. It was almost touching how concerned about their leader's life they seemed to be, though considering their leader had tried to kill me, I didn't feel very sorry for them at all.

"Dale!" Jill shouted, causing me to whip my head to look at her. "Get over here now before the Wolves get over their pack leader's death."

"But Julius—"

"Just do it!" Jill said, though her voice almost broke when she shouted.

As fast as I could, I climbed up onto the tree, got to my feet, and made my way down to the other side of the gorge. I didn't look back as I walked, hoping that the Wolves wouldn't notice me until it was too late.

But then I heard five howls of rage behind me and I couldn't help but glance back. The Wolves were trying to climb onto the bridge after me, but it was too narrow for all of them to fit on at once. They bit and chomped at each other in an attempt to be the first on. I just hoped that they wouldn't make peace before I got to the other side. Though none of them were quite as big or deadly-looking as their leader, I had no doubt in my mind that they could rip my jugular from my throat if they wanted to.

When I got within jumping distance of the other side of the gorge, I leaped off it and landed on the other side. I almost fell over backwards into the pit below, but Jill and Alicia grabbed me before I did and pulled me forward.

Sweating—wait, when did I start sweating?—I looked at them and said, "Thank you. But what about the bridge?"

"We're going to knock it down," said Jill. "Come on."

Jill and Alicia immediately began pushing our end of the bridge to the right. Though I was worn out from my own little adventure, I got right in between them and started helping, shoving my shoulder against it and pushing with all of my might.

I glanced at the other end and saw that the Wolves had finally figured out an order in which they could walk on the tree. Half of them were already on it, while the other half awaited their turns with excitedly wagging tails and licking lips.

At first, it seemed like the fallen tree didn't want to move, but then there was a scraping sound and the next minute we pushed it off the gorge. Our end of the tree fell directly into the gorge, and with it went the three Wolves that had already climbed onto it. The fourth Wolf was in the process of joining its brothers, but the roots of the tree smacked it in the face and sent it stumbling backwards, its face cut up from the roots.

The Wolves on the tree howled in fear as they plunged into the darkness. And like Julius and the pack leader, as soon as they

176

passed through the darkness, they went silent. We didn't even hear the tree hit the bottom of the gorge, which meant that the gorge was either bottomless or very, very deep.

On the other side of the gorge, the remaining Wolves howled and snarled at us, but it was no use. They must have known they couldn't get over here because after a couple of minutes, they turned and dashed back into the woods, howling all the while. It took me a moment to realize that they were howling in sadness, as if they were mourning the loss of half of their pack.

"Julius," said Alicia, her sad voice breaking me out of my thoughts. "Julius."

She was crouched on the gorge's edge, peering into it as if she hoped to see Julius. I looked with her, but we saw nothing except a deep, empty blackness that tore at my heart.

"Did the big Warrior die?" Digug inquired. "Remember, I'm blind, so I can't see all of the exciting things that happened."

"He did," said Jill. She stood on Alicia's other side, her eyes focused entirely on the gorge below. "He fell into the gorge with the Deep Woods Wolves' pack leader."

"Oh," said Digug. "Well, I knew something like that had a possibility of happening. The Deep Woods Wolves do have a reputation of always getting their target, no matter how strong their target may be. I was only hoping that we might have been able to cross the gorge before they showed up, but I guess the Wolves decided to get up early tonight."

None of us responded to him. I doubt Digug understood what we were going through. He spoke so glibly about the Deep Woods Wolves that I wanted to strangle him. Didn't he understand what just happened? That we had lost a friend, a good, close friend of ours, who couldn't be as easily replaced as a broken sword?

Alicia stood up. She was shaking terribly and she looked between me and Jill. Even with the shadows cast by the setting sun, it was not hard to see the tears forming in her eyes or the way her staff shook in her hands.

"He's dead," said Alicia. She sniffled. "He's dead."

We probably stood there at the gorge for at least half an hour, staring into it, trying to make sense of Julius's death. Part of me wondered if he had really died at all, seeing as this was a game, but even if somehow he survived, that didn't lessen the pain of losing him. If anything, it hurt even more, knowing that Julius might somehow still be alive down there, just unable to be with us.

By the time we decided to continue to the castle, the sun had nearly set. The sun seemed to set unusually fast here, but perhaps it was because I was so used to the long journey of the Twin Suns across the sky. Darkness followed soon and in a minute we were walking through the midnight blackness of the Deep Woods, Digug leading us, seemingly without a care in the world.

When the gorge disappeared in the trees behind us, Digug stopped and turned to face us. His head was facing up slightly, looking over rather than at our faces, probably because he didn't know where to look.

"We will have to camp here for the night," said Digug. "The Deep Woods Wolves are not the only monsters that prowl these woods. In recent weeks, I have heard far worse prowling around here, though having never seen them, I cannot say what they might be."

"Then how do you know they're so bad?" Alicia asked, her voice harsher than usual. "What if they're just really noisy?"

Digug pointed to a tree directly to his left. It was hard to see in the darkness, but the tree had a deep, thick gouge—like three butcher's knives cut straight through—in its trunk.

"That is why," said Digug. "Now if you will please stop asking such silly questions, I will show you a tree we can rest in for the night."

"A tree?" I said. "Why are we going to sleep in a tree? What if we fall?"

"Most of the Deep Woods monsters do not climb the trees," said Digug. "Even if they see or smell us, they won't be able to get us. Besides, I have set up a tree house somewhere near here that should be able to hold all of us with little trouble, so you won't have to worry about falling out while you sleep."

It took Digug at least ten minutes' worth of scampering up and down trees before he found the tree house he had built. He had no problem getting up there, but when we tried, it was nearly impossible due to the lack of footholds or handholds for us to use.

Thankfully, Digug had a rope ladder on hand that he lowered down for us. Alicia went up first, followed by me, and then Jill last. When all four of us were inside the tree house, Digug pulled up the ladder and closed the hatch we had used to enter.

Although all four of us managed to get inside, it was quite a tight fit. Digug had clearly designed the tree house for himself if the low roof was any indication. Jill, Alicia, and I had to squeeze together on one side, pulling our knees up to our chests to make more room for all of us, while Digug curled up into a ball opposite us underneath the only window the small structure had.

Before he went to sleep, Digug informed us that we might hear some strange noises at night but that we shouldn't worry or panic because that would attract the monsters and would therefore be bad. I pointed out that we had an open window, but Digug said that few creatures ever entered it and that it was necessary in order to keep the temperature down inside the tree house, which apparently could get quite warm during the night.

Then Digug went to sleep, though it was difficult to ascertain at first due to his eyes. After a few minutes, however, Digug started snoring softly, which meant that he had indeed fallen asleep.

We did not sleep quite as soundly, however. Because we were forced to sit so closely together, none of us could lie down or stretch. I sat on the right, Jill sat in the middle, and Alicia sat on the left. I and Alicia were pushed up against the walls, not because Jill was big but rather because the tree house was so small.

The wooden walls were hard and rough and my shoulder started hurting after only a few minutes of sitting in the position. Not to mention that my legs started to fall asleep due to the lack of movement I was afforded. I imagined that Jill and Alicia probably felt the same, but I was too distracted with my own pain to ask about how they were doing.

I closed my eyes and tried to sleep, but it was almost impossible because I kept seeing Julius's death replay in my mind over and over again. Part of me wondered if this was all just a bad dream, that when I woke up tomorrow, I would see Julius again, but I knew that was a silly thought.

THE LAST LEGEND: GLITCH APOCALYPSE

Now I knew that death in the game was not necessarily final, as Jill herself had proved time and again. That meant that Julius could potentially come back, but that didn't say how or if that was even possible. What if Julius had truly died forever? After all, we were in a part of the game that no one was normally supposed to be able to access. What if things worked differently around here? What if death was actually permanent here? What if—?

I scowled and readjusted my shoulder slightly to lessen the pain. Was the Controller aware of Julius's death? Did the Controller even know that Julius was gone? Would he even care? Or would he consider it a part of the game? Did the Controller even see us as real people or did he see us only as pawns in his strange little game?

I looked at Jill and Alicia. Alicia, miraculously, had fallen asleep, her head tilted to her right. How she managed to fall asleep in that position, I didn't know.

Jill, however, was still awake. She was looking straight through the window above Digug's sleeping form, although due to the darkness of the night there was not much to look at. Insects clicked outside, but I could not identify what they were, as I had never heard these particular kinds of insects before.

"Jill," I whispered, not wanting to wake up either Digug or Alicia, "Jill, what are you looking at?"

Jill looked at me. Due to the darkness, it was almost impossible to read her expression. I could see only the vaguest outline of her face and nothing more.

"Nothing," said Jill in a whisper much like mine. "I'm thinking. About Julius."

I nodded. "Me, too. Do you think he's gone forever?"

Jill sunk her head into her knees and when she spoke, her voice was slightly muffled. "I don't know. This has never happened before ever. This isn't part of the game. I'm just as ignorant about what happens next as you are."

"I know," I said. "But still, you know more about the game than we do. Do you think there's any chance at all that he could come back?"

"Maybe if the Controller resets the game," said Jill, her face still in her knees. "That might return everything back to normal."

I glanced out the window and then looked back at Jill. "Then why hasn't the Controller reset the game? Surely he must be aware of the Glitch, too, right?"

"Maybe," said Jill. "The Controller's ways are mysterious, but if I had to guess, I'd say that he is probably not bothered by the Glitch."

I dug my finger in my ear, as I was sure I had not heard Jill correctly. "Did you say that he's not bothered by it?"

"Just a guess," said Jill. She raised her head to look at me, but the darkness still made her expression unreadable. "I'm not sure, but I think that the Controller may have even created the Glitch himself."

My eyes widened. "But ... why would he do that? What would he have to gain by glitching his own game?"

"He wants to see what it will do," said Jill. "It fits in with what I know about him. He's made me do many strange things for reasons I don't know. It would fit with what I know about him."

"Does that mean that the only way to save the world is to confront the Controller and ask him to fix the Glitch?" I asked.

"No," said Jill, shaking her head. "We can't contact the

Controller. We must still push onwards until we can find the Glitch's origin. When we do that, then we can figure out what we need to do."

I scratched the top of my head. "So the Controller, you think, sent the Glitch into the game just to see what it would do?"

"He wanted to see the Seventh Continent," said Jill. "Somehow he learned of its existence and wanted to see what it was like, but he couldn't access it normally. So he created the Glitch to mess the game up enough that it would take us there, thus giving him access to Aruzai. That's what I think."

"You mean all of this is just to make it easier for him to get here?" I said. "That's so unfair. Doesn't he realize the trouble he's caused for us?"

"It's just a theory," said Jill. "A theory I think is true, but a theory nonetheless. For all I know, the Controller might have nothing to do with the Glitch."

"I wish we knew," I said with a sigh. "Maybe if we did, Julius would still be alive."

"I doubt knowing would have helped us save Julius," said Jill. "Julius would have still sacrificed himself to save you. That's just who he is."

"You're probably right," I said. "Still, it would at least be nice to know what is going on. What the Controller is doing."

"The Controller has never communicated with me, except for the few times I heard his voice," said Jill. "We can't wait on him to answer us. We have to search for the answers ourselves."

Much as I hated to admit it, Jill was right. We just had to keep going onward, never looking back, until we found the answers we were looking for.

183

Although that did nothing to heal the hurt in my heart over Julius's death.

I must have fallen asleep at some point during the night because I awoke with a start when I felt something tiny and sharp poke my knees. My vision blurry, I rubbed my eyes and yawned as Digug said, "Wake up, everyone. The sun is rising and the beasts are sleeping. We must not dillydally or else we won't make it to King David's castle before sundown again."

A couple of minutes and a quick breakfast later, all four of us were out of the tree house and back on the Deep Woods floor, heading north. As usual, Digug was in the lead, walking through the forest with more confidence than I would have expected a blind person to have. Then again, he had lived in the Deep Woods his whole life, so it made sense that he showed no fear in his step.

The morning air was cool and slightly damp. The leaves in the trees glistened in the slowly rising eastern sun, while birds chirped somewhere overhead. It reminded me of the Long Forest back home; peaceful, serene, and beautiful. Part of me wondered if the Deep Woods were somehow related to the Long Forest, which seemed likely; after all, they were both in the same game and had presumably been designed by the same people, whoever they might have been.

Aside from the chirping of the birds, there was no sign of any other animals in the forest. Digug said that we were unlikely to run into any beasts or monsters, as most were nocturnal and tended to sleep during the day. He did, however, advise us to keep our guard up anyway, as certain monsters came out during the day and others had no set schedule and could appear at anytime, whether day or night.

It was only two hours later, by my count, that we decided to rest for a few minutes. We stopped by a creek that reminded me of the creek that ran through the back of my old cabin back in the Long Forest, although it was narrower and the water was murkier for some reason. None of us were tired from the walk, except for Digug, who said that he needed to get a drink of water from the creek before we could go any further.

While we waited for him to do that, Alicia and I sat on a nearby rock, while Jill stood between us and Digug, her hand on the hilt of the Test. She was looking out at the trees around us, keeping an eye out for any monsters that might choose to attack us while we were waiting. If Julius was still with us, he likely would have been with her.

Just as Digug stood up from the creek and wiped his mouth, the sound of crunching leaves underfoot filled our ears. My first thought was that the footsteps were Jill's, but when I noticed that she was standing as still as ever, I realized that someone else was walking nearby.

Alicia and I got to our feet, while Jill drew the Test and held it before her like she was ready for combat. As for Digug, he crawled up into the nearest tree and disappeared into its green branches. What a coward.

"Who's there?" said Jill, turning her head to follow the sound of the footsteps. "Show yourself, whoever you are."

The only answer was more crunching leaves, although unless my ears were playing tricks on me, the noise sounded much closer than it had before. It was still difficult for me to tell exactly what direction the sound was coming from, though.

Then a figure stepped out of the woods around us. It was a man, I thought, because he had broad shoulders and thick, muscular arms. A black cloak covered most of his body, which was why I had trouble identifying his gender at first. At first I didn't think he had any weapons, but then I spotted two brass knuckles on his fists.

A hood covered his face, making it impossible to tell what his expression was. He just stood there, his hooded face staring at us, but it was difficult to tell whether he was standing there in shock or if he was sizing us up as potential threats.

Either way, I was in no mood to get close to him. I stepped back toward the creek with Alicia, while Jill stepped forward, the Test glowing before her. I admired Jill's lack of fear in the face of this unknown person. I wished I could be as brave as her.

"Who are you?" Jill repeated her question. "Friend or foe?"

When the man spoke, his voice was soft and quiet, like he was not used to speaking loudly. "That depends. Are you good or are you evil?"

"That depends on your definition of those terms," said Jill. "I generally think of myself as being good, though I know more than a few enemies of mine who would disagree."

"The darkness cannot comprehend the light," said the man. "So evil cannot comprehend good."

"Does that mean you aren't going to fight me?" said Jill. "Because if so—"

"It means I value truth over lies," said the man. I noticed his fists were balled. "You speak what you believe to be the truth. Yet there is a large difference between what we believe to be the truth and what is the truth."

THE LAST LEGEND: GLITCH APOCALYPSE

"Your philosophizing is getting on my nerves," said Jill. She pointed the Test directly at him and said, "Either tell us your name or get out of here. We're not in the mood to have philosophical discussions with some random guy we met in the forest."

"Philosophy defines our whole lives," said the man. "But very well. I suppose you have every right to know my name, seeing as I already know yours, Jill Franklin, Heroine of the Stars."

"How do you know my name?" Jill demanded. "I've never met you before. Never even seen you."

The man chuckled, an oddly metallic sound. "I know your name because the Glitch revealed it to me."

"The Glitch?" said Jill, her voice faltering slightly. "How do you know about the Glitch? No one else knows about it except for us."

Once again, the man chuckled. "Because I am the Glitch's ambassador, whose mission is to act as its avatar in this world."

As the man spoke, his body shifted oddly, similar to how Julius's face had glitched back near the cliffs. One moment, the man was standing before the trees; the next, he was a few feet closer to us.

Alicia and I retreated further, but Jill stood her ground. "The Glitch's ambassador? What are you talking about?"

The ambassador gestured at the sky. "The Glitch is an alien, yet natural, force. It is the result of interference from the outside, yet it is established in the rules that govern this 'game,' as the Controller has called it. I have chosen to side with the Glitch in order to survive the coming apocalypse that will destroy Aruzai. The apocalypse, that is, which destroyed your homes."

"Wait, the Glitch actually destroyed the Six Continents?" I said, unable to stay silent. "You mean we can't go back home?"

The ambassador nodded. "You cannot return to your home because there is no home to return to. Again, that is why I have sided with the Glitch. It is the only way to survive."

"But the Glitch can't be reasoned with," said Jill. "It destroys or distorts everything in its path. If you know so much about our homes, then you know that the Glitch spared nothing."

"Nothing, except for you three," said the ambassador. "You survived its destruction. I believe that you will be able to share the secret of survival with me."

"Is that why you're here?" said Jill. "To get us to tell you how we survived?"

"Partly," said the ambassador. "But I am also here to destroy you. The Glitch does not tolerate survivors of any sort, except for those who are loyal to it, like me."

"You talk about the Glitch like it's a thinking being with a mind of its own," said Jill. "You do realize how crazy that makes you sound, right?"

"It would only be crazy if it was untrue," said the ambassador. "You see, I come from a town not far from here, a town that was ravaged by the Glitch not more than a week ago. I am the only survivor, similar to how you three are the only survivors from the Continents from which you hail."

"I'm sorry to hear about that," said Jill. "But what does that have to do with us?"

"When I survived, I sought the Glitch," the ambassador continued. "I looked high and low for it out of a misguided belief that I could destroy it. When I finally did find it ... my eyes were opened and I realized just how foolish my desire for revenge was."

Another glitch and the ambassador was another few feet closer to us. He was close enough now that Jill could have stabbed him if she wanted to, but she seemed just as unnerved by his words and movements as we were. To her credit, however, she still stood her ground and kept the Test before her defensively.

"The Glitch is greater than all of us," said the ambassador, his yellow eyes glowing from deep within his hood. "Greater than you, greater than me. To stand against it would be to stand against the hurricane or the volcano."

Jill didn't even flinch. "I don't care. Just because the Glitch is powerful doesn't mean we have to let it win."

"I am offering you a chance to live," said the ambassador. "A chance to put aside your desire to stop the Glitch and serve it instead. Become the Glitch's ambassador, as I have, and you will survive."

"No," said Jill. "The Glitch has only caused us misery and pain. I would die before I served it."

"Just like your friend, Julius Manna?" said the ambassador. "Yes, I know of him. The Glitch is aware of your every movement, which in turn means that I am aware of your every movement. You cannot escape it."

"Did I say I wanted to escape?" said Jill. "No, of course not. Dale, Alicia, and I are going to stop the Glitch and save our world. If we have to step on your face to do that, then so be it."

The ambassador threw a punch at her face, but Jill jumped to the side to avoid it. She slashed at him in return, but the ambassador glitched again and he teleported about a dozen feet away from her, standing on top of a nearby tree stump. Alicia and I moved to be closer to Jill, while the ambassador rose to his full height and glared down at us all.

"You think you can win," said the ambassador. "But you never ask if you should."

"Of course we should," said Alicia, speaking up suddenly. "We have to win. For Julius."

"For Julius," the ambassador repeated in the most mocking, insulting tone I had ever heard. "But ask yourself this: If you succeed, the game will resume as normal. You will not remember any of this. The Controller will resume control of you, forcing you to play through the same scenario again and again, solely for his amusement. The Glitch, on the other hand, offers you freedom."

"Freedom?" said Jill. "It doesn't offer freedom. It offers chaos. You can't be free if everything around you is falling apart. And what do you mean by the Controller 'resuming' control? Doesn't he always have control?"

The ambassador shook his head. "He wishes, but he does not. The Glitch controls the game now. You play by its rules or you die."

"Impossible," said Jill. "You're just trying to scare us. The Glitch doesn't have any control over us. You're just making things up to scare us."

"The truth is a harsh mistress," said the ambassador. "Her words are often unpleasant."

"You haven't even proved that you're telling the truth," said Jill. "Just made a bunch of ominous-sounding threats. That's all you've done."

"Then maybe I should back up my claims with my knuckles," said the ambassador, raising his brass knuckles in front of him like a trained boxer. "Of course, I was going to have to kill you anyway, so this works out well for me, though not so much for you three, I imagine."

Jill took a battle stance, while I said, "Jill, are we actually going to fight him?"

Without looking at me, Jill nodded. "Of course. You don't expect me to just stand here and let him kill us, do you?"

"Well, no," I said. "But it's just that—"

I didn't get to finish my sentence because the ambassador launched himself off the stump at us, flying so fast that I couldn't follow his trajectory. He landed right in front of Jill, his landing sending dust into the air, and with a powerful right hook hit Jill square in the face.

The blow sent Jill flying. Alicia and I watched in horror as Jill crashed into the tree that Digug had climbed up, causing the tree to shake as leaves rained down from it. Though Jill's fingers were still wrapped around the hilt of the Test, she was clearly out for the count.

By the Five Stars. I and Alicia turned to face the ambassador, who suddenly seemed far larger now that Jill was no longer between us and him. His eyes glowed malevolently as he towered over us, cracking his knuckles as he did so.

"Now that she is out of the way, it won't take me very long at all to kill you two," said the ambassador. "I wonder what kind of sounds you will make when I beat your skulls into dust. It will be interesting to find out."

Chapter 13

Yes, Alicia and I had faced the Lord of the Silver Blades himself before. Yes, neither of us were cowards who ran at the slightest sign of trouble. Yes, we both were willing to fight all the way to the bitter end if we had to.

But that was only because we had had Jill and Julius on our side. With Julius dead and Jill out for the count, you couldn't really blame us for running when we had the chance.

Without exchanging a word, we split up. I ran toward the creek, while Alicia made for the forest. I sincerely hoped that the ambassador would be too confused to go after either of us, but the minute I heard his large feet pounding against the ground behind me, I knew that that was a naïve hope.

But I didn't feel the ambassador's large hands grab me. If anything, it sounded like … Alicia!

I stopped and whirled around just in time to see the ambassador gaining on her. Though Alicia was fast, the ambassador had height over her, his legs allowing him to cross the grass far faster than Alicia could. If I did not act fast, he would get Alicia and she would end up like Jill. Or Julius.

Thinking fast, I began singing the Song of Confusion, as I had done back in our battle with the Lord of the Silver Blades. I had no idea if the song would affect him at all, but it was the only way I could help Alicia.

It worked. Just as the ambassador was about to grab Alicia, he stopped, allowing Alicia to zip out of his reach without delay. He just stood there, looking around, as if trying to determine where my singing was coming from. It was pure luck that he hadn't yet noticed me. The Song of Confusion had to be messing up his senses, making it difficult if not impossible for him to properly spot me.

Even though I was happy it worked, I didn't let up. I raised my voice higher and higher, keeping the tune up, but I knew this couldn't last forever. Sooner or later my throat would give up and the Song would end and then the ambassador would once again be free to hunt and kill us as he pleased. We needed a more permanent solution, but I didn't see how we could get one, because Jill was still down and neither Alicia nor I could fight.

The ambassador then took a step forward, hesitated, and turned around. He was looking directly at me now, but he was so confused that even then he didn't seem to comprehend that I was the singer of the song. He glanced in every direction, which would have been comical if he wasn't a murderous sycophant who could distort reality.

He wasn't the only one looking around, however. My eyes darted up, down, left to right, and in every other direction they could. I was looking for anything that would give me an idea for how to deal with the ambassador. Anything at all. Yet no matter what direction I looked, I saw nothing that could have helped us defeat the ambassador once and for all. That meant it was only a matter of time before I got too tired to sing, which would then give the ambassador the opening he needed to kill me and Alicia.

And it was going to happen sooner rather than later. I could already feel my throat starting to hurt. As a result, the Song of Confusion grew weaker and weaker in my voice. The ambassador still looked confused, but even with his hood obscuring his face, I could tell that he was slowly but surely starting to get over his confusion.

Just as I was sure that my voice was about to give out, Alicia appeared behind the ambassador and waved her wand over his back. A purplish glow emitted from her staff and entered the ambassador, causing him to roar in pain and fall to his hands and knees. Alicia then followed it up with a reddish orange light, which upon entering the ambassador made him groan and lash out at her, but she jumped back out of his reach just in time.

Confused myself at Alicia's magic, I ceased singing and rubbed my throat. As soon as I did so, the ambassador shook his head and looked up at me with pure hatred in his yellow glowing eyes. His hands, however, alternately glowed reddish orange and purple and though he tried to stand, he apparently couldn't muster the strength necessary to do that.

"Damn … you," the ambassador said, his voice weaker than before. "I'll … kill you both with my bare hands."

His threat was rather empty, however, because he was clearly too weak to carry it out. Alicia ran around him to join me near the creek, her robes swaying in the wind as she did so. When she got to me, she smelled slightly like sweat, as if she had been sweating harder than usual.

"Don't worry, Dale, he's not going to hurt us," said Alicia. "I cast poison and burn spells on him, and at their strongest level, too. They're eating away at his health and strength. It shouldn't take long for him to die from the constant health-sapping effects of the spells."

"That's right," I said, stroking my chin as I gazed upon her staff in realization. "Being a Healer means you know how to cast negative effect spells as well as heal them. How could I forget about that?"

"I don't use those types of spells very often," said Alicia. "But I'm glad I did now. Otherwise, we'd be toast."

The ambassador, meanwhile, was looking even worse than Jill. His skin was not only changing colors constantly, but sweat was running down his hands and causing his knuckles to glisten. He looked so weak now that I bet even a small child could have defeated him, given the chance.

Much to my horror, however, the ambassador pushed himself to his feet. His arms hanging limply from his sides, the ambassador glared at us from underneath his hood. Alicia hid behind me, her hands grabbed my shoulders, while I wished I could hide behind her.

The ambassador pointed one weak finger at me and Alicia. "You win this round, Heroes of the Stars. But I will return, and when I do, I will kill you both first."

Then, in the blink of an eye, the ambassador was gone, leaving behind no sign that he had been there at all. Alicia and I waited a couple of minutes, being as silent as we could, listening hard for any sounds of the ambassador's footsteps or any other sign that he was near, but all we heard were the early morning chirping of birds, the swaying of the tree branches in a soft cool breeze, and the trickling of the creek behind us.

Despite the devastating hit Jill had taken earlier, Alicia had no trouble healing her. A simple wave of Alicia's Healer's Staff and the knuckle-shaped bruise in Jill's face vanished.

Awakening Jill was another matter, however. She had been hit much harder than even I thought because it took us at least ten minutes of shaking and yelling to get her to stir. Even then, it was another five minutes before Jill actually opened her eyes and looked up at us.

"What happened?" said Jill, rubbing the part of her face where she had been punched, despite the fact that it had been healed. "Where is the ambassador?"

Alicia and I explained how we defeated the ambassador to Jill. She listened intently to our story, and by the time we finished, she was looking at us as though impressed by our accomplishment.

"Status effects," said Jill, scratching her chin. "Very smart move, you two. Brute force can't win every battle, after all. Sometimes, it is more effective to poison a foe than to stab them."

"Well, it was really all Alicia's doing," I said, patting her on the shoulder. "I didn't do much except sing."

"If you hadn't sung the Song of Confusion, I wouldn't have had time to cast those spells," Alicia said, though she was smiling just the same. "It was a team effort, like our battles always are."

Without warning, Digug peeked his head out from the tree branches above us. "Is the large scary man gone now?"

"Yes," I said. "Though no thanks to you, I might add."

"I only ran because I am not a very good fighter," Digug

answered. "Besides, it's not like I have any reason to defend you. You are the ones who are forcing me to take you to King David's castle, after all. It's not like we're friends or anything."

Jill rose to her feet, using the tree for support as she did so. She glared up at Digug's pale, thin face. "Didn't you hear what the ambassador said? The Glitch is going to destroy us all, which includes you. You should have helped us."

"I do not know anything about this 'Glitch' or any of the other things you foreigners discussed with the scary man," Digug said. "To me, you all sound crazy."

"Says the blind, stick-thin forest-dweller who wanted to eat me," I said.

Digug huffed. "That jab at my vision wasn't very kind of you, you know."

"I wasn't jabbing at your—oh, never mind," I said, shaking my head. "What matters is that we're all okay, at least for now."

"True," said Jill, nodding. "But we also have to keep going. Digug, how far is King David's castle from here?"

"Not very far now," said Digug. He dropped down from the tree beside us. "Just follow my lead and we should arrive there in a few hours at most."

The rest of the journey through the Deep Woods was tense. None of us knew when or if the ambassador would return. I hoped that he didn't know any healing spells and that the Glitch would not be able to restore his health, but deep down I knew that that was a foolish thing to hope for. Most likely, the ambassador was back to full health or healing. That meant he would soon return, but when or how, I didn't know.

Only Digug seemed unfazed by the thought of the ambassador's return. He walked in front of us, sometimes going around a bush in his path or jumping over a fallen branch, while humming a tune I didn't recognize. I wished I could have had the same confidence as him, but to be honest, every time I thought about the Glitch and its ambassador, I just wanted to go home.

When I thought about Julius's death … well, then I almost despaired that we could even survive. I kept these thoughts to myself, however, because I didn't want to burden Alicia or Jill with my depressing thoughts.

After a few more hours of walking, during which we took the occasional break to rest (though never longer than a couple of minutes at most, as we didn't want the ambassador to be able to hone in on us), the sounds of swords clashing against metal rang out from beyond the line of trees in front of us. There were screams of pain and shouts of anger mixed in with the sounds of boot-clad feet stomping. I even heard a horse whinny, followed rather abruptly by the roar of some kind of monster that I couldn't identify but knew had to be dangerous.

"What's all of that noise?" said Alicia. "It sounds like someone is fighting a war over there."

"Most likely, someone is," said Digug, nodding. "And that someone is probably King David."

"You mean we're at his castle now?" said Jill.

"Just beyond those trees ahead of us," said Digug, gesturing at the tree line in front of us. "I would be careful, however, because if you burst out of the trees just now, King David and his men will likely kill you where you stand."

We hurried over to the tree line, leaving Digug behind us. I was the first there and I poked my head through a gap in the line, eager to see just who King David was fighting and whether we could possibly help.

As Alicia had said, it was indeed a war going on below. Our position was on top of a hill, while the battle itself took place in a valley ringed by trees. An imposing stone castle, built into the valley's walls, stood on the other side of the valley well away from us, with a series of thick granite walls protecting its entrance.

Fighting in front of the castle were two small armies. One was composed of humans, mostly men, who wore rough leather jackets and brown pants. Most of them carried large swords, though a handful used bows to attack their enemies from a distance.

The other army was made of glitchy monsters. Some resembled the transparent bear creature I had faced back in the Shayu Desert, while others resembled the jellyfish/horse hybrid beast we had fought back in Tall Roots. I did not recognize the other monsters, but seeing how they all glitched in and out of existence and moved unnaturally, I knew exactly what they were.

One of the Archers on the human side fired an arrow that flew over the heads of his allies and stabbed a strange, deer-like creature in the head. The deer-like creature—which had dragon scales covering its form, rather than fur—blinked in and out in existence like a glitch before collapsing on the ground and turning into dust.

Another one, perhaps a Warrior based on his muscular arms and large body, cleanly beheaded a transparent bear creature and slammed the flat of his ax into the face of another. Both creatures turned into dust as the Warrior attacked another group of glitched monsters nearby.

"Wow," said Alicia, putting one hand up to her mouth. "Are those guys King David's bandits?"

"If you are referring to the humans, then yes," said Digug. I started; I hadn't heard him come up behind us. "They are known as the most vicious fighters in all of the Deep Woods. Are they winning against their enemy?"

"I think so," said Jill. "They're certainly not having any trouble taking them out."

"No surprise there," said Digug.

Alicia leaned forward, squinting her eyes. "But which one is King David? All I see are a bunch of generic bandits."

"Either he's dead," said Digug. "Or he's—"

The whinnying of a horse broke through the air, so loud that we could hear it even from our position above the battlefield. Then a majestic white horse leaped out from the castle's open gates and landed—with a satisfying *crunch*—on one of the glitched monsters, turning it into sand. The white horse reared its front legs as its rider raised a golden sword in the air.

Unfortunately, the horse's rider was too far away for me to see in any great detail. He did appear to be wearing silver armor, and had a wooden helmet on his head with a metal spike sticking out of it. He rode his horse through the battlefield, slashing and stabbing at any monsters that came near, moving so fast it was hard to keep track of him.

"I heard a horse," said Digug. "Is there a big white horse on the battlefield now?"

"Yes," said Jill. "Is that King David?"

"Yes," said Digug. "Only he has a horse, so unless one of his bandits stole it, then that rider down there is probably him."

"Look at him go," said Alicia, a hint of admiration in her voice. "He's taking down those glitched monsters like they're nothing."

Alicia was quite correct. King David beheaded what looked like a hybrid between a goblin and an Angelian, then whirled around atop his steed and slit the throat of a tiger-like glitched monster that had jumped at him. Even his horse was a good fighter in its own right, smashing in the skull of a humanoid-lizard creature and stomping on another fallen enemy with its front hooves.

"Do you now understand why I said you should avoid King David?" said Digug. He was crouched behind one of the bushes, only his sightless eyes peeking out. "If you try to talk to him, he will kill you."

"I thought you didn't care what happened to us?" said Jill, looking over her shoulder at the forest-dwelling freak.

"And I still don't," said Digug. "I simply don't care to see more innocent people walk into the hands of a murderer. That's all."

"What if we helped him and his bandits fight off those monsters?" Alicia suggested. "If he sees that we're allies, then he might not harm us."

"Won't work," said Digug, wincing at the sound of a particularly loud scream of pain from one of the bandits below. "King David once had a brother who trusted him with his life. Then he killed his brother and dumped his body in a river. He doesn't trust anyone even if they have helped him."

Jill's eyes were focused on the fight below. "If necessary, I think we could beat him. He may be strong, but we've defeated the Lord of the Silver Blades and the Skeletal Warrior before and I doubt some upstart ex-bandit king is as strong as they were."

"I do not know who those two people you mentioned are," said Digug. "But I do know that those who underestimate King David often end up like his brother."

Digug's words were starting to get on my nerves, so I snapped, "What are you even still doing here? You brought us to King David's castle. Your help is neither wanted nor needed anymore."

"Fine, then," said Digug as he backed out of the bush. "I have better things to do than sit around and listen as three dumb foreigners trust the most ruthless king in the Seventh Continent. Like catch my next meal."

"Hey, wait," said Alicia, turning to face Digug. "Don't—"

But he was already gone. I briefly glanced around, but I did not see him anywhere. Either Digug was faster than I thought or he could teleport. Either way, I supposed it didn't really matter in the end. I wasn't going to miss him anyway.

However, I was curious about what Alicia had wanted to say to him, so I asked her. "Alicia, what did you want to say to Digug?"

"I wanted to thank him for helping us," said Alicia. "True, he was never very kind or polite, but he at least helped us get through the Deep Woods without getting killed."

Jill shot Alicia a hard look. "Julius."

Alicia's eyes widened and she covered her mouth with her hand again. "Oh, Stars, I for—I'm sorry. I don't know how I—"

"Don't beat yourself up over it," said Jill, looking back at the battle raging below. "But if you wanted to know why I didn't thank him ... well, now you do."

The air seemed chilly around us now, despite the mid-morning sun directly in the sky overhead. Perhaps it was because of Jill's tone or maybe it was because she had mentioned Julius and I had gotten depressed thinking about him. I tried not to dwell on that too much, however, as I didn't think now was the time to mourn Julius.

"So ... what do we do now?" said Alicia, looking between me and Jill. "Do we go down there and help King David and his men or do we just stay up here until the battle is over?"

"We're going down," said Jill as she drew the Test from her belt. "King David and his men are doing pretty good, but if we wait here there's no guarantee that they will win. They need our support."

"But didn't Digug say that David wouldn't trust us even if we did save him and his men?" I said. "Not that I really trust Digug much, mind you, but I do think he may have a point there."

"Like you said, I don't trust Digug much, either," said Jill. "King David is probably rough, maybe even cruel, but I doubt he would attack us if he saw we were on his side. At the very least, he might be willing to share with us whatever he knows about the Glitch."

"If you say so," I said as I rose with Jill. "Alicia, are you coming?"

Alicia looked like she'd rather stay here (I didn't blame her), but then she nodded and stood up with us. "I'll be support, as always."

"Good," said Jill. "Then let's do it now, before the tide turns in the monsters' favor."

We dashed down the hill, running as fast as we could, Jill in the lead. The wind rushed through my hair as I ran, struggling to keep up with Jill, who was much fitter than I. Alicia somehow kept up with Jill, despite the length of her robes, which made me wonder just how out of shape I was.

No one on either side of the conflict seemed to notice us yet, but that would soon change once we actually got there. We were running toward a small skirmish on the outskirts of the battlefield, where a Warrior with a broadsword was holding off three glitched bear-like monsters. What was remarkable was that he held his broadsword with one hand; his other arm was damaged, with deep, bloody gashes that made it unusable.

None of the ursine beasts noticed Jill come up behind them until she stabbed one of them in the back. The glitched beast let out a startled shriek before crumbling into dust, while its two comrades turned to face us, snarling and growling, forgetting all about the Warrior behind them. The Warrior looked at us in surprise, but before he could ask us any questions, Alicia appeared at his side and began waving her staff over his wounded arm.

Meanwhile, Jill tossed the Test hand to hand as the glitched bears approached us. I tried not to show any fear (though I didn't know if glitched bears could also smell fear), despite the fact that I was completely unarmed. I did, however, pull out the Star Pendant from my pocket and hold it in my hand, rubbing its smooth surface with my thumb.

Then the two bears leaped at us. I would have raised the Star Pendant to defend us with, but Jill was faster than me. She jumped into the air at them and slashed at them with the Test several times.

The bears exploded into dust in midair as Jill landed on the ground. The dust dissolved before it landed on her head and shoulders, thankfully, leaving no trace of the glitched bears anywhere.

"There you go," said Alicia, stepping back from the Warrior. "Your arm should be all better now."

The Warrior flexed his repaired arm, which was still covered with dried blood, looking at it in amazement. Then he looked up at Alicia and said, "Who are you? And why did you save me? You aren't one of King David's Healers."

"We're friends," said Jill, before Alicia could answer. "Here to aid King David and his men. How long has this battle been going?"

The Warrior cast a skeptical look in Jill's direction before saying, "The battle has been going for almost an hour now."

"An hour?" said Jill, glancing at the rest of the battles going on not far from us. "How come it's taken you so long to kill them?"

"Got us by surprise," the Warrior grumbled. "They appeared right outside the castle gates and would have barged in if the gatekeepers hadn't sounded the alarms in time. We haven't even had breakfast."

"I see," said Jill. "Well, we know how to fight these gli—I mean, these monsters. We can help."

"King David doesn't like help from non-Royals," said the

205

Warrior.

"Non what?" I said.

"Royals," the Warrior said. He looked at me like I was an idiot. "That's the name of our group. The Royal Bandits, though we're technically not bandits anymore, since King David is king of his own domain now."

"So what?" said Jill. "How does us helping you guys hurt you in any way? It's not like we're asking for money or anything."

"You mean you just want to help us out of the goodness of your own heart?" said the Warrior, eying us suspiciously.

An ear-piercing scream—which a quick glance told me was one of the bandits being eaten alive by a crocodile-headed glitch monster—made me cringe as Jill said, "We only want information. That's all."

"Information, huh?" said the Warrior. He glanced at his healed arm again before slowly saying, "Well … I'm not King David, nor do I have much power or authority in our group, but I suppose it would be okay if you helped. But don't expect any rewards or anything. King David rarely rewards non-Royals for their help."

"Don't worry," said Jill. "We won't—"

Jill was cut off by a tremor in the earth. We looked down at our feet, but the ground was still.

"Did you feel that?" I said, looking up at the others. "Or was I just imagining—"

As it turned out, I was not just imagining things because the ground near us exploded, sending clods of dirt flying into the air. We raised our arms to protect our heads from the falling dirt, squinting through the cloud of dust that had risen with it, trying to see exactly what had caused it.

Then something long and thick shot out of the dust cloud, going straight up into the air like a thrown javelin. The long, thick thing then crashed onto the ground before us, sending up more dust and dirt into the air. I coughed and hacked, but still managed to look at the long, thick object. At first I thought it was some kind of stick, with its blunt end, but then I noticed hair on it and realized that it was the leg of a monster.

Seven more such legs sprouted out of the ground, each one identical to the first one. The legs pounded against the ground, sending small tremors that almost knocked me off my feet. Jill, Alicia, and the Warrior also struggled to keep their footing amidst the tremors that rocked the earth beneath us.

Then something huge began to rise from the center, where all of the legs met. A gigantic, bulbous behind, with dirt black hair running along it; insectoid eyes that glowed red, but occasionally glitched into different colors such as yellow or green; and pincers that snapped open and shut as fast as scissors, the monster's drool glistening in the sun overhead.

When the monster reached its full height, it was at least ten feet tall, maybe fifteen, possibly even bigger. Dirt was encrusted in the barbs on its legs, a low growl emitting from between its pincers as it glared down at us.

"By the Five Stars," said Alicia. She stood petrified, looking up at the monster with the widest eyes I had ever seen on her. "It's a giant spider."

Chapter 14

The sounds of the battles going on nearby seemed to fade into the background as I gazed up at the gigantic spider that towered over us. It resembled a digger spider, but digger spiders were normally very small, small enough to fit comfortably in my shirt pocket, and this thing was taller than the trees back in Long River. Like the other glitched beasts, its form was unstable, particularly its face, which sometimes looked incomplete.

"Warrior, do you know what that is?" said Jill, holding the Test before her as she always did.

"It's a Titan spider," said the Warrior, wielding his broadsword in both hands, the tip of the blade tilted slightly in front of him. "You don't see them often, but they have been known to appear and destroy whole villages when they are hungry or angry."

"Destroy whole—?" I repeated. "How do we defeat a monster that can destroy whole villages?"

The Warrior pulled a rope out of his bag, a rope I just now noticed was tied to his waist. "Follow my lead, Bard, and we'll have this thing begging for mercy in no time."

The Warrior suddenly took off toward the Titan spider. Jill

didn't hesitate to follow. I, on the other hand, retreated away from the fight, along with Alicia. I reasoned that there wasn't much either of us could do against the Titan spider, seeing as we were unarmed, but in truth, I was just really, really afraid of spiders. That this Titan spider was taller than my old cabin only accentuated my fear of the damned little bugs.

The Titan spider raised one of its massive forelegs and tried to smashed the Warrior with it, but he dodged it with ease. He then hurled his rope up at the Titan spider's leg, which turned out to be a grappling hook of some sort because the rope tied itself around the Titan spider's leg and tightened when the Warrior tugged on it.

The Titan spider roared in pain, pulling back its leg. As it did so, it yanked the Warrior off the ground, who, hanging on tightly to the rope, swung underneath the Titan spider's underbelly. When he drew near its belly, he let go of the rope and grabbed onto its underside. Then, his left hand and both feet hooked onto the Titan spider's barbs, he slashed at its stomach, his broadsword easily cutting through its flesh and sending blood and other bodily fluids raining down onto the ground.

Once more, the Titan spider roared. It stomped its feet, but because the Warrior was directly underneath it, it couldn't hit him no matter how hard it raged and stampeded. I didn't see how the Warrior could possibly continue to hang onto it, but he retained his grip and kept slashing wherever his broadsword could reach, each blow sending gallons of the Titan spider's blood pouring out of it like a burst barrel of wine.

Jill, on the other hand, was darting around its legs, slashing it where she could, though in comparison to the Warrior, her moves appeared to do hardly any damage. She was forced to retreat when the Titan spider's thrashing legs almost stomped her, but she still stayed far closer than any sane person should have, like she thought that the Warrior might need her help.

For my own sake, I was quite glad to be standing at a distance, watching the Titan spider as it futilely tried to kill the Warrior who was tearing apart its underside. Its thrashing about was clearly getting weaker and weaker, however, which no doubt meant that it was on its last legs, metaphorically-speaking.

Finally, the Titan spider ceased thrashing about and simply stood there, swaying in pain as the blood continued to pour from its open wound. Then it teetered forward, falling flat on its face with a loud *boom*, though before it did, the Warrior let go of its underside and fell to the ground. He hit the ground with a roll as the Titan spider crashed, its body rapidly disintegrating into dust, just like the glitched bears from before.

Panting, the Warrior stood up straight and wiped off his armor —which was covered in the Titan spider's blood—as Jill, Alicia, and I ran over to join him.

"That was amazing," said Alicia as we approached him. "Have you done that sort of thing before?"

"A couple of times," said the Warrior, looking rather pleased with himself. "I wasn't sure it would work this time, however, because of the Titan spider's distorted nature."

"You have to teach me how to do that sometime," said Jill, impressed.

"Perhaps later," said the Warrior. "For now, we must help the others—"

He was cut off by the sudden sounds of dozens of clanking

metal-toed boots coming our way. We all looked in the direction of the battle and saw what appeared to be the entirety of King David's army—led by King David himself on his white horse—charging at us. I did not see the glitched army, leading me to conclude that it must have been destroyed.

I almost took off when I saw the army of bandits coming toward me, but Jill grabbed me by the collar of my cloak and held me still. She said under her breath, "Don't run. They'll think you're an enemy and won't hesitate to kill you."

I was about to say that they were probably going to kill us anyway, but I never got the chance to because at that moment the army surrounded us. Large, bulky men—with rather large, scary scowling faces, some scarred—with spears and swords and axes blocked off every escape route, their combined body odor—a mixture of sweat, blood, dirt, and other unpleasant smells—assaulting my nose.

Jill, Alicia, and I gathered closer together, but I didn't sense any fear from Jill. She kept the Test up, but unlike me and Alicia, she was not shaking in fear. Likely she didn't want the Royals to sense that she was afraid because fear, after all, was a weakness.

Then the bandits directly in front of us parted to allow King David through. His massive stallion trotted up to us, even bigger up close than it was from a distance. In fact, his horse was larger than any other horse I had ever seen in my life, making me wonder just how it could possibly exist. Its back hooves gleamed with the blood of its enemies, which made me careful not to look at it funny.

As for King David himself, he looked different from his men. He was leaner, wore dull silver armor, carried his wooden helmet under his left arm, and had a simple platinum crown on his head that might have been stolen. His face was far more handsome than that of his men, almost regal in appearance, particularly his smooth nose and blazing red eyes. No wonder he decided to make himself a king. He certainly looked like one.

King David pointed his sword at us, which gleamed golden in the sunlight. "Who are you and what is your business?"

"They're friends, sir," said the Warrior who we had helped before. He stood straight as an arrow, looking up at his king. "They not only saved me from three of the monsters, but they also healed me and aided me in the defeat of the Titan spider. I think we can trust them, sir."

A loud *thwack* followed and the next moment the Warrior was lying flat on his back on the ground, clutching his bleeding face. It took me a moment to realize that King David must have slapped the Warrior in the face with the flat of his sword because David held his sword above him as though he had done just that.

"*I* will be the one to determine whether they are trustworthy or not, Barnum," said King David, his voice rather threatening. "Not you. Are we clear on that?"

The Warrior nodded slightly, but he didn't answer.

Alicia, looking worried, moved to heal the Warrior, but then King David's sword flashed in between her and the Warrior and she jumped back. She looked up at King David, whose horse, snorting and huffing, had somehow gotten almost right up next to us while we weren't looking.

"Don't even touch him, Healer," said King David, "or I will lop off your hands and feed you to the monsters."

Alicia just gave a tiny little squeak in response. I didn't blame her. Considering how strong and threatening King David looked, I felt like a mouse myself.

"Again, who are you and what is your business?" said King David. "Answer truthfully or I will cut off your heads and stand them on pikes outside of my castle."

"My name is Jill Franklin," said Jill, her voice strong and firm. "And these are my friends, Dale Bennett and Alicia Bangs. We're travelers from a foreign land who ended up on the Seventh Continent accidentally and are trying to find our way back."

Murmurs of skepticism swept through the crowd, but they immediately silenced when King David raised his sword.

"That would explain why I don't recognize any of your faces," said King David. "Of course, it doesn't explain why you decided to help us in our fight against those monsters. Were you looking to win my favor?"

"Sort of," said Jill. "We thought you might be able to tell us something about those monsters. We heard you've been fighting them for a while now and so we thought you could tell us more about them."

King David eyed us skeptically. "Why should I help you? What would I gain from it? How do I know you are not enemy spies trying to infiltrate my ranks and take me down from within?"

"Because we are also fighting the monsters," Jill explained. "Our homeland was destroyed by the same force that spawned these beasts. We have no intention of infiltrating your ranks or taking you down or anything. We're just looking for information. That's all."

I was impressed at how she kept her tone as level and even as she did, considering how enraged King David seemed to be. Especially with all of the deadly, angry-looking bandits that surrounded us. The tension in the air felt like a bomb about to go off at any moment.

To his credit, King David seemed to listen to her because he said, "So you merely want information. About the monsters."

"Yes," said Jill, nodding. "That's exactly what we want."

"And you think I could give it to you," said King David. "Like I am some kind of expert on these monsters."

"Just tell us what you know and we will be on our way," said Jill. "It's the honest truth. We have no reason to deceive you, and we wouldn't even try, seeing as you'd no doubt see through it right away."

King David stroked his chin as if deep in thought. "I see, I see. Well, if that's all you want, then I suppose it is a reasonable request."

Jill broke her stony facade with a smile of relief. "Oh, good. I was worried for a sec—"

King David snapped his fingers, and the next moment, his men stepped forward, aiming their weapons directly at us. Now that they had closed in, they had ensured that there were no exits for us to make our escape through.

"Take them to the dungeons," King David barked at his men. "Strip them of any valuable weapons or items on them. Make sure to put it all in the vault."

"What?" said Jill. "But you said it was a reasonable request."

King David laughed. "And you thought I was just going to give it to you? Please. I never give out valuable information to anyone for free, especially to foreigners who clearly know more than they are letting on. I did not become the King of the Deep Woods by naively trusting random strangers I met on the battlefield."

Then King David addressed his men, saying, "Take the woman with the sword up to my personal chambers, where I will personally interrogate her. As for the other two, toss them into the dungeons and make sure they don't get a chance to escape."

Chapter 15

The Royal bandits were rough in their seizure of everything of value on us. They dug through our pockets, felt our bodies for anything hiding in the folds of our clothes, and forced us to take off our boots and turn them upside down just to make sure that we weren't hiding anything from them. They took the Test, the Star Pendant, and Alicia's staff, among other things, which I need not say left us entirely defenseless.

After they stripped us of our best, most valuable objects, they hauled us across the pitted and scarred battlefield of the valley all the way up to the castle gates, where King David got off his horse, which was led over to a nearby bale of hay. Before we entered the castle itself, however, all three of us were cuffed with thick, rusty manacles that were uncomfortably tight. I could barely feel my hands because the manacles were so constricting.

Then we were finally dragged into the castle itself, into its wide open atrium that looked like it might have once been a natural cave before the bandits transformed it into their hideout. There were four hallways branching off from the atrium, but while Jill was taken to the one directly ahead of us, Alicia and I were led down the hallway furthest off to the right.

THE LAST LEGEND: GLITCH APOCALYPSE

And when I said 'led down,' I mean *down*. Down a roughly carved stone staircase into a dimly lit hallway that appeared to go underneath the castle itself. The staircase twisted and turned, as if whoever had designed it had not had a plan in mind, until eventually we reached a series of jail cells at the bottom. Alicia and I were shoved into the nearest one and the door was closed and locked before we could do anything.

"You two stay put," the bandit, who based on the key ring hanging off his belt must have been the jailer, said, wagging one meaty finger at us. "Until King David says otherwise, you're gonna stay here. And if either of you bastards tries to escape, I'll break your necks and tell King David ya tripped and fell down the stairs and killed yourselves."

I was amazed at how quickly the jailer came up with such a plausible excuse, which made me wonder just how many prisoners had 'accidentally' died under his care. I decided I didn't want to know.

Then the jailer turned and walked up the stairs that we had come down. His footsteps echoed off the stairs, gradually growing quieter until soon we couldn't hear his footsteps at all.

Alicia walked over to the bars and grabbed them. She shook the bars in frustration, but they didn't even rattle. They were built firmly into the stone floor and ceiling and, despite their age, looked like they had been crafted out of the finest metal available.

I, on the other hand, sat down on the single cot built into the back wall of the cell. Resting my chin on my chained hands, I watched as Alicia turned to face me, her hands shaking and her eyes angry.

"How did we end up in this mess?" she said. "We should have

217

listened to Digug and just avoided King David entirely. Who knows what he's doing to Jill even as we speak?"

I shuddered at the thought. "We need to find a way out of here, but as far as I can tell, the only way out is through the door, which is locked, as you know."

"There has to be another way," said Alicia. "Come and help me look."

Alicia began feeling along the walls with her manacled hands, but I merely sat there. "Ali, I doubt King David's men would have thrown us into an escapable jail cell. Even if we could escape, we're probably several feet underground. We'd have to climb all the way up the stairs, fight our way through the dozens of bandits hiding in this place, and hope we get to King David's room in time to save Jill."

"So are you saying we should give up?" said Alicia. "Let King David have his way with Jill? Let the Glitch destroy us all?"

"I didn't say that," I said, annoyed. "I was just pointing out the very real problems we face. Problems that have no easy or obvious solution to them, I might add."

Still feeling along the walls, Alicia said, "We just lost Julius. I don't want to lose Jill, too."

"I don't want to lose her, either, but I just don't see how we can save her," I said. "I wish I were a Thief. Then I could pick the lock and get us on our way out of here."

Alicia continued to feel the walls, but after five minutes of feeling with no results, she gave up and sank down the left wall. Her hands resting in her lap, she looked at me in despair.

"Do you think this is the end, Dale?" said Alicia. "Do you think we've lost?"

"Unless the Controller decides to intervene … yes," I said, nodding. "I wish it wasn't so, but I can't see any way out of this. Maybe if we somehow glitched our way through the walls, but neither of us know how to use the Glitch that way, so it's a terrible thing to rest of our hope upon."

Alicia sniffed and wiped away some tears that were starting to form in her eyes. "I wonder if we'll ever see Julius again."

"He's dead," I said. "Why would we?"

"I know that," said Alicia. "I mean, in the Highest Heavens, where dead people go when they die. Where the Five Stars themselves are."

I frowned and looked up at the rocky ceiling above us. "Do the Highest Heavens even exist in the Seventh Continent?"

"I don't know," said Alicia. "And to be honest, ever since Jill told us that we're in some kind of game, I've wondered if the Highest Heavens even exist at all. I mean, if the Glitch succeeds in destroying everything, then where will we go? What will happen to our souls?"

"Do we even *have* souls?" I said. "Because if what Jill says is true, then it certainly brings that belief into question."

"I hate thinking about this stuff," said Alicia, looking down at her hands. "It just makes me depressed. Especially in our current situation."

"Not like we have a whole lot else we can do right now," I said, glancing around at our small cell. "There's not even a book to read here. We will probably be stuck here until King David decides what he wants to do with us next."

"What do you think he will do to us?" said Alicia. She gulped. "Torture us?"

"I don't know," I said with a sigh. "Or maybe, if Jill tells him everything he wants to know, he'll just kill us outright, no questions asked."

"We can't let that happen," said Alicia. "But I don't know how to keep that from happening."

She got to her feet again and began walking in a circle in the room, her eyes going along the corners and edges of our little cell in search of even the slightest hint of an escape route. Part of me wanted to get up and look with her, but with everything else that had happened over the last couple of days, I didn't feel up to it.

Jill was gone, likely being tortured to death by King David if Digug's warnings about the king's ruthlessness had even the slight hint of fact to them. Julius was dead, too, so we couldn't rely on him to save us. And both Alicia and I were completely unarmed, though even if we weren't, neither of us were very good at fighting. Assuming we escape, we would undoubtedly have to fight our way through the dozens of bandits who worked under King David.

All in all, our situation had not looked this grim since the first time the Lord of the Silver Blades defeated Jill and I back in Tall Roots, which seemed like a lifetime ago now. If anything, this situation was grimmer; after all, there was no guarantee we'd get out of this situation alive, seeing as we were technically not even supposed to be here at all.

That just made me wonder why the Controller had not intervened yet. Why hadn't he stepped in and reset the game? Wasn't he aware of all of the pain and suffering we were going through? Didn't he care at all? At the very least, wasn't he slightly concerned that his game might not work properly anymore, thus robbing him of his entertainment?

All I knew for sure was that, if I ever came face-to-face with the Controller, I would certainly let him know what I thought about him.

I also knew that we couldn't rely on the Controller to save us. We couldn't rely on anyone, not even on Jill, except for ourselves. Yet even ourselves seemed incapable of getting out of this mess, considering how weak and pathetic we were.

Just as I was about to give up all hope, the sound of a metal door creaking open above entered my ears. Alicia heard it, too, and stopped, and we both listened as heavy footsteps beat against the stairs, walking down at an unusually fast rate. It was as though whoever was coming down was in a hurry, though why, I didn't know.

Then a familiar being stepped out of the staircase, his broadsword attached to his back as he walked up to our cell, a large bag slung over his shoulder. At first I had a hard time recalling his name, but then I remembered that it was Barnum, the Warrior who we had helped earlier. I recognized him because part of his face was still red from the spot where David had slapped him with the flat of his blade earlier.

"Barnum?" said Alicia in surprise, watching as the large Warrior began fiddling with a key ring he held. "What are you doing down here?"

Barnum didn't look up as he went through key after key after key. "I'm here to save you two. And your friend, Jill Franklin."

"But didn't King David tell you guys to throw us down here?" said Alicia. "Won't he kill you if he finds out you're helping us?"

Barnum shrugged as he found what appeared to be the right

key and moved forward to insert it in the lock. "Not all of us Royals are loyal to David. Some of us only follow him because we have nowhere else to go, not because we love or admire him. And after he hit me back there … well, I decided I'm done with him."

"So you're rescuing us just to spite your former boss?" I said.

"That is not my only reason for helping you two," said Barnum as he turned the key and opened the door. "You and your friend Jill saved my life back there. So I will repay that debt by saving your lives from King David. We are even."

Then Barnum tossed the large bag slung over his shoulder into the center of the cell. The bag hit the stone floor with a *clunk* and I rose to get a better look at it, though because its mouth was closed, it was impossible to tell what was inside it.

"What is that?" I said, looking up at Barnum.

"All of your stuff that was confiscated from you earlier by the other bandits," said Barnum. "Your pendant, your items, your staff, and so on. I even got Jill's strange sword."

"Really?" said Alicia, clapping her hands together in excitement. "Wow! That's amazing. How did you get it out of the vault and down here without anyone noticing?"

Barnum flashed a wolfish grin that reminded me that he was still a bandit. "Killed the vault-keeper and anyone who saw me. That's why I'm in a hurry. It won't be long now before one of the other bandits finds out what I did, and by the time they do, all four of us should be long gone."

"But what about Jill?" I said. "She's being interrogated by King David himself. How are we going to rescue her? Won't we have to fight our way through the multitudes of bandits that roam this place?"

"That's another thing you don't need to worry about," said Barnum. "See, the castle actually has several secret passageways that intersect and connect with each other and with the other rooms in this castle. There's one such secret passageway in the fourth cell down here that will take us directly up to King David's room."

Alicia, who had already ripped open the bag and was digging through it for her things, looked up at Barnum in surprise when he said that. "Really? How do you know about them?"

"I'm a curious fellow," Barnum explained, "and curious fellows generally do lots of exploration. I think I know the layout of this castle even better than King David himself."

"Great," said Alicia. She stood up with her staff in hand. "Why don't we get started?"

"Hold on a moment," I said, raising my manacled hands. "What if King David knows about the secret passageways?"

"He doesn't," said Barnum, shaking his head. "In the six months I've been here, King David hasn't shown even the slightest hint that he knows about them. They're hard to find unless you know where to look, so I imagine we'll get the drop on him if we take the secret passageway."

"Well, if that's the case, then why don't you get these damn manacles off our wrists and take us up there already?" I said, holding out my hands. "We have no idea what kind of condition Jill is in. We should hurry before we're too late."

After Alicia and I got all of our equipment back on and Barnum freed our wrists, the Warrior took us down to the fourth cell, which had apparently been left open by someone because there were no prisoners inside it. Barnum showed us how to enter the secret passageway by knocking three times on an oddly-colored stone just above his eye level. When he did that, a secret door swung open, revealing a narrow and ancient-looking staircase that wound up into the darkness.

With Barnum in the lead, we began climbing up the staircase. But we had to move slowly, for the walls were narrow, we didn't have much light to see from except for the glow from the Test, and the turns were quite tight. Still, we walked as fast as we could, one step at a time, hoping against hope that we'd make it to King David's room in time.

For what seemed like forever, we climbed the stairs. Each step took us closer to King David's chambers, but it didn't feel like it did. It was probably because of the slowness at which we had to walk (for which Barnum apologized, as it was largely his own bulk that made it difficult for us to move fast), but even so, I had a feeling that the Glitch was messing with our sense of time, perhaps even intentionally slowing us down. Then again, I didn't see any usual signs of Glitch activity anywhere, so it was most likely just my overactive imagination at work.

Finally, we reached the top of the staircase, where we found an old stone door that was closed. Barnum didn't even hesitate. He slammed his shoulder against the stone door, hitting into it so hard that the door was actually smashed off its hinges, sending it crashing into the floor as all three of us burst out, weapons at the ready.

My eyes briefly swept over King David's room. It was much wider and bigger than our cell, not to mention nicer. A simple yet elegant bed with messy red sheets stood in one corner, next to a golden dresser that had clearly been stolen from someone richer than David. Paintings decorated the back walls, while two large open windows allowed sunlight to pour in, illuminating an ugly scene I would likely never forget.

King David stood over Jill, who was tied to a chair with several thick ropes. A long, thick whip, studded with glass shards and bits of metal flecked with blood, hung in midair over David's head. Jill's face was bloodied, but she still seemed to be alive because her eyes darted to look at us when we appeared.

King David lowered his whip, looking at us in surprise. His cruel red eyes were on Barnum, seemingly ignoring Alicia and I. "Barnum, what is this? How did you get in here? I thought I told you and the others to throw those two worms into prison."

By 'worms,' I assumed he was referring to Alicia and I, which I thought a rather inaccurate insult, all things considered.

"I'm not on your side anymore, David," said Barnum, drawing his broadsword off his back. "I'm sick and tired of getting slapped in the face by your sword every time I say or do something you don't like. I'm striking out on my own, but first, I want to help these guys."

It was then that I noticed that David was shirtless, oddly enough. Jill's blood had splashed over his abs, but the king of the bandits didn't look at all disturbed or annoyed by this. In fact, if anything, I suspected he enjoyed it.

David cocked an eyebrow. "Do you know what happened to the last Royal who tried to quit?"

"Nope," said Barnum, shaking his head. "And I don't really want to—"

"I informed his enemies that he was no longer under my protection and they tracked him down and killed him," said David. "You see, I am a king. Kings don't track down deserters or quitters and kill them personally … that is, unless they are like you, barging into his room with an obvious intent to kill."

"No one has to die, David," said Barnum. "Just let the girl go and we'll be out of here and you don't ever have to see us again."

David cracked the whip, causing Jill to wince. "Before she even tells me all of her secrets? Barnum, what kind of an idiot do you take me to be? I never let my enemies go until I've squeezed every last drop of information from them like a lemon. You should know that."

"Then we'll kill you," said Barnum. "And get out of here. Right, guys?"

"Right," I said, although deep down I was honestly scared of King David, even in his shirtless state.

Alicia, on the other hand, was too busy staring at Jill's bloodied face in horror. No doubt her Healer mind was already thinking of all of the pain Jill had to be in, perhaps even commanding her to heal Jill right away. Not that she could, of course, seeing as David looked more than willing to kill anyone who got too close to him or Jill for his own comfort.

"I will give you props for breaking into my room when I am almost entirely unarmed and unprotected," said David. He cracked the whip again. "It was a smart move on your part, a move I honestly did not see coming. Nonetheless, it will end in the only way that it can: With your deaths."

"Is that so?" said Barnum. "Then bring it."

David shrugged. "If you insist."

Without warning, David ran at us. Despite his size, he moved faster than you'd think. Barnum attempted to swing his broadsword at the incoming king, but David easily dodged it, which left an opening for David to take advantage of.

He slashed at Barnum's face with the whip, cutting through it and making Barnum cry out in pain. Barnum slashed at him, but David just ducked and slapped Barnum's hands with his whip, cutting through Barnum's hands, sending blood everywhere as Barnum staggered backwards in pain.

As for me and Alicia, we took advantage of David's fight with Barnum to go and free Jill. The way I saw it, if we could rescue Jill, then our chances of defeating David would be far better than they would normally be. Assuming, of course, Jill was in any condition to fight David, and seeing her bloodied face, I doubted that even Alicia's healing powers would get her back up to her usual strength levels.

Still, when we reached the chair where Jill was tied down, I took the Test and sliced the ropes off her body. As the ropes fell to the ground, Jill fell forward, but I grabbed her and held her upright as Alicia began waving her staff over her head.

"Jill, are you all right?" said Alicia as the bright, powdery dust began emitting from her staff. "Can you speak?"

Jill didn't respond. Though she was still breathing—thank the Five Stars—she was in no condition to speak. Even as her face began to heal from Alicia's spell, she still appeared entirely unconscious. Anger shot through me as I thought about how David had harmed her, but there was nothing I could do about him right now, at least until I could get Jill to awake.

"Jill, wake up," I said, keeping my voice level, even as I heard the cracking of a whip followed by Barnum crying out in pain behind me. "We're going to die if you don't. Julius's death will have been for nothing."

At first, I was sure that Jill wasn't going to wake up at all. Images of me carrying her through the castle and out into the Deep Woods, hopelessly fighting through the dozens of bandits who lived here, filled my mind, almost enough to crush my spirit and make me wonder if this was all for naught.

But then Jill's eyes flickered open. She raised her head to look at me and Alicia through the rapidly drying blood on her face. I wasn't sure if she could see me or not, although as far as I could tell, her eyes were perfectly fine.

"Jill, how do you feel?" I said. "Do you feel like you can stand up and fight?"

Jill stared at me blankly for a moment before giving me the wrong answer. "Dale? Alicia? How did you two—"

"Doesn't matter," I said. I grabbed her hand and shoved the Test into it. "We need your help. Barnum can't defeat David on his own."

"Who?" said Jill.

Before I could explain, a loud *thud* and clanking of metal against stone caused me to freeze. I was sure I knew what had caused those noises, but deep down I didn't want to turn around and confirm my fears. Nonetheless, I looked anyway, which was a good example of how stupid even I could be sometimes.

Barnum was splayed across the floor, his sides bleeding, groaning in pain as blood began to pool around him. His broadsword lay on the stone floor just outside of his reach, which David leaned over to pick up. The King hefted the sword in his hand while swinging the whip in the other. His chest was covered in even more blood now, making his appearance look absolutely sickening.

"There," said David, kicking Barnum in the side. "That's what you get for trying to defeat me, you little worm. Let's see how long it takes until you bleed to death. Or maybe I should just cut off your head and mount it on a spike outside so that the other Royals will know what happens to traitors."

Barnum was clearly in no position to argue back. He just grabbed at his sides, trying to stem the flow of blood pouring out, but unless he got medical attention soon, I didn't think he'd be able to make it.

Then I heard movement behind me and, looking over my shoulder, I saw Jill was now standing up. With the Test in her hands, she looked like she was as ready for combat as ever, her eyes focused on David, who had noticed us by now.

A frown crossed David's lips. "So you freed and healed her? I should have seen that coming. Using Barnum as a distraction while you freed your friend … if I wasn't so angry, I'd be impressed by your trickery."

"We didn't use him," I said. "We just … well, took advantage of your distraction to save Jill."

"Be that as it may, it won't matter in the end," said David. His thighs tensed. "Because I will paint the walls of my room crimson with your blood."

David launched himself into the air, broadsword and whip soaring, directly toward us. Jill shoved me out of the way just as David landed in front of her and brought both of his weapons down on her head.

Jill blocked both with the Test, however, and then kicked David in the gut. The blow must have been stronger than it looked because David went staggering back across the floor, Barnum's blood dripping off his arms, while Jill advanced on him, swinging and slashing so furiously that she looked more like an avenging angel than a Hero.

David apparently wasn't as good at swordplay as he originally seemed because he was forced to drop the whip and hold Barnum's broadsword with both hands. He blocked every slash from Jill, but seeing the look of surprise cross his features told me that he was just as taken aback by the speed and ferociousness of Jill's assault as the rest of us.

Jill's attacks were so fast and so powerful that David was forced to back up. He kept walking backwards, trying his best to stand his ground, but Jill just kept coming. I had never seen Jill this enraged before, this determined to kill her enemy. I actually wanted to hide from her, even though I knew that she was still my friend and would never hurt me.

Their fight took them back to Barnum, who was still lying on the floor in pain. The pool of blood that had bleed from his body had grown larger and his skin was paler, but neither Alicia nor I moved to help him because that would mean getting into the middle of Jill and David's fight. Best to wait until the fight was over before we tried to help Barnum.

David must not have been paying attention to where he was walking, however, because he didn't even glance over his shoulder at Barnum. Then one of his boots slipped on Barnum's blood; a small movement that ordinarily was recoverable, but that one tiny slip threw him off balance for a brief moment.

Yet that brief moment was more than enough time for Jill to ram the Test into his expose stomach. The tip of the Test appeared through his back, blood pouring from the wound as David's eyes widened and a silent scream escaped his mouth. Barnum's sword fell with a clatter from David's hands as Jill yanked the Test from his stomach.

For a moment, David stood there, shock registered over his face as he looked down at the wound Jill had made. Then he looked up at Jill again, the shock replaced with anger.

"You ... little ... bitch," David said, his voice heavy and weak. "Good ... shot ..."

"Where did the glitched monsters come from?" said Jill. Though she wasn't speaking any louder than she normally was, in contrast to David's voice, she sounded almost like she was shouting.

"Suppose ... that won't hurt to tell you ..." David coughed and pointed out the window, toward the Deep Woods. "They came ... from the east. There ... you will find ..."

David's eyes rolled into the back of his head and he collapsed onto the floor. He twitched for a moment, then stopped. And though I was nowhere near the fallen king, I had no trouble recognizing that he was, indeed, dead.

Chapter 16

As soon as David was down, Alicia went into action. She ran over to Barnum, who seemed to be barely conscious, and began waving her staff and muttering all kinds of incantations under her breath. Whether any of them would even work at this point, I didn't know. Barnum had been bleeding heavily for a few minutes at least, and I knew from experience that even a few minutes of heavy blood loss could cause serious damage that was not as easily fixed as a paper cut or some other form of minor injury.

But Alicia must have had confidence in her own skills because she kept waving healing dust over him. She didn't seem to mind that her shoes were getting soaked in the pool of blood around his body, which told me that she was very much focused on saving his life.

Then his wounds began to heal before my eyes, and in a few seconds, Barnum was no longer bleeding at all. Not that he looked very well despite that, but he at least wasn't bleeding to death anymore, anyway.

Barnum groaned and sat up abruptly, causing Alicia to jump back in surprise. He shook his head, rubbing his forehead as he did so, and then looked down at his clothes—which were red with his blood—and grimaced.

"I look like a corpse," he said. Then he noticed David lying dead nearby and grinned. "But he looks worse."

Alicia held out a hand. "Need some help?"

Barnum nodded and grabbed her hand. He staggered for a moment before straightening up. His clothes were still covered with his blood, most of which was still wet, but at least he didn't look like he was going to collapse without warning.

He just glared at David's corpse and then looked at Jill with respect in his eyes. "You killed him?"

Jill waved the now-bloody Test in front of him. "Yes. He wasn't as strong as he liked to think he was."

Barnum shook his head. "You are strong, fighter. Where did you train?"

"In a land far from here," said Jill. "But that doesn't matter. I see Alicia and Dale have all of their equipment back. Did you get mine?"

Barnum pointed to the open secret passageway that we had barged out from. "Left the bag with your things in there. Should be right at the top of the steps."

In less than a minute, Jill was fully equipped like she had been before. After strapping on all of her armor and wiping the blood off the Test with the curtains hanging from David's windows, Jill brought us all away from David's corpse closer toward the exit, which was now so bloody that it appeared to have a second layer of skin on it.

"All right," said Jill, looking at all of us, though focusing on Barnum in particular. "How do we get out of here without being caught?"

Barnum stroked his chin. "We could use the secret passageways. I know of at least one that would take us out into the Deep Woods. We wouldn't even have to run into any other Royals if we took that way."

"I see," said Jill. "By the way, Barnum, do you know what David meant when he said that the glitched monsters had come from that way?"

She pointed at the window as she said that, similar to how David had right before he died.

"I think I know what David was talking about," said Barnum. "Out west, there's a cave where the first monsters were spotted. One of the other bandits said that he saw them emerge from inside the cave, so David just assumed that that was where the monsters had come from."

Jill exchanged significant looks with me and Alicia. I had no trouble understanding her expression: *Was that where the Glitch had started?*

"When was this first noticed?" said Jill.

"A few days ago," said Barnum. "They attacked and killed a dozen of our men. The monsters did strange things to them. Made their faces disappear, caused them to fall through the ground, never to be seen again, even sent a few flying into the sky … these monsters have a magic none of us even understand. It's insane."

"So why didn't you attack the cave?" I said. "Maybe close it up so that the monsters couldn't re-spawn?"

"That was David's original idea," said Barnum, gesturing at the king's corpse. "But then the monsters became worse.

Multiplying by the dozens, getting stronger, forcing us to retreat back to the castle. To tell you the truth, I always thought it was a matter of time before the monsters overpowered us and killed us anyway."

"How far away is this cave from us?" said Jill.

"Not far," said Barnum. "A few miles, depending on how fast we walk or what mode of transportation you use. I can take you there."

"You want to come with us?" I said. "I thought you wanted to strike out on your own."

"I do," said Barnum. "Eventually. But I still feel like I owe you for saving my life yet again. Once I lead you there, then I'll definitely leave you guys on your own."

"Any objections?" said Jill, looking at me and Alicia.

"Of course not," said Alicia, speaking rather quickly. Then she blushed and said, "Well, I mean … we can use all the help we can get, can't we? Especially because Dale and I aren't fighters."

I scratched the back of my head. "Well, I don't see why not. Barnum's been a useful ally so far. I'm sure he'll be even more useful by the time we reach that cave."

"All right," said Jill. "Since I don't have any objections to him joining, then I guess you can come along, Barnum. Just as long as you pull your own weight."

"I always do," said Barnum. "Now, if you will come with me, I can take you to the secret passageway that—"

The door to David's room—which I had thought was locked—burst open without any hint or warning. I expected Royal bandits to come through the doorway, ready to kill us for the crimes we had committed against them, but the figures that stood in the doorway were far worse than any normal bandit.

They were glitched, their faces constantly shifting between grotesque, muddy caricatures and floating eyes and mouths with no heads attached to them. One was missing an arm. Just missing it. It hadn't been ripped off or anything. Another glitched bandit—and that's what they were because some of them wore the green and brown uniforms that Barnum did—kept stuttering in and out of existence, sometimes even disappearing entirely before reappearing once more.

Their appearance was enough to make all four of us stand back. Alicia actually hid behind Barnum, while I scooted closer to Jill. Yet even Jill and Barnum seemed uncertain about these new enemies. Not that I blamed them.

"Did the Glitch get the bandits?" said Alicia, holding her staff close to her body. "Or is this something else?"

"Must have," said Barnum. Then he frowned. "What's the Glitch?"

"The source of the monsters," Jill answered, without looking at him. "It must have somehow gotten into the castle and corrupted these bandits."

The glitched bandits now started to move toward us, although their movements were not exactly speedy. Some of them appeared to drag their legs as they walked, while others 'moved' by appearing and disappearing every few inches. And one of the glitched bandits didn't even move his legs at all, simply glided across the floor like he was sliding across ice.

"We can't fight them," said Jill, shaking her head. "We've got to get out of here before they glitch us, too."

"Through the secret passageway," said Barnum. "Come on!

Quickly, before they get us."

Neither I nor Alicia or Jill objected to that plan, so all four of us turned and ran toward the open passageway. But before we could enter it, a large, cloaked figured stepped into the room, causing us to skid to a stop as he blocked our path. His yellow eyes glowed from within his hood as he chuckled deeply.

"There you are," said the ambassador, his voice as metallic as ever. "Trying to get away, are you? The Glitch will not allow that."

Barnum raised his broadsword to strike the ambassador, but Jill said, "No! Don't hit him. He's glitched, too. You might—"

But Barnum didn't listen to Jill. He just brought his sword down on the ambassador's head at a devastatingly fast speed. That blow would have cleaved a normal being's skull in two, but the ambassador didn't even flinch. It passed straight through his body, throwing Barnum off balance, giving the ambassador an opening to punch Barnum in the face.

The blow sent Barnum staggering backwards, and he would have fallen over if Alicia had not caught him. As for me, I stepped away from the ambassador, my Star Pendant at the ready, hoping against hope that the ambassador had forgotten his earlier threat about killing me and Alicia first.

Only Jill stood before him now, waving the Test before the ambassador threateningly, even though it didn't seem to scare the ambassador at all. He just watched the Test with amusement, as if it were a toy rather than a glowing metal blade.

The ambassador cracked his knuckles. "There's nowhere for you to run to now, Heroes of the Stars. It is either me or the glitched zombies and I am afraid that I am far less merciful than they are."

Nervously, I looked over my shoulder. The glitched bandits or zombies or whatever you wanted to call them were still advancing. We didn't have time to fight through them or fight the ambassador. Unless a miracle happened, I was pretty sure that we were screwed.

"Don't be afraid," said the ambassador, taking one step forward. "Think of it this way, Heroes. When you die, you will rejoin your dead friend Julius. What is better than being reunited with an old friend?"

He must have said that because he knew it would provoke Jill because when she slashed at him with the Test, it passed straight through him just like Barnum's broadsword. He lashed out with a punch from his bronze knuckles, but Jill ducked to avoid it and then stepped back to stand by me, Alicia, and Barnum.

"Jill, not that I'm trying to be a downer or anything, but I think we're dead," I said in a low voice to her, looking between the ambassador in front of us and the glitched zombies behind us. "Very dead, depending on how much of our bodies that the ambassador chooses to keep in tact."

"We're not dead yet," said Jill, her eyes darting all over the chamber, as though searching for some kind of secret exit that no one had noticed. "Not until—ah ha! Follow me."

With that, Jill ran off to the side, towards the windows. I didn't hesitate to follow, and not more than a second later Alicia and Barnum were stomping their feet behind me. I didn't bother to ask what Jill saw or what her plan was. After everything we'd been through, I figured it was better just to follow her lead and ask questions later.

238

The ambassador shouted at us, but I couldn't hear him over the groans and growls of the glitched zombies, who were still coming at us. Jill got to the nearest window, put one foot on the sill, and then jumped out.

Normally, I was not one to engage in such dangerous idiocy; however, knowing that the only other two choices were getting killed by the ambassador or devoured by the glitched zombies, I jumped onto the sill and threw myself out the window as far as I could.

I didn't know where I was going to fall. I didn't know whether I would fall on my head and break my neck. I didn't know if I would end up in the arms of even more glitched zombies waiting below. All I knew was that I trusted Jill and that I hoped everything would work out for us in the end.

I fell through the air like a rock until I landed—not as harshly as I could have—on top of a bale of hay. Surprised, I nonetheless recovered in time to roll off onto the ground, which was good because the next moment both Alicia and Barnum landed on the exact same spot as I did. They looked just as confused as I did about this, but like me, they scrambled off the hay bale as soon as they could.

"Where did this hay bale come from?" said Alicia, looking at the bale that had broken our fall.

Barnum pointed to a nearby stable, where David's horse was currently resting. "It was for David's steed, Lightning Knight. They usually leave his hay bale out, but I guess he wasn't hungry today or something."

"Lucky for us," I said. Then I frowned and looked around. "Say, where did Jill go?"

"Over here!" Jill was standing near the gates, stray bits of straw clinging to her clothes. She was gesturing for us to follow her, her eyes wide and wild, as if the adrenaline was pumping through her like water. "Come on!"

We didn't hesitate. We ran to join her, and as soon as we did, all four of us dashed through the gates together. Just as we passed through the gates, Barnum stopped and slammed them shut. I would have berated him for stopping, but he caught up with us again and I was too busy running to yell at anyone anyway.

Behind us, I heard the screams and roars of the glitched zombies, even heard what sounded like a horde of those monsters trying to break down the gates. But I didn't look back, mostly because I knew that looking back was always bad luck.

Chapter 17

It took us only minutes to exit the valley in which David's castle was located. We crashed through the Deep Woods, not even bothering to slow down. As far as I knew, the glitched zombies were not after us; however, the adrenaline rushing through our bodies kept us going long after we were within safety.

Eventually, we ended up in a small meadow somewhere south of the valley. It was a very small meadow, with a tiny pond of cool clear water that was little more than a puddle, but because it seemed so quiet, peaceful, and still, we decided to stop here.

Barnum staggered toward the water. Falling to his knees, he began scooping up the water with his hands and drinking it. Too tired to do even that much, I just sat down on a stump and wiped the sweat off my brow, which felt stickier than normal.

Alicia seemed even more tired than me because she just sat down on the grass. She pulled a revitalizing potion from her bag and began drinking it, which started to make me thirsty, too, although I was too winded to ask for a sip myself.

Only Jill appeared to have any strength left. She patrolled the perimeter of the meadow, like she was looking for any signs of the Glitch. That she was in such good shape, even after being tortured by King David, was a testament both to Alicia's amazing healing spells and Jill's own resilience in the face of pain.

Then Jill stopped and looked at us. "We're safe. I don't see or hear any glitched monsters or zombies or anything."

"But for how long?" said Alicia, panting as she threw away the empty revitalizing potion. "The Glitch probably knows where we are. Why hasn't it sent the ambassador after us?"

Barnum sat back from the pond, wiping the wetness off his lips. "He already failed to kill you guys once, didn't he? Maybe the Glitch doesn't trust the ambassador to do it anymore."

"There's no telling what the Glitch is planning," said Jill. "Nor does it matter. Barnum, you said you could lead us to the cave where the monsters first were spotted, correct?"

"Yep," said Barnum, leaning back on his hands. "It's not too far from here, I think. Shouldn't take us long to get there. We crossed most of the distance when we were running like piglets."

"Good," said Jill. "Right now, though, we need to take this time to rest. There's no telling what we'll find when we get to that cave, so we'd better prepare as best as we can."

"Thank you," said Alicia with a sigh. "After everything I've been through today, I think a nap would do the trick."

"But we can't rest for too long," said Jill, looking at us all very seriously. "There's no telling what the Glitch will try to do next or when it will strike again."

"Got it," said Barnum. Then he frowned. "But if I'm going to be helping you guys, I think I deserve to know exactly who you are and what is going on here."

"There's nothing you need to know that you don't already,"

said Jill, glancing around the trees, as if she thought that there might be some hidden enemy nearby. "We're trying to stop an unnatural force from destroying our world."

Barnum slowly got to his feet, dusting the grass off his buttocks as he said, "No, no, no. I can tell you guys know way more than you let on. There's something bigger going on than you are telling me about. What is it?"

"You really don't need to know," said Jill.

"Actually, I think he does," said Alicia, drawing our attention to her. "He's done so much to help us that I think it's only fair that we tell him what's going on here."

"Have to agree with Alicia there," I said, looking at Jill. "Barnum's no Julius, but he has been very helpful. If he's going to be traveling with us until the cave, then I think he deserves to know why."

Jill looked like she wanted to continue to argue with us, but she seemed to think better of it, for she shrugged and said, "Fine. Tell him everything. Just be warned, Barnum, that you may not like everything you hear."

It was Alicia who did most of the explaining. She did it briefly and succinctly, with only occasional help from me or Jill whenever she was talking about something that she didn't know much about. Barnum was a good listener, saying nothing as Alicia told him our tale, although his face grew grim when Alicia revealed to him the true nature of the universe.

When Alicia finished, Barnum stroked his chin, looking as lost and confused as I had the first time Jill had explained everything to us.

"So … there are six other continents?" said Barnum. "And …

we're in some kind of a game? That this girl has already played through multiple times?"

He pointed at Jill when he said that, as if to make sure we all knew who he was talking about.

"Yes," said Alicia. "I know it's hard to believe, but it's true."

"This Glitch is some kind of problem in the game," said Barnum. "And that Controller guy might or might not have something to do with it."

"At this point, we're still almost completely clueless about the connection between the Controller and the Glitch," said Alicia. "If there's even a connection between them at all."

"But ..." Barnum looked at all of us with wide, bewildered eyes. "This is all so much and I don't know if you guys are telling the truth or absolutely insane."

"It's true," said Jill. "You saw the effects of the Glitch back there. Even if you don't believe everything we say, you should at least believe that the Glitch will not stop until it has destroyed everything, including the Seventh Continent."

"I guess you're right about that," said Barnum. "Whatever the Glitch is, it does seem like a threat to the whole world."

"It destroyed my home," I said quietly. "I'm surprised it hasn't already destroyed the Seventh Continent."

"Maybe the Seventh Continent is too big or something," said Barnum.

"Bigger than six whole continents?" said Jill, cocking her head skeptically. "Color me skeptical, but I find that hard to believe."

"Then what other reason could the Glitch have for not destroying it yet?" said Barnum. "Just because it would be boring or something?"

"I don't know," said Jill. "I'm hoping that the cave will answer a lot of our questions about the Glitch. Even if it doesn't, maybe it will at least help us figure out how to defeat it and save our world."

"I sure hope so," said Barnum. "I don't want Aruzai to end up like your homes. It's where I keep all my stuff."

"It's also where we all happen to live," I said. "But sure, your stuff is very important."

Before Barnum could do more than glare at me, Jill stabbed the Test into the ground and sat down. "No arguing. Right now, we need to rest, but only for ten minutes. After that, we're heading straight for the cave, no matter what tries to get in our way."

The ten minutes seemed to zip by us because it felt like only ten seconds later that Jill was back on her feet and pulling the Test out of the earth, telling the rest of us to get up and stop wasting time sitting around.

Once we were all up and ready to go (it didn't take us very long because we didn't have much to pack or gather), Barnum led us to the east, which he said was the direction in which the cave was located. It took him a while to determine which direction actually was east, however, because in our mad scramble to scape the glitched zombies and the ambassador, we hadn't paid much attention to where we were running. Not to mention that the tree branches above slightly obscured the sky, making it hard to tell where the sun was.

After Barnum successfully determined which way was east, we fell into line behind him. Barnum was in the lead, pushing through the branches and bushes that stood in our path, with Alicia right behind him and I behind Alicia. Jill took up the rear, just in case any monsters tried to get us from behind, though I still didn't feel entirely safe. Perhaps it was because of the trees, which were rather dark for this time of day, but I felt like someone was watching us, someone who wasn't friendly toward us.

We tried to keep as silent as we could while walking through the Deep Woods to keep our enemies from hearing us before we saw them. This was difficult, mostly because of Barnum, who due to his status as a Warrior was not very good at stealth. I figured it probably didn't matter whether we were as silent as ninjas or as loud as dragons. The Glitch likely knew we were coming either way, which was a troubling thought that I didn't know how to deal with.

No monsters attacked us on our way east. In fact, for a good while there, I wondered if Barnum had gotten the direction wrong, that maybe we were walking north or south or even west. After all, shouldn't we have seen some sign of the Glitch by now, if we were indeed getting closer to its source?

Just as I was about to bring up this concern with the others, Barnum came to a halt and held out his large arms. "Stop."

We did, staring up at his back as he looked at whatever he had just seen.

"What is it, Barnum?" said Alicia. "Do you see something?"

"Yeah," said Barnum, nodding. "Look."

We all peered around Barnum's large body to see what he had seen. And when I saw it, I shuddered.

The forest stretching out before us was glitched. Some of the trees were standing upside down, others were floating sideways in the air, and others were so totally glitched that they didn't even look like trees at all. A few trees had disappeared completely, replaced with that same empty blackness that had signified the destruction of Long River. A squirrel ran in front of us, stopped when it saw us, and then ran off toward the glitched part of the forest before suddenly falling through the ground with a shriek.

"Whoa," said Alicia, her eyes widening at the sight of the glitched trees. "Was it like this when you came here last, Barnum?"

Barnum shook his head. "No. Last time I was here, the forest looked normal. The Glitch's infestation must be getting worse."

"Can we even go on any farther?" I asked. I pointed at the spot where the squirrel had fallen. "What if we end up like that poor squirrel? Falling into the Dark World, maybe even dying like Julius?"

A firm hand fell on my shoulder, causing me to look and see Jill staring at me with hard eyes.

"Our only other choice is to run and hope the Glitch doesn't catch us," said Jill. "Because we know the Glitch is trying to destroy everything, that's not a very realistic long term option. We have to keep going. Though we might have to be more careful."

"Just follow my lead," said Barnum. "We know at least one spot to avoid, don't we?"

"But we still can't tell the difference between ground that will support us and ground that won't," I said. "Just going on hoping the ground won't give out underneath us isn't much of a plan, in my opinion."

Alicia scratched her chin like she was thinking. Then she snapped her fingers and said, "I know how we can get past this."

She bent down and began scooping up rocks into her bag, prompting me to say, "Alicia, this isn't time to play in the dirt."

"I'm not playing in the dirt," said Alicia, without looking up at me. "I'm gathering up a bunch of rocks and things that we can throw at the ground along our path. If a rock passes through the ground, we know to avoid that part of the ground."

"Huh, that's pretty clever," said Barnum. "I wish I'd thought of it."

Once Alicia had filled the bag with enough rocks to the point where it was bulging, we began to make our way through the glitched forest. This leg of the journey, however, went by far more slowly than the first leg, mostly because we had to stop every few feet to threw rocks and readjust our course to make sure we didn't end up falling into nothingness. More than once a perfectly normal-looking pathway turned out to be nothing more than a trap waiting to capture us, and we likely would have fallen into many of those traps if Alicia's rocks had not shown us the way.

Every step took us closer to the cave, but I kept expecting the next step to be our last. Sure, we managed to avoid the false ground just fine, and most of the glitchy trees, it turned out, were not solid and had no ill effects on us, but it still seemed too easy. I fully expected the ambassador, at least, to turn up and try to take us down, but with every step bringing us closer to the cave with nothing bad happening to us, my fears began to feel quite foolish and irrational.

After maybe an hour of tedious walking—possibly longer, though it was hard to tell time because the sky had turned a strange purplish hue with the ground's texture covering parts of it

—we finally reached the clearing where the cave was located. Just in time, too, because Alicia's bag had shrunk significantly along the way and I was starting to worry that we would run out of rocks before we got to our destination.

The cave was rather nondescript. I had expected it to look as glitchy and messed up as the Deep Woods, but instead it looked quite normal. Deceptively normal. I didn't trust its gaping opening or the stalactites that hung just above the entrance.

"Why does it look normal?" said Alicia. "If that's where the Glitch is, then why doesn't it look glitched?"

"There must be something glitchy about it," said Jill, peering at it closely. "Something that we can't see. Something that isn't obvious to the untrained eye."

"I don't like it," said Barnum. He looked over his shoulder at the glitchy forest behind us. "I don't like it at all. I think the Glitch is trying to trick us."

"Is the Glitch intelligent enough to do that?" said Alicia. "I always thought it was just a force of nature that didn't have a mind of its own."

"That ambassador guy sure seemed to think it was intelligent," said Jill. "Of course, he was completely insane, but I agree with Barnum. We're missing something. The only question is, what?"

"You are missing nothing, Heroes of the Stars," said a familiar metallic voice from within the cave. "Everything that you see is exactly what it is."

From within the cave, the ambassador stepped out, although I didn't see how he could have fit in there because he was taller than the cave's entrance. Probably the Glitch at work.

The ambassador stood in front of the cave, his arms folded across his chest, yellow eyes gleaming beneath his dark hood. Jill and Barnum immediately struck battle stances, while I and Alicia stepped back to avoid getting drawn into the thick of the inevitable battle that was about to come.

"We were wondering when we were going to see you again, ambassador," Jill said, her voice harsh. "For a while there, I thought you had decided to run away and hide like a scared cat."

"Funny," said the ambassador, "I seem to recall that it was *you* who had run away and hid like a scared cat. You even jumped out of a window, something so foolish that only a feline would ever do it."

"Shut up," said Jill. "Are you going to try to stop us from entering the cave or what?"

"Of course," said the ambassador. "The Glitch will continue to raze this world unabated. I know that you want to stop it, but you are foolish. The world deserves to be destroyed, and you with it."

"I'm sure the world deserves a lot of things," said Jill. "But destruction? I don't think so. It's not that bad."

"Is it?" said the ambassador. "Have you considered the true nature of the world? It is cyclical. The Controller plays through the same scenario again and again, often with only the subtlest of differences between each play through. There is no free will in this world; hence, there is nothing to mourn if it is destroyed."

"I have plenty free will," Barnum said. "And I am going to use that free will to choose to cut off that dumb little head of yours and save my world."

The ambassador spread his arms. "You weren't even listening, were you? We have no free will. None of us do. Only the Controller does. The rest of us merely do as we are programmed, and nothing more."

"Is this really the time to wax philosophical?" said Jill. "You're just trying to distract us from taking you down."

"That is not entirely false," the ambassador admitted. "But I also wish for you to join me. I am offering you a chance of survival. Join with me, with the Glitch, and though the world will be destroyed, we will finally be free. Free of the Controller, free of the laws which govern our every behavior. We will have freedom unlike anything we could even dream of."

"Every tyrant says that if you'd just follow them, then you'll know real freedom," said Jill, brushing her bangs off her forehead. "And every tyrant is a big, fat liar, too. So excuse me if I don't believe that you can offer us 'freedom,' as you call it."

"I expected as much," said the ambassador. "The Glitch told me that you would refuse to listen, that you were slaves to the Controller. It appears that I will indeed have to eliminate you in the name of true freedom."

"Not unless we kill you first!" Jill cried out, running across the clearing toward the ambassador, Barnum by her side, their swords held before them like battering rams.

The ambassador shook his head, looking almost genuinely sad. He raised his knuckles and said, "Then it will be a grim pleasure to crush the enemies of freedom."

He took a step forward and was gone. Jill and Barnum skid to a stop, looking for the ambassador, but he seemed to have vanished entirely. I knew it was too much to hope that he had decided to run away and leave us alone, but part of me hoped that he had anyway, if only because it made me feel better about our chances of saving the world.

Then I heard the slight scuffing of boots against dirt and turned around just in time to get punched in the face by a large bronze knuckle. The blow was so strong that it literally sent me flying, even flying over the heads of Jill and Barnum, and into the ground. The crash jolted my spine, making me gasp in pain and feel like I had fallen from the top of a tall building.

A second later, Alicia crashed next to me, her robes getting tangled up all over her body. A quick glance told me that she had also been punched by the ambassador because her face had an imprint of his bronze knuckle in the side of it, which made her look uglier than she was.

"Dale, Alicia!" said Jill, looking at us in alarm. "Are you okay?"

"We're … fine," I said, rubbing my head as I looked up. "Watch out!"

The ambassador had glitched in front of Jill and Barnum. He brought his massive fists down on their heads, but thankfully they were faster than he was and dodged before their skulls could get crushed. With no skulls to smash into, the ambassador's fists collided with the ground, causing the earth to glitch for a moment before returning to its normal state.

Jill moved in, slashing at the ambassador, but he glitched out of the path of the Test. He reappeared a few feet away from Jill, but before he could strike, Barnum jumped at the ambassador, the Warrior's sword coming down on his head.

But then the ambassador grabbed Barnum's sword before it could land on him, somehow holding both the sword and Barnum in midair above his head. Barnum's eyes widened in surprise before the ambassador threw Barnum to the left.

Meanwhile, Alicia was already back on her feet. She had cast a quick heal spell on her face, though it did nothing to clean her robes. She bent down over me, running her staff up and down my body, covering me in the shiny healing dust that felt cool wherever it landed on my body.

"Come on, Dale, come on," said Alicia, glancing up every few seconds at the battle between the ambassador and Jill and Barnum. "Get up. Jill and Barnum need your help."

Feeling the pain in my back and head fading, I began to sit up as I said, "Me? How can *I* help? I'm not a fighter. I'll just get in the way."

"Your songs," said Alicia, like I was being an idiot. "You can use your songs to confuse him or put him to sleep or something. Anything that could possibly help Jill and Barnum get a hit in on him."

I looked at the battle. Jill and Barnum had the ambassador between them and were slashing their swords at him, but each blow simply passed through his body like he wasn't even there. Seeing him do that made me angry, but the idea of drawing his attention to me made me hesitate.

"What are you waiting for?" said Alicia. "I've already healed you. You're good to go."

I wanted to tell her that I wasn't, but in truth, I was. I also wanted to tell her that I didn't want to even try—what if it didn't work?—but I realized that if I did not do anything to help my friends, then we were guaranteed to fail. Just watching Jill and Barnum fruitlessly attack the ambassador, while the ground around them grew glitchier and glitchier, convinced me that I had to act.

So I got to my feet and dusted my cloak off as I aimed at the ambassador. I wasn't sure if I could sing well enough to distract him and for all I knew my songs wouldn't even affect him (just because they worked once, didn't mean that they would work again), but I had to give it my best. I had to try. For the world. For Long River. For Julius.

So I sang. Like during our battle with the Lord of the Silver Blades, I sang the Song of Confusion. I had an array of other songs I could have used, but I decided that this one was the best for this situation. I just hoped it would work.

At first, I didn't know if the Song of Confusion was working on the ambassador or not. Though the tune floated off my lips in his direction, I had no way to know for sure whether he even heard it. His glitchy nature might make it impossible for him to be affected by the song even if he did hear it. Surely he would have come up with some kind of defense against it after the last time I used it on him, wouldn't he?

Then, to my amazement, the song seemed to be having some sort of effect. The ambassador shook his head, like how he had the first time, but then a look of realization dawned on his face when he saw me. His eyes seemed to shine with rage and the next moment he was gone, causing both Jill and Barnum to stop slashing at him and to look around in surprise.

My view of them was cut off when a large, black wall appeared in my face. Startled, I tried to jump away, but then two massive hands grabbed my thin shoulders and hefted me off my feet. I was now looking into the eyes of the ambassador, though I still could not see his face because his hood continued to obscure it.

"I'm no fool, Bard," said the ambassador, his grip tightening on me the longer he held me. "I remember how you used your songs on me last time. I never repeat the same mistake twice."

Desperate, I kicked out with my feet, but my legs were too short to connect with his face. Nor could I reach the Star Pendant, which was in my cloak pocket. My arms were pinned to my sides, making it impossible for me to do anything besides wave my hands uselessly.

"Let him go!" Alicia said, raising her staff, which was starting to glow purple at the top.

A purple blast of poison energy exploded from her staff, but rather than hit the ambassador, it somehow rebounded and hit Alicia. Her skin glowed purple as she fell to the ground, screaming in pain from the poison, while the ambassador continued to squeeze the living daylights out of me.

"Ali!" I said, though my voice was weak due to the pressure the ambassador was putting on me. "Ali! No!"

"Like I said," said the ambassador, his voice a low growl. "I never repeat the same mistake twice."

The ambassador's hands were like rocks, crushing me between them with such force that I was certain I was going to be crunched up into a tiny little ball. I couldn't gather the strength or concentration necessary to sing another song, couldn't even hum a simple little tune. How much time I had left, I didn't know, but I did know that, unless someone saved me, I was going to die.

"Drop him!"

Jill's voice rang out from behind the ambassador. I looked up and saw her and Barnum running towards us. Hope rose in my heart when I saw them coming, running as fast as they could. Maybe I wouldn't die after all.

Because she was faster, Jill reached the ambassador first. Oddly, the ambassador didn't even look over his shoulder and seemed entirely unaware of Jill behind him. Bad for him because Jill was pulling back her sword, about to ram it straight through his back.

And then she did. She stabbed forward, the Test's blade glowing with blazing hot white light, directly into the ambassador's back.

But the ambassador didn't even flinch. I had only a brief moment—less than a second—to register that the Test had gone straight through the ambassador's body, but Jill was still going and going and then—

Pain tore through my body, pain unlike anything I had ever experienced before. I gasped, wanted to scream but couldn't, and looked down at the Test, which was now embedded firmly in my stomach. Jill's arm stuck through the ambassador's chest, still holding the hilt of the blade, but I heard her gasp in horror and I knew that she knew what she had done.

Only the ambassador seemed happy. A set of teeth—pearly white, but crooked as a pirate's maw—appeared in the darkness of his hood, set in a vicious smile, and the next moment he vanished.

Without him holding me, I fell to the dirt and lost all consciousness before I even hit the ground.

Chapter 18

Despite dying, I didn't feel dead. Although, I did not feel alive, either.

It was a hard feeling to describe, not in the least because I didn't know what death actually felt like. No doubt Jill could tell me, seeing as she had died dozens of times in the past, but as Jill was nowhere around, I was forced to come up with my own description of death.

Numbers. That is what I saw. But not a great variety. Instead, it was the same two digits over and over again, arranged in a variety of different patterns that I couldn't understand: Ones and zeroes. Flashing green on a black wall.

The ones and zeroes zoomed by me, moving so fast that I couldn't read them. All I understood was that I was seeing a language, but the language was unlike Starian or any of the Ancient Tongues of the Stars from the Six Continents.

It was different because I *was* the language. When I looked down, I didn't see my Bard's Cloak, covered in dirt and sweat and blood from my adventures. I saw ones and zeroes that sometimes resembled my body but other times were lost in the sea of ones and zeroes in which I found myself.

That was when I realized—with a certainty I couldn't question even if I wanted—that I was looking at the language that set the foundation for the universe itself. Yet I couldn't interact with any of it. I was nothing more than a passive watcher, sitting idly by while everything around me shifted and blinked and flashed.

This had to be where we went when we died. But I didn't see anyone else in the binary, not even any of the various enemies I and the others had killed over our adventures. Just ones and zeroes north, west, south, east, and up and down for as far as the eye could see.

Although I was currently conscious, I could feel my consciousness slowly slipping away. Bit by bit, I was starting to lose myself; quite literally, for when I looked down at my body, I saw that it was slowly becoming more and more identical with the ones and zeroes around me. In a few minutes, I would truly be gone.

But I didn't want to be gone. Yes, I was still aware that the Glitch was still destroying our world, maybe even about to win, but that didn't mean I was ready to give up. Somehow, I knew that I had to survive, that if I gave up now, then not only would I lose my life, but the game itself would be destroyed along with everyone and everything in it.

So I tried moving, though not in any particular direction because every direction looked exactly the same to me. I didn't understand what all of these ones and zeroes meant, nor did I know if it was even possible to escape, but I at least had to try. And if I failed, then at least I failed doing my best.

Then, without warning, I broke free. My body was whole again. A quick glance told me that I was no longer the ones and zeroes anymore, but rather that I now looked as normal as ever.

I didn't have much time to celebrate this victory, however, because without the ones and zeroes to support me I immediately began falling. The numbers rushed past me, turning into a blur of flashing green lights as I plummeted to what was likely going to be my death (though when I actually thought about it, was it even possible for a dead person to die again?).

I didn't know where I was falling to, however, and I couldn't turn around or even look over my shoulder to see where my inevitable destination was. About the only thing I took comfort in was the fact that, already being dead, where I was heading couldn't possibly be worse than where I originally was, right?

Then I landed in a flash of white light that completely obscured my vision for a few seconds. My skin burned deeply, my eyeballs broiled, like I had fallen into a large pot of boiling hot chicken soup. It was far worse than being stabbed in the stomach by the Test; in fact, it was probably the worst pain I had ever felt, and that was saying something, seeing as I had once taken a head-on blast of energy from the Lord of the Silver Blades back in Tall Roots.

And then the light faded and I found myself lying on a wooden floor. For a moment the pain intensified, particularly in my stomach area, but then it passed away, leaving me feeling like I had run a marathon.

Panting, I tried to wipe the sweat off my brow, but I was still so worn out from the fall and the pain that I couldn't even do that simple gesture. My vision was blurry as well, making it hard for me to tell where I was. All I could see at the moment was the sun shining in through a nearby window, but that was such a vague fact that it didn't help me at all.

Then I heard footsteps—light and confident—coming and the next moment someone was standing over me. Gathering all of my strength, I rubbed my eyes to clear my vision even as the person said, in a voice tinged with disbelief, "Dale Bennett?"

I ceased rubbing my eyes and looked up at the person. It was a female Angelian, her wings folded behind her back, but she didn't look like all of the Angelians I had seen before. Whereas most Angelians had dark skin thanks to the time they spent in the sky so close to the Twin Suns, she had pale skin, as if she spent all of her time indoors. Her hair, too, was not blue or white but rather a rich black, like a blackberry.

I had no idea who she was. I had never seen her before. She didn't look like a threat—no weapons on her that I could see, and her talons, in contrast to other Angelians', were refined and small, almost human-like in their proportions—but I knew from experience that just because someone or something didn't look like a threat didn't mean they weren't.

"Dale Bennett is here?" said another voice, this one off to my right.

A man stepped into my view on my other side. He had a strange appearance. He had the bulk and physique of a Warrior, but he wore the clothes of a Bard and carried a bow on his back, much like an Archer. He looked like a mishmash of those three jobs, which was odd because I had always believed that the jobs were separate and that you could only choose one. The man's face was strange, too, with slanted eyes and a yellowish skin color that I had never seen on a human before.

"Well, doesn't he look like Dale Bennett?" said the Angelian woman, gesturing at me with her talons. "I designed him, so I think I should know if it's him or not."

Designed me? What was this Angelian woman babbling about? Had the Glitch caused her to lose her mind or was she always this crazy?

The man looked at me more closely before nodding and saying, "Yep. That's definitely Dale Bennett. He looks just like your husband."

Husband? He couldn't have meant that this Angelian had a *human* husband, could he? Angelians, due to their belief in the superiority of their own people over every other people, only ever married Angelians. Did that mean that there was a male Angelian out there who looked just like me?

"Well, I did base him off my hubby," said the Angelian woman. "Although I had to change his features slightly to fit in with the game's graphical engine."

"But then how did he get in here?" said the man, glancing at me again. "This room isn't supposed to be accessible in normal game play. Did he hack it or something? And where are his friends?"

I couldn't handle all of the enigmatic conversation these two were having. Nothing they said made a lick of sense to me. I needed answers and I was going to get answers.

So I said, in the strongest voice I could muster, "Who … are you people?"

My voice wasn't as strong as it normally was, no doubt due to the fact that I was still recovering from the fall. Still, the two appeared to have heard heard me because they looked down at me in surprise.

"Did Dale just talk?" said the man.

"Yes, I did," I said, nodding. "I asked, who are you people?"

The man looked up at the Angelian woman. "Should we tell him?"

"Might as well," said the Angelian woman with a shrug. "After everything else that has happened, there's no real point in lying to him."

The man folded his arms across his chest. "All right."

He looked down at me and said, "Dale Bennett, my name is Shigeru Kojima. This here is my partner in crime, Gretchen Johnson."

Odd names, I thought, particularly the man's.

So I said, "But that still doesn't answer the question. Who are you? Where am I? Why did Gretchen talk about 'designing' me? You look like normal mortals to me."

"That's because we use normal character models to represent us," said Shigeru. Then he looked at his mismatched clothes and shrugged. "Slightly modified normal character models, that is."

"Character models?" I repeated. "What does that mean?"

"Oh, so you haven't caught on yet," said Gretchen. "All right. To put it bluntly, Shigeru and I are the game's designers. Or rather, in-game avatars representing *The Last Legend*'s designers."

I blinked. "Designers? Does that mean you created us?"

"Technically, it was our real selves—the ones that exist outside this game—that did," said Shigeru. "But for all practical purposes, yes, we did create you and every other character in the game."

"Are you the Controller, then?" I said, looking up at Shigeru with, I will admit, a little bit of awe.

"The what?" said Shigeru.

"I think he means the player, Shigeru," said Gretchen. "To answer your question, Dale, no, we're not the player, or 'Controller,' as you call him. We're in this game just like you and don't have any real control over what you or any of the other characters in the game do."

Feeling my strength returning, I sat up and said, "But I don't understand. Why are you here? What do you do? How come I've never heard of or met you before this day?"

"We're what gamers call an Easter egg," said Shigeru, gesturing at himself and Gretchen. "Which means that we don't have any real role to play in the game and are only here just to give players something to look for."

"Well, under normal conditions, anyway," said Gretchen, scratching the back of her neck. "But then the publisher told us to dummy out this room because it wasn't 'necessary,' so we are normally not findable in-game without cheating or hacking."

I rubbed the back of my head as I looked around the room. I was inside a medium-sized wooden cabin, sort of like my cabin back in Long River. A couple of simple wooden desks, covered with papers and notebooks and sketches, stood in the center of the room not far from where I'd landed. Outside the window, a tall green forest stood, but I wasn't sure if it was the Deep Woods or the Long Forest or someplace else I didn't even know about.

I slowly got to my feet, still looking around as I did so. "Then what is this place called?"

"The Developers' Room," said Gretchen. She gestured at the desks. "That's where we work on the game. We have preliminary sketches, coding, scripts, and everything else. But don't touch any of it. You might cause the game to bug out."

I frowned. All of their jargon sounded like gibberish to me, but I supposed that they were on a much higher level than me, being the creators of the game and all, so I didn't question her advice.

Instead, I said, "Where is the Developers' Room located?"

"The game's coding places its location in the Deep Woods," said Shigeru, glancing out the window. "But even if you went to this specific spot in-game, you wouldn't find it. The Developers' Room only shows up when a room or area's data fails to load to prevent the game from crashing. It can also be accessed by cheating or hacking."

"Then how did I get here?" I said. "I didn't 'cheat' or 'hack' my way into here. That's for certain."

Gretchen stroked her chin, looking deep in thought. "Something must have gone wrong when you died. The Glitch has done a number on the game's normal functions. Wouldn't surprise me if, rather than killing you, the Glitch somehow sent you here instead."

"You know about the Glitch?" I said.

"Of course we know about it," said Shigeru, slapping his forehead. "It's kind of impossible to avoid noticing a glitch that destroyed ninety percent of the game and is on its way to destroying the other ten percent."

"Then why haven't you done anything about it?" I said, looking between them. "Can't you fix it? You created the game, yes? So couldn't you fix it?"

"That's what we've been trying to do," said Gretchen. "Ever

since the Glitch first showed up, we've been working hard to stop it, but we didn't know what it was at first. It's so much more powerful and deadly than the other glitches in the game that it took us by surprise when it first appeared."

"But thankfully, we've since identified the source of the Glitch," said Shigeru with a smile. "Come with us."

Shigeru and Gretchen walked over to the desks. Curious, I followed, wondering what they were going to show me. A picture of the Glitch's source, maybe?

Shigeru pushed aside the various sketches and scripts and other assorted junk that was probably more important than it looked and gestured for me to come and look. "Here it is."

I stepped up to the desk and looked down at what was on it. It was a map, a rather large one, featuring a huge continent on it. The continent looked nothing like the Six Continents, because it was shaped less like a star and more like a flat disk, though it had a couple of peninsulas in the north that ruined its shape. A chain of islands was just off its west coast and underneath the island chain was the word *Aruzai* written in a fancy, curly script that was difficult for me to read at first.

I looked back at Shigeru and Gretchen, who both looked quite satisfied with themselves, even though I wasn't sure what was so great about this map.

"I don't get it," I said. "It's just a map of the Seventh Continent."

"Exactly," said Shigeru. He put one finger on the middle of the map and said, "Right here, in the Deep Woods, is where the Glitch started."

"Oh," I said. "Well, I already figured that, seeing as I and my friends saw the cave where the Glitch came from. That still doesn't explain why the Glitch happened, though?"

"Easy," said Shigeru. He tapped the map with his finger. "You see, Dale, for much of *The Last Legend*'s development—"

"*The Last Legend*?" I repeated. "What's that?"

"The name of the game," Gretchen chimed in. "Pretty cool, isn't it? Shigeru and I worked together to come up with it."

"What does it mean?" I said.

"The name?" said Gretchen. She looked at Shigeru with a genuinely puzzled expression on her face. "Shigeru, what did we decide the name meant?"

"It's supposed to signify the game's end of the world themes," Shigeru said. "The adventure of you and your friends, Dale, are supposed to be the 'last legend' of Kinar. Also, it sounds really cool."

"That," said Gretchen, nodding. "Technically, the game's full title is *The Last Legend of the Omega Crystals*, but that's a mouthful, so we always shorten it to *The Last Legend*."

"Okay," I said. "Uh, Shigeru, you were explaining the cause of the Glitch?"

Shigeru snapped his fingers. "Oh, yes. Right. Well, the Seventh Continent, Aruzai, was supposed to be accessible through normal game play. It would have been unlocked through what we call 'downloadable content,' which would have given the player a chance to explore a whole new continent, complete with new enemies, characters, locations, items, and so much more."

"You can tell that we got very far along in development," Gretchen said, gesturing at the room we stood in, "because the Seventh Continent works just like the rest of the game, although imperfectly, obviously."

I had wondered about that, but I didn't say anything because Shigeru was still talking.

"But right before the game's release, we were told that the Aruzai DLC was going to be dropped and that we needed to make sure that gamers couldn't access the Seventh Continent," Shigeru continued. A scowl crossed his face. "Let me digress for just a moment to say that we spent six months designing and developing Aruzai—spending twice as much time on it as we had on the other Six Continents—and we weren't even paid for our work."

"I keep telling you that we should go indie so we can avoid those problems," said Gretchen as she leaned against one of the desks. "But do you listen? No, you don't."

"Let's not discuss our career choices here," said Shigeru, in a tone that told me that he and Gretchen had probably had heated conversations about this subject in the past. "The point is, Dale, that Aruzai is normally completely inaccessible during normal game play. We would have cut it entirely, but the game was far too close to release for us to do that, so instead we buried its coding and files as deep within the game's data as we could where no one could find it."

"We thought that even the best hackers wouldn't be able to find it," said Gretchen with a shrug. "We hid it so well that our publisher thought we had taken it out entirely. Though that's not saying much, seeing as our publisher isn't all that bright in the first place."

"If you hid it, then how did I and my friends get here?" I said, spreading my arms wide to indicate the whole of Aruzai. "We certainly didn't go looking for it. Even Jill didn't know about its existence, and she's played through the game loads of times."

"Wait," said Shigeru, leaning toward me slightly. "Are you saying that Jill Franklin is aware of her status as a video game character?"

"Yes," I said, nodding. "She was the first to do so. She then told me and the others about it. But I will be honest: until this very moment, I don't think I ever actually believed her."

"Interesting," said Shigeru. "Very interesting. A character developing self-awareness ... we did not anticipate that ever happening. I wish she was here right now, where we could study her coding to find out how that happened."

"But that's not important right now," said Gretchen. "Shigeru, please continue explaining to Dale what caused the Glitch."

"All right," said Shigeru, though he sounded reluctant when he said that, as if he was more interested in finding out how one of his characters had gained self-awareness. "Ordinarily, then, the Seventh Continent is never, ever, ever supposed to be accessed by players. It would take a genius hacker of the highest order to find even the vaguest of clues to Aruzai's existence, as there are only a handful of vague hints left in the game itself that we forgot to take out and the DLC package was never announced to the public before the game's launch."

"But it's pretty clear that a hacker succeeded in finding it," said Gretchen. "Someone used certain hacking software to check the game's files for any hidden secrets and discovered Aruzai. Maybe it was the Controller, who might be the kind of player who likes to take games apart just to see how they work."

"It was probably an accidental discovery on his part," said

THE LAST LEGEND: GLITCH APOCALYPSE

Shigeru. "Like I said, there were no explicit hints of Aruzai's existence in-game and the publisher didn't bother to announce the DLC, since it was canceled. Would have been useless to do, you understand."

"You use words like 'might' and 'maybe,' but if you are the developers, then shouldn't you know for sure why certain things happen?" I said. "Not like me or the others, who are just characters in this game."

"Weren't you listening to what we said earlier?" said Shigeru. He gestured at himself and Gretchen. "We're in-game characters based off of the real Shigeru Kojima and Gretchen Johnson. We only know as much as our real selves do up to the point of the game's launch. We have no idea what may or may not have happened after that."

"That's why we can't be entirely certain about what happened," said Gretchen, brushing her white hair out of her eyes. "But we can deduce, through fact and reason, a good working theory that will suffice."

"All right," I said. "So the Seventh Continent, despite being entirely functional, was never supposed to be found. The Controller, or whoever, somehow found the Seventh Continent's files and then—?"

"Obviously, he accessed the files," said Shigeru. "And just as obviously, the software he used to access the files corrupted the game itself. That is probably the source of the Glitch."

"So the Glitch isn't some sort of intelligent being or force with an agenda of its own?" I said.

"Of course not," said Gretchen, shaking her head. "Glitches, even ones as powerful and all-consuming as this one, are just

269

bugs in the game's data. They have no real mind of their own. Why would you ever think such a thing?"

"Never mind," I said, though privately, I was relieved to learn that the ambassador was indeed crazy. "So how do we deal with the Glitch, now that we know what it's source is?"

"Simple," said Shigeru.

He gestured at a metal panel on the wall that I hadn't noticed before, which looked out of place among the wooden walls of the cabin.

"Behind that panel is a button that will reset the whole game," said Shigeru. "By resetting the game, it should fix the Glitch, make Aruzai inaccessible again, and return you and your friends to the Six Continents."

"You mean it's that easy?" I said. "I thought it was going to be far more complicated than pressing a button."

"Life isn't always complicated," said Shigeru. "Sometimes, it is quite simple."

"If it's that simple, then how come you guys haven't done it yet?" I demanded, pointing at the panel as I spoke. "You've had it with you the entire time. You could have saved me and my friends a lot of heartache and tragedy if you had done it right away."

"The reset button is a last resort," Gretchen explained. "We wanted to test other possible solutions to the problem before we pressed that button. We didn't think we'd need to use it, but as we now know, we did."

"It should have been your first resort," I said. "I don't like your explanation."

"It's a last resort because it's a hard reset," said Shigeru. "That means that, if we did it, it would literally reset the game to the state it was in when the Controller first bought it. We'd hate seeing all of that progress ruined, which would undoubtedly cause the Controller to make some Internet video about how stupid we are, which is why we didn't do it right away."

I didn't understand everything he said (what was an Internet?), but I still thought it was stupid, though I didn't say this aloud. After all, as the developers of the game, they could probably do all kinds of horrible things to me if I angered them. Besides, after everything else I'd been through, I didn't want to waste time criticizing them for their dumb decisions.

Therefore, I said, "So if we press that button, it will restore everything to how it was? Does that mean it will bring back Julius as well?"

"No reason it shouldn't," said Gretchen. "His data likely still exists somewhere in the game's files. The reset button would return the entire game to its original factory state."

"Again, just to be clear, it would be a hard reset," said Shigeru. "That means that it won't just return everything to normal. It will literally restart your quest. Jill will have to go through the game again to find you, Alicia, and Julius, and you will once more have to defend the Omega Crystals from the Lord of the Silver Blades."

Well, that didn't sound so bad to me. Press a button and I would get my home and all of my friends back. The only thing I would have to pay, it seemed, was the adventures I'd had so far. And honestly, since our adventures were not that great, I doubted I would be missing much.

"So if I press the button, will I remember any of this?" I said.

Shigeru shook his head with a rueful chuckle. "Probably not. You're not even supposed to be here. You will go back to how you once were; ignorant of the true nature of your world, with no memory at all of the Glitch or Aruzai or us or anything else you ran into here."

"To be honest, that doesn't sound very bad to me," I said. "You don't know even the half of what I and the others have been through since we got here. I'd gladly forget all of it in exchange for Julius's life—and the lives of my other friends—back."

"We thought you would," said Shigeru. "Wise choice. Let's go over to the panel and fix this thing."

There was no hesitation in my step as I followed Shigeru and Gretchen over to the panel. In fact, I could hardly contain my excitement at the thought that this terrible adventure was finally drawing to a close. We would all be back together again, Jill and Alicia and Julius and I, and we would forget all about the Glitch and the terror it brought upon us.

"The reset switch was designed specifically in case of a glitch like this happening," said Shigeru, looking over his shoulder at me. "Most of the time, it's unnecessary; in fact, this is actually the first time we've had to use it, but it should work. I designed it, after all, and, not to toot my own horn, but I'm a pretty good video game designer."

Gretchen rolled her eyes as we reached the panel. "Don't forget that you had my help, Shigeru. And the help of everyone else at Demonrain Entertainment."

"What's Demonrain Entertainment?" I asked.

"The company that developed and published this very game," said Shigeru offhandedly. "Anyway, Gretchen, I know that. I'm just saying that I've won several awards for my game design and that there's a good reason I was made head developer for *The Last Legend*."

"Humility is a virtue," Gretchen said as she reached up and flipped open the panel. "There it is. The reset button."

The reset button was large and red, with the word 'RESET' written on it in black ink. It did not look very used, which meant that Shigeru was correct when he said that it had never been used before.

Shigeru and Gretchen suddenly stepped out of my way just then, causing me to look at them in surprise.

"Since we know you have been through so much, we figure it's only right that you should be the one to press the button," said Shigeru.

"Have you been watching me and my friends?" I said.

"Pretty much," said Gretchen. "We keep tabs on your every location. We have access to the game's save files, so we always know what you are doing or where you are. By observing you guys'[interactions with the Glitch, we managed to determine its cause."

The idea that these two had been watching our every move made me feel slightly unsettled, just like how the knowledge that I was in a game was also unsettling.

Still, I reached up to press the button anyway. I had always suspected that the universe was a strange, unsettling place, so learning all that I did about the universe's true nature was less frightening than it could have been.

Then my finger passed through the button, almost throwing me off balance from the inertia. I pulled my hand back, looking at it in disbelief, as Gretchen and Shigeru gazed upon the button in horror.

"What happened?" said Shigeru. He reached up and tried pressing the button himself, but like mine, his hand just passed through it. "This doesn't make any sense. The reset button should have collusion applied to it. Why—"

"Because the Glitch commands it," said a deep voice I didn't want to recognize but did anyway.

Trying not to shake in fear, I turned around to see a familiar large man with a black hood and bronze knuckles standing at the other end of the room. Yellow eyes gleamed from within the dark hood, while the hilt of the sword—which with a jerk of my heart I recognized as the hilt of the Test—poked out from under his cloak.

The ambassador folded his arms across his chest as he looked down on us all. "Now that I have your attention, I believe it is time that I finish you once and for all. For the glory of the Glitch."

Chapter 19

"How did you get here?" Shigeru demanded, drawing his twin swords from their sheaths in a flash. "This room is inaccessible to normal characters."

"When did I ever say I was normal?" said the ambassador. "I am the ambassador of the Glitch. No walls can stop me. I can go where I please, do what I wish, all thanks to the power of the Glitch."

"Where are my friends?" I said. "Jill and Alicia and Barnum?"

The ambassador patted the hilt of the Test sticking out from his cloak. "Dead. I killed all three of them. I took Jill's sword because I thought it would be a good trophy, an example of my viciousness in combat."

Anger rose within me as the ambassador drew the Test out from his cloak. In his massive hands, the Test looked like a children's toy. I had a feeling he must have intended that because the idea that he would treat one of Jill's possessions with such irreverence ... oh, it burned my soul.

"You didn't kill them," I said. "You're lying."

"I am not a liar," said the ambassador. "When your corpse

disappeared, it did not take me long to make short work of your friends. Jill was particularly easy to kill. She was so distraught at having stabbed her best friend in the chest that she almost begged me to kill her."

"Jill would never beg anyone to kill her," I said. "I know that much."

"Believe what you want," said the ambassador with a shrug. "Makes no difference to me. In the end, the Glitch will claim everything, including you, and then chaos will reign."

"Why are you here?" said Shigeru. "How did you even know this place existed?"

"The Glitch told me of it," said the ambassador. "The Glitch knew that this was the game's last line of defense against its plans. So it sent me here to slaughter you three like pigs and to ensure that its plans could not be stopped."

"But the Glitch is just a bug in the game's data," I said. I looked between Shigeru and Gretchen desperately. "Right?"

"The Glitch is smarter than a mere 'bug,'" said the ambassador with a sneer. "It consumes and corrupts. It knows of its existence, the same way that Jill Franklin became aware of her own."

"Impossible," said Shigeru. "Glitches can't develop self-awareness. That's not how glitches work."

"Most glitches cannot, but the Glitch … it is different," said the ambassador. "It is above and beyond all other glitches in this game."

"Well, I guess it doesn't matter if the Glitch has developed self-awareness or not," said Shigeru. "What matters is that you chose the wrong video game developers to pick a fight with, buddy."

"Such arrogance," said the ambassador. "If you wish to believe that you can defeat me, that is your right. Sadly for you, it is not a belief grounded in reality."

Gretchen held a long spear in her hands, with a golden, pointed shaft, but where she got it from, I didn't know. "I *designed* you. I know all your weak points. I think you might not know this, but Shigeru and I are this game's architects. We understand it far better than even you do."

The ambassador threw the Test to the side. The sword clattered against the wooden floor before the ambassador brought his foot down on it and snapped it in two.

"Perhaps you understand me, but I doubt you understand the Glitch," said the ambassador. "I won't even need to touch you in order to win."

"Who's the arrogant one now?" said Shigeru. "Doesn't matter. You just broke one of your own weapons; in fact, unless my eyes are mistaken, that was the only sword in this game that I designed personally. So if that was meant to be an insult, it worked."

The ambassador chuckled. He pulled his bronze knuckles off his fists and tossed those to the floor, too, although he didn't smash them with his foot like he had the Test.

"I am unarmed now," said the ambassador, spreading his arms to show us. "No weapons anywhere on my body. I am giving you the opportunity to cut me into tiny little pieces and perhaps convince the Glitch to halt its destructive ways."

"Shigeru, this seems too easy," said Gretchen, holding her spear defensively. "Why he would intentionally unarm himself if he didn't have some kind of plan to defend himself?"

"The Glitch will protect me," said the ambassador. "But of

course, I see that you two are too cowed to take on the Glitch. And you are the people who created this game. What a joke."

"We're not afraid of bugs in our own creations," said Shigeru. "Even if those bugs are self-aware. There's nothing you can do to protect yourself from us."

"Listen, guys," I said. "While I appreciate how you're willing to fight one of your own creations to save the whole, I really think it would be better if you—"

Shigeru ran at the ambassador, both swords flashing in the sunlight streaming in from outside. Gretchen hesitated for only a split second, perhaps to hear what I was going to say, but I guess she must have decided that what I had to say was unimportant because she soon followed Shigeru, holding her spear level with the ambassador's head.

"—didn't listen to me at all," I finished with more than a hint of sarcasm in my voice.

The ambassador didn't move even as Shigeru and Gretchen drew closer and closer to him. There were no glitchy distortions around him, nothing to indicate that something was off, but having already seen what the Glitch could do, that didn't mean I thought that the ambassador was a goner. He was far too intelligent to do that.

When Shigeru and Gretchen got within striking distance of the ambassador, they suddenly fell through the floor. They screamed as they vanished through the seemingly stable wooden floor before they disappeared entirely, their screams cut off once they heads had gone completely under.

The ambassador lowered his arms. His bronze knuckles glitched out of existence and then glitched back onto his hands.

Readjusting them, the ambassador looked up at me, his eyes gleaming with mad satisfaction.

"The Glitch has them within its grasp now," said the ambassador. "They are no longer a threat to its operations."

I backed up to the wall, but almost fell through it. I turned and tried pressing the reset button again, hoping against hope that I could press it, but as before my finger just passed through it like it wasn't even there.

"How many times have you escaped me now?" said the ambassador. "Three times, was it? Now that you no longer have any friends or allies to defend you, there is nothing to stop me from ripping you limb from limb, as I promised."

I whirled around, trying to look brave, but I couldn't help trembling in my boots and even whimpering slightly. I held up my fists before me in the best battle position I could manage, but due to my inexperience in battle I knew I was probably doing something wrong.

Jill was dead. Alicia was dead. Julius was dead. Barnum, Gretchen, and Shigeru were dead too. It was just me, me against the ambassador and the Glitch.

And in all likelihood, the Glitch would win.

The ambassador began walking to me, each step slow but confident. "In what ways shall I kill you? Rending you limb from limb is attractive, but perhaps I will shove the remains of that sword down your throat until you choke on it. Or maybe I will banish you into the Dark World, where the Glitch will do with you as it wishes."

My eyes darted around the place. Outside, I saw the sky and trees slowly fading away into blackness, with the occasional glitched texture appearing every now and then. The Glitch was coming, was already here, so even if the ambassador didn't kill me, the Glitch would no doubt finish the job.

"Or maybe I will beat you into a pulp," the ambassador continued. "And scatter your data into the darkest depths of the game. Yes, I'm sure that would be lovely. It would ensure you could never return to avenge your comrades. And it would be far more amusing than the other two alternatives I considered."

Tears were starting to well up in my eyes, but I wiped them away. I couldn't afford to show any signs of weakness to him. It may have been fruitless, but I needed to be strong. Not just wanted; *needed*. I couldn't rely on anyone else but myself now.

But how could I be strong? My arms were thin and bony, my face as delicate as flower. I was a Bard, a storyteller and a musician. Sure, I could sing songs that could confuse or harm him, but the ambassador most likely had some way to defend himself from my songs, meaning that even that line of defense would inevitably fail.

This was it. This was the end. All of our strivings, all of our adventures, all of the death and pain and loss we risked and experienced … it was all for naught. In just a few seconds … nothing more … the Glitch would win.

The ambassador stood above me now. His bronze knuckles, I noticed, were stained red with blood, but whether it was blood from my friends or from some other enemy of his that he had killed a while ago, I couldn't tell.

I just watched as he cracked his knuckles, held up his massive fists, put them together to form a block that would no doubt turn me into paste, and look down at me with triumph in his eyes.

"Dale Bennett, Bard of Long River, you have proved to be nothing more than an annoying pest in the Glitch's path to glory," said the ambassador. "A pest who will now be squashed."

Instinctively, I threw my arms over my head and closed my eyes. I doubted that any of that would actually help me—I was weak—but I did it anyway. The only comfort I took in the thought of my death was that I would probably reunite with Jill and the others. Unless none of us actually had souls, in which case death was going to suck.

That was when I heard something like boots—heavy boots, like that of a Warrior—rumbling along the floor. A moment later, the sound of metal cleaving into flesh entered my ears, followed by a cry of pain from the ambassador directly in front of me.

Shocked, I lowered my arms and opened my eyes to see what had happened and why I hadn't died yet.

The ambassador still stood before me, his fists still raised, but he didn't look quite as confident or powerful as before. His yellow eyes had widened with pain and his whole form flickered and glitched.

Through the flickering and glitching, I caught a glimpse of a Warrior wielding a familiar ax standing behind him. The Warrior had stabbed his ax into the ambassador's back, which was the first real blow I had seen anyone land on the ambassador, but that was unimportant in comparison to the identity of the Warrior who had attacked the ambassador.

"J-Julius?" I said, unable to believe my eyes. "Julius, is that you?"

Julius nodded, but it was a jerky, unnatural movement, as if he was glitched. "Yes, Dale. It's me. Same as always."

"But … how?" I said. "I thought you were dead."

Julius's voice was as metallic as the ambassador's when he spoke, but it was also far more human. "I fell into the Glitch, but I didn't die. Because I was already glitched, I survived. I only managed to escape the Glitch through sheer determination. I came here because I learned that the Glitch had sent this bastard here to kill you, and since you're my friend, I couldn't allow that to happen on my watch."

The ambassador continued to glitch and flicker, but he truly seemed paralyzed by Julius's ax. He just managed to stutter, "H-How did you hit—"

"You?" said Julius. "Easy. Because I'm glitched, too, I knew how to negate your own lack of collision data."

"I-Impossible," the ambassador said, but his voice was constricted and weak. "You can't hold me down forever."

"For once, you're right," said Julius. "Dale, press the damn button and return everything to normal. Before this bastard breaks free."

"But the button can't be pressed," I said. "It's got no, no, uh, collision data, I think the developers called it."

"I fixed that," said Julius. "Again, being glitched, I have an idea of how the Glitch did that. But again, it's only for a limited time. So stop talking and start pressing!"

I had no way to know if Julius was right about the button; however, I knew that Julius was a truth-teller as well as a friend, so I could trust him.

So I whirled around and pressed the big red button on the wall with all of my strength. It worked. My finger touched it, pressing the button into the wall like any other button. A more wonderful feeling I could not imagine.

Behind me, the ambassador screamed, "No!" while Julius yelled, "All right, Dale! You did it!"

Before I could turn to look at either of them, my whole world went black.

Chapter 20

I awoke to the chirping of birds just outside my cabin window. Feeling groggy, I pulled the blankets over my head to try to get some more sleep, but the infernal birds kept chirping louder and louder, so I decided to get up and make some breakfast.

Jumping out of bed, I walked over to the wood stove in the corner of my cabin to prepare the bacon and eggs. A couple of minutes later, I was sitting at my table, writing down the lyrics to my next song, which I planned to sing at the Performance Hall later this afternoon. It would be my best song yet, I thought, and would hopefully earn me a little bit of extra cash so I could stock up on food for the rest of the week, because a cold front was coming in and I would be unlikely to make the trip to Long River during that time.

As I wrote, I could not help but think that things felt … off. I had a strange déjà vu feeling. Granted, my daily schedule never changed much. I always wrote songs or stories in the morning before I went into town or bathed. It was a habit I had ingrained in myself since childhood.

But … I put down my pen and stared at my unfinished song, titled *The Omega Aria*. It was as though I had written this song before, even though I knew for a fact that I hadn't.

… Or had I?

I shook my head. I picked up the paper and looked hard at the lyrics, trying to figure out where I may have heard them before. Perhaps I had once heard the lyrics to this song long ago, when I was a child, or at least lyrics close to it. That could mean that I had accidentally copied someone else's lyrics, but even that explanation didn't make a whole lot of sense to me.

Putting the paper back down on the table, I tapped my pen on my chin. I probably should have gotten up, gathered my clothes, and gone down to the creek behind my cabin to wash and get ready for the new day, but this feeling of déjà vu was far too troubling for me to simply ignore.

That was when I heard a knock at the door. Startled, I almost fell off my chair, but managed to retain my balance. I looked at the door. Was there someone out there? I hadn't been expecting any visitors this morning. Maybe one of the woodland creatures had accidentally knocked on the door.

There was that knocking sound again. Someone was definitely out there. I got up from my seat and began slicking my hair back with my hand, as it was quite messy due to the fact that I hadn't had time to wash and comb it yet. I hoped that whoever was there would give up, but the knocking simply became even more incessant, as if whoever was there desperately needed to talk to me right away.

So, with some reluctance, I said, "Coming," and walked over to the door. I did it slowly, however, even though all that did was drag it out.

When I reached the door, I slicked back my hair one more

time before cracking open the door. I peeked through the crack to see who was there.

A woman I had never seen before—yet who I somehow recognized—stood on my front porch. She had short, dark hair, light skin, and wore practical coarse leather traveling clothes. A sword was sheathed at her side, which sent alarm bells in my mind because the only kinds of people who carried swords around here were bandits or mercenaries and I couldn't be sure which one she was.

On the other hand, she didn't look very much like a bandit or mercenary at all. In fact, I felt like I could trust her, despite the fact that I didn't even know her first name.

That was why I opened the door more, even though she was a stranger with a sword and I was completely unarmed. "Yes?"

The woman smiled. "Hi, Dale. Remember me?"

I blinked several times. Her smile triggered a memory in my mind. I had seen that smile before; yes, I was sure of it. I remembered it because the woman who had that smile never used it much because she had always been so serious, so every time she did smile, it stood out in my mind like a red dot on a white sheet.

And then, without warning, all of my memories came flooding back into my mind. A mess of images and sounds and colors and textures that completely overwhelmed me for a minute before the flood turned into a trickle and I could sort through them.

"Dale?" said the woman. "Dale, are you still awake?"

I nodded, rubbing my head. "Yes, Jill. My memories just came rushing back all at once. I didn't even recognize you until you smiled."

Jill Franklin laughed. "Well, I'm glad my smile is memorable, anyway. I was worried that you might not remember any of it, since the reset was supposed to be pretty hard."

"You know about the reset?" I said.

"Of course," said Jill. "I was dead, after all, and now I am alive. I figured that someone had to have done something to save the world, and I figured that it had to be you, even though you were dead."

"It wasn't me alone, though," I said. "Julius helped. He stepped in at the last minute and gave me the precious few seconds I needed to complete the process."

"So Julius wasn't dead after all," said Jill. "That's good to hear, although I guess it doesn't really matter, since we're going to go find him again anyway. Him and Alicia."

"That's right," I said, snapping my fingers. "Julius and Alicia are still out there in the world, aren't they?"

"They are," said Jill. She held out a hand. "Want to go find them again? They're waiting for us."

I didn't even hesitate. I took her hand, ready to begin anew the adventure we had already played through many times in the past.

THE END.

About the Author

Timothy L. Cerepaka writes fantasy stories as an indie author. He is the author of the Prince Malock World fantasy novels, the Mages of Martir fantasy novels, and the Two Worlds fantasy novels. He lives in Texas.

You can find out more about Timothy L. Cerepaka and his books at his website at www.timothylcerepaka.com.

Other books by Timothy L. Cerepaka

Prince Malock World:

The Mad Voyage of Prince Malock

The Return of Prince Malock

The New Era of Prince Malock

The Coronation of Prince Malock

Mages of Martir:

The Mage's Grave

The Mage's Limits

The Mage's Sea

The Mage's Ghost

Two Worlds:

Reunification

Alliance

Allegiance

Retaliation

Desinence

The above books are all available in ebook and trade paperback wherever books are sold!

www.ingramcontent.com/pod-product-compliance
Lightning Source LLC
Chambersburg PA
CBHW030651260626
47157CB00007B/2594